AUTUMN RUN

They sat together, Emily trying to hold on and Patch trying to let her. They hid their faces on a shoulder of the other. "I know it's difficult," Emily whispered. "But can you tell me? Did she say anything? Anything before…?"

Patch shook himself free. As he walked away, he heard his daughter's final declaration. It was something he'd tried to shush away, just before climbing the deck to get the life raft. The words echoed in his head as he recalled the horror in her eyes and the smoke-soiled tears he'd failed to wipe away.

"Daddy, I'm so sorry I ruined your boat."

AUTUMN RUN

M Alan Bahr

Especially for Joe:

To Lori

Prologue

Maybe we understand love best when we lose what we love most.

- From Kit Lerner's Journal

Patch ignored the squawk of his plane's stall alarm and bucked a shifting crosswind. The Cessna heaved and fishtailed as though fitted to a warped track across the sky. Two dozen feet over an alpine lake and angled all but crabwise by the gale, he brought the nose up and felt the floats reach forward. Seconds later he eased back on the throttle and the plane caught choppy water that left the windshield awash with spray.

He turned on the wipers and headed for a rocky beach at the foot of slate-colored mountains. Near the base of a haulout his client was packing gear and taking down an orange tent. Patch coasted to shore where ice shattered in his path and the floats scraped coarse gravel. He opened the door and leaned outside, his body all gaunt lines and restless angles. His long graying hair tossed about in the cold wind.

"Let's be quick," he hollered. "Bad weather's on its way."

What he didn't say was the notion most on his mind—that he should have put his foot down and stuck with their original takeout plan. They were pushing their luck to be in the air with a storm brewing. The client stumbled over loose shale to the water's edge. His jeans and fleece jacket were grimy with campfire ash and dried blood. He carried a full pack that he hoisted up to Patch.

"Thanks for the extra days," he said. "I got a nice bull— three brow tines, big rack."

Patch nodded congratulations, but thought: A moose that size won't be an easy haul. He looked at the hunter's sweat-stained face, his tired eyes and greasy hair, and guessed the man had missed more than his morning coffee. "You don't seem too excited," he said. "In fact, you look like hell."

"Nothing that a hot shower and a meal won't fix."

Patch set the pack down and folded his arms. "Even so, we'll be traveling through rough weather. Find a bag or a piece of tarp, anything, and stick close to it. Okay?"

The man nodded.

They stowed the quartered moose and the remaining gear and Patch shoved the plane off. He guessed at the distance to the opposite shore and considered the altitude needed to ferry into the pass. He fed the engine and heard the moose rack and meat shift in the pod below. With the float rudders down to hold direction, Patch squared off into the squall. The wind moaned and tossed rivulets of water over the plane's cowling and windshield. He powered through the chop, breaking the water's suction by raising first one float, then the other. The shore loomed menacingly close, but he eked enough lift to rise and take to the sky.

"Damn," he said, "we're packing a load."

They circled out of the narrow neck of the draw and into clouds that gathered between the mountains. Wet snow fell at times, as did rain. Patch took his bearings from the brief moments when the sky opened and he could see terrain. He settled into a rhythm marked by the pitch and keel of flight and bad weather.

Halfway through the pass, the fog thinned and a river appeared flowing through a pastel carpet of tundra. Patch saw a speck of color that he puzzled over until it disappeared behind a hummock of ground. He tilted the yoke and the plane lurched and came about. The stall warning droned briefly.

"What are you doing?" the client asked.

"I might have seen a tent down there."

The plane held its circle, at various times propelled crosswise, abreast, and headfirst into the storm. Each moment exposed them to a separate and distinct battering. The client covered his face with wind-chapped hands and groaned.

"Got a bag?" Patch asked.

"I forgot."

Patch scanned the cockpit and snatched a map from above his visor. He snapped the paper open. "Here," he said before handing it over.

The man retched and coughed, then he retched some more. Patch cracked open his window and searched the tundra again, his face as impassive as the boulders that littered each mountainside. Suddenly he straightened in his seat.

"Oh, hell. Somebody's down there."

The passenger strained to look out the pilot-side window. "You're not going to land, are you? You said we were overweight."

"Sure, but we can lose what's in the cargo pod. A man's life takes precedence over a game carcass." Patch ignored the man's look of concern and searched for water big enough to support a landing. "The river looks shallow," he whispered.

The plane reeled as if it had struck and broke through a wall. Once again the client bent over the paper in his lap. The stench of vomit filled the plane. "What should I do with this?" he asked, holding out the sagging paper.

"Hang on. I'm taking a closer look."

The plane dipped again, this time without holding a circle. The stall light and buzzer came on and didn't shut off. They plunged and bobbed and fell again. The client dropped the soaked map at his feet and looked forward with wide, startled eyes.

"Please, can't you just call somebody?"

Patch pulled the plane out of its sharp descent and felt his stomach fall through the seat. They were over the river now, tracking it. "I'm not within radio distance," he said.

"Maybe you can wait until we get home?"

"We're in Alaska, Mister. No one's walking out of this storm." The clouds had darkened and snow swirled with dizzying effect. Despite his earlier claim, Patch grasped the radio transmitter and spoke into it. Only white noise came in reply.

"Maybe he plans to float out," the client said.

Patch shook his head. "Did you see a canoe or a raft? And for your information Kaknu is nearly two-hundred miles away—one hell of a walk in muskeg and bad weather. I doubt you'd want to hike it."

The river drew closer, until its rocky bottom came into view and the curved bank ahead surprised Patch with its proximity and steep rise. Inches from touching down he knew the effort would ground them—maybe even do worse. He pulled the throttle back, risking a stall. The client gritted his teeth and closed his eyes just as the plane grazed the spruce tops along the far ridge.

"You're going to kill us," he said.

No, Patch thought, but we might be leaving a man to die. As he maneuvered the plane up and away, he stole anxious glances into the river valley from where they'd come. He pleaded silently, don't let this happen—please, not again—but it was too late. At a height above the mountains Patch turned for a final look and saw an opaque wall of haze that reached from ground to sky. Where the clouds passed, he knew, winter was claiming its territory and leaving the land desolate.

Chapter 1

*I think of heaven as a place without time, where
people can go from one age to another and undo
all their sins.*

- From Kit Lerner's Journal

For the rest of winter, each killing freeze and snowstorm
drew Patch's thoughts across Cook Inlet and pestered him with
two questions: What happened to the fellow on the Killborn?
And what would I have done, if it had been me out there? The
second question was especially unyielding. It put his mind in
the middle of that frozen valley, alone and starving, and haunted
him with a range of nightmarish possibilities.

Patch counted the reasons he'd left the traveler behind—bad
weather and concern for a client's safety at the top of his list—
still he pored over maps of the area and considered other actions
he might have taken. Though he continued to believe his

decision had been sound, he couldn't shake what he believed to be an ideal: When someone was in danger, a man pulled out all stops and did *something*. To hell with what was or wasn't possible.

So when spring broke early, Patch was itching to see the Killborn River again. Before the last icicle dropped from the eaves outside his apartment window, he called a local ground service and had his Cessna 185 delivered to a slip on a lake near the airport. A few mornings later he stared west from Bluff Street and saw Mount Illiamna on the far side of the inlet. It towered above the other mountains, a curl of smoke rising from it. Not a breeze in the air, he told himself, it's time to go.

At the airport Patch stood before his plane and tried to recall how he'd arrived there. He'd been too preoccupied to remember the drive along the bluff, past the rows of spruce and occasional views of the mudflats and river mouth. He couldn't remember entering the padlocked gate and skirting the asphalt runway to where his plane waited in a man-made reservoir. His mind had been on the Killborn River, where his thoughts had been for most of winter.

The Cessna was on floats again, no longer a swan with chicken feet, but a sleek and elegant piece of machinery. Patch shoved it out of its slip and the shore ice didn't break so much as bend and disappear with a suck and a black swirl. He grabbed a strut and, with only the vaguest of plans, pulled himself into the cockpit. Minutes later he was in the air, sweeping west over a glacier-fed sea that he still found beguiling, though it had snatched from him everything he'd truly loved.

From the opposite shore he tracked a crooked draw through steep mountains until the terrain opened as if he'd passed through a door. The snowbound plain stretched to the horizon, with jagged cracks and turquoise pools decorating the landscape. Patch saw the signs of breakup and grunted with satisfaction. In combination with an empty cargo pod, he hoped the high water would allow him to land.

Even so, the watershed seemed to stretch forever, with nooks and crannies everywhere. He could as easily find an eyelash in a coal bin than locate a camp he'd spotted only once in bad weather, but Patch had to try. He owed himself that much for the beating his speculation and second-guessing had cost him all winter. In spite of that, he recognized an irony in the task: If the man *had* walked out alive, what evidence would remain to prove it? The best Patch could hope for was to learn that the tent had been moved. At least then he might accept the possibility that all had gone well.

A half hour went by and he began to review landmarks in his mind: a wide pass through another range of mountains, a bend in the pass, a knuckle of ridge along the bend's inseam, the river passing before the face of the knuckle, and a gravel spit jutting into the river. The tent, he recalled, had sat on a knoll a short distance up the bank, but all the reckoning went unneeded when the bend appeared and he identified it in his bones for the disquiet it put in the deepest part of him. Anxious now, and with eyes flitting between bank and horizon, he followed the river to where a portion of it rippled over a shallow bar. Patch figured the spit, which had been high and dry in the fall, would be covered by spring melt. He circled twice, searching for anything unusual: a bit of color, an indentation against the white background, animal tracks. When he saw what might pass for a snow-covered knoll, he knew he had to land.

The normally tea-colored river was full of pale sediment and blocks of ice, but a pool of black water gathered below the riffles. Further downstream forested hills flanked both banks and led the stream along lazy curves. Patch countered back and studied the dark stretch again. A direct path required a steep descent, but he saw no better alternative. He banked hard to lose altitude and leveled after clearing a stand of spruce. The water came up fast and gave him little time to maneuver. Rolling from wingtip to wingtip, he cut back on the throttle and eased off on the flaps. The plane lit hard and dug into the river's back. Patch slammed forward against his safety restraints and winced in anticipation of what might follow, but the impact ended almost instantly.

"Damn," he said. "It shouldn't have been that easy." Then the question he'd already resolved after vacillating all winter resurrected itself. Could I have landed back then? No, he told himself, and you know the reasons why.

Patch goosed the plane upstream and ran aground where riffles marked the spit and a slurry of ice and water tumbled as it passed. Before he could talk himself out of the effort, he leaped from the cockpit and stumbled a dozen feet through calf-high flow to shore. He tied the plane to a clump of willows and walked up the bank, shivering and cursing from the cold.

The top layer of snow was frozen and held his weight. He stopped at the crest of the ridge and the wind moaned. It seemed to take on substance, like fine grit, in his lungs. He drew his parka tighter around him and turned where he stood. All around him the mountains glistened, as if sprinkled with crushed glass, and he measured them as a last view of the world. So this, he thought, is what it looks like from down here and he judged its grandeur as surpassed only by its isolation.

He lowered his gaze, when a shallow bowl in the snow caught his eye. Patch stared at the spot, wondering if it marked the place he'd come to find. Not likely, he told himself, I couldn't have just walked up to it, but the light left a peculiar shadow there, so he stomped at the frozen crust and knelt to dig. Wavering between hope and dread, he pushed away the broken wedges of snow and scratched out a hole. Suddenly, his hand brushed something slick that sprang back against his touch. An orange rainfly appeared and he pulled at it. Wet now with sweat and numb from the cold, he found the tent's entryway and worked the zipper without success. He thought to cut it with a knife, but decided not to damage the material. Instead he scraped the zipper free of ice and wrestled with it again.

Gradually the flap opened, but Patch hesitated to enter. He stood, as if looking for witnesses, but only saw ravens gathered near shallow water. They'd come to pick on dead salmon—the previous autumn's run of silvers—exposed now by retreating ice. Patch considered his own familiarity with death. He could warm his hands in the guts of a freshly downed caribou with no other thought than what might be for dinner, but the situation was different here. He caught himself hoping—and it shamed him somehow—that he wouldn't smell the death inside. Worried that he might get sick, Patch assured himself: Whatever is in there is frozen.

17

Beneath the domed ceiling of the tent, sunlight filtered through the nylon fabric and cast a red glow. He waited for his eyes to focus and a number of objects seemed to rise from the shadows: a pack with its frost-covered contents partially spilt and a sleeping bag half hidden by the sagging far wall. He drew the sleeping bag toward him, but he heard the crack of breaking ice and dropped it as if it had bit him. The bag was too heavy to be empty and, when one end came off the pad, he smelled urine. There was another odor, too, like the scent of freezer-burned fish.

Patch sat on his haunches, shaking from a mix of cold and profound regret, and considered his next steps. He should call the authorities—that seemed obvious—but what would he say? In his mind he played out the conversation to its end and knew there would be questions, the most likely one: Who is he?

A pair of boots stood at the head of the sleeping bag. Patch pulled them clear of the tent wall and a belt pack—the kind that old farts on cruise boats wore—slid out, tangled in the laces. He dropped the boots, grasped the belt pack and unzipped the pocket. A plastic bag, containing a camera and several rolls of film, tumbled out. He rummaged through the poke and extracted a wad of money, a penknife, and several ballpoint pens. The remaining contents he dumped and scattered on the floor, hoping the object of his search would be there, but it wasn't. Once more he turned his attention to the belt pack and noticed a separate compartment inside. He opened it and took a slow breath.

In addition to a driver's license, there was a second form of ID. He pulled them free and held them up where the sun penetrated most directly. He blinked at the license photo and leaned toward the tent wall, seeking more light. To Patch's dismay, his first impression had been right. He saw a delicate face, fair skin, short but curled hair.

"Oh, hell," he whispered and the rush of emotion was more than he could bear. He whirled on his knees, stuck his head outside and vomited until it hurt.

The license had belonged to a woman, a fact that settled like a bitter weight in his gut. He verified her date of birth and shut his eyes to it, thinking: That's how old my girl would have been. For the eight years since Amanda's passing, she'd never wandered far from his thoughts. Now, here was another female to grieve over.

Her address was an Anchorage street location that he committed to memory. Her vital statistics read: blond hair, green eyes, five-foot three-inches tall, and a hundred and ten pounds. The summary didn't include, however, other features that Patch observed in the photo and found endearing: the way she tucked her hair behind her ears, her small upturned nose, and the hint of freckles on her face. From the second ID the same woman's face stared back at him. An inscription above the photograph read: University of California, Berkeley.

He took inventory of the tent and sought order in the jumble. Every object spoke of a long winter and last mortal acts. There were burned cans of Sterno, an empty bag of instant oatmeal, a toothbrush in a cup, a Coleman lantern, a deck of playing cards, and a leather-bound Bible. He held each item carefully as though it were a priceless relic and imagined its role in the hell to which she'd succumbed: the final minute of light, the last morsel of food, faith questioned and lost.

Patch sought other more fitting tributes to the woman and ran a hand along the edge of the tent. On his knees he explored hidden corners and carefully avoided the sleeping bag that, like a shroud, melded with the contour of a body inside. Toward the entryway he struck something solid that moved. He gripped the object and raised it to his face. At first he thought it was another book, but the truth of it made him gasp.

"I'll be damned," he said. "She kept a diary."

Patch cracked it open, seeing it as a way to hear from the dead and offer a dozen heart-felt replies—goodbye and I'm sorry, among them—but in the dim light he couldn't read the tiny cursive marks. He crawled out of the tent and walked to the riverbank. On a frozen ridge he sat and read the inside front cover. The first words seemed to be a curious dedication, likely written near the end of the woman's life in a hand subject to fits of instability.

> *When you find this, give it to my mom. She'll want to know what happened.*

###

When you find this...

The more Patch considered those four words, the more they seemed like an accusation. She'd been a student at a prestigious university—inspired, he assumed, by precise language and reasoned arguments. He imagined her final days and saw a

20

young woman confined to a sleeping bag. With little hope of deliverance and nothing more enduring than the ideas she could express in a journal, she selected her words deliberately.

Patch considered the phrase and a thought mushroomed in his head. The woman had been aware of him, even known he would come. No matter how hard he tried to shake the notion, he couldn't. If it weren't true, she would have used a term more open to chance—a phrase, like: If someone finds this….

He continued to sit on the bank of the Killborn, leafing through the journal's pages. It was a collection of random ideas, some expressed with forethought, others declared spontaneously. The first entry was dated nearly six years prior and there was a long gap after the earliest postings. He didn't read so much as hear a woman's voice speak the phrases his eyes fell upon. The first entry began: I think I'm pregnant.

Patch wanted to delve further, but he looked at the sky and gauged only three hours of daylight remaining. He forded the shallow water and placed the book on the front passenger seat of his aircraft. Staring at the hard binding and loose-leaf pages, he mumbled, "What am I going to do with you?"

Patch sloshed back through the shallows and entered the tent on hands and knees. He gathered the woman's possessions and stuffed them quickly into the pack. In the dim light Patch—who hadn't uttered a prayer in years—knelt before the body. Though he felt awkward doing it, he folded his arms the way he'd been taught in Sunday school and spoke in a hush, not sure to whom he was speaking.

"I'm sorry about what happened here. I wish I could've helped, but you saw the weather. It wasn't in the cards."

He thought of that first blizzard of fall, how it had continued for five consecutive days and delayed the search and rescue flights that followed. A state trooper had offered words of solace then: "You must've spotted a local who made it home ahead of foul weather." But Patch had seen jeopardy take its ultimate toll before and knew better. Something in the waving figure had suggested desperation.

He touched the edge of the sleeping bag and tugged down on the opening. A knit cap showed, followed by a curl of blond hair and puffy yellowing skin. The body was curled and on its side, chin on chest. Patch didn't have a clear view to the woman's face, but saw more than what he'd bargained for: an eye closed to the cold, lips dried and broken, jaw clenched.

"I'll take you home," he said, replacing the cover. "At least your mom will get you back and she'll learn what happened to you. That's more than I got. And I'll make sure she gets your diary, too. I promise."

Patch shuddered to think how the young woman's parents might take the news. "Your poor mom," he said, recalling the way Emily had been torn apart by their daughter's calamity. "There's nothing worse in this world than losing a child."

He'd barely spoken when the shadow of a raven passed overhead. The black swirl of wings seemed to wake him and he hauled the pack outside. He left it on the riverbank and returned to the knoll. After collapsing the tent over the sleeping bag, he tossed the folded poles inside and wrapped the nylon fabric around the body. Patch worked his arms under the bundle and picked it up as though carrying a child to bed. The entire burden weighed less than a hundred and twenty pounds, but the material was slick and allowed the body to shift. Down the hill he marched, then through the river's slurry to the cargo pod under the plane's fuselage. He laid the bundle inside and returned to stow the backpack, but before closing the hatch cover, he fished out the film and camera and put them in his pocket.

On his way home the journal bounced on the passenger seat beside him as if it were eager to share its secrets. Patch tried to ignore it until he was within radio distance of the airport. By then shadows had emerged from beneath rocks and tree boughs. Their dark fingers stretched across his flight path and obscured the crags and crevasses over which he passed. Finally forced to make a decision, he slipped the journal beneath his seat and gave instructions to ground control.

A state trooper in a squad car and a paramedic in an ambulance met Patch at the reservoir. They tied down the plane and worked silently to empty its cargo pod and carry the body to the ambulance. The trooper sealed the backpack and placed it in the trunk of his car. He took off his hat and wiped his brow.

"You got a look at her, I guess?" he said.

Patch shrugged. "She was huddled in her bedding, but I saw enough." He decided to say no more, remembering the queasiness he'd felt and his reluctance to disturb the woman's rest.

A moment of silence passed until the trooper cleared his throat. "My dispatcher said you identified her—that you mentioned a name."

"I did: Kit Lerner. She's from Anchorage. You'll find her driver's license in the pack."

"Hmm. That's the name we checked out, but there's no file on her—missing person, or otherwise."

The paramedic scratched his head. "A lady out there alone and no one to even notice she was gone. That's a hell of a way to go."

"I don't get it," Patch said and his limbs felt frozen and heavy. "I'd have thought her mother would be frantic."

"You know that for a fact?" the trooper asked.

Patch realized that he'd almost mentioned the journal and its reference to Kit's mother. "Not really. She was young—only twenty—and a college student. I just assumed."

"Well, it's a hell of world and some parents would just as soon eat their young."

The conversation broke down into a series of affirming grunts and shaking heads, before the trooper marked its conclusion by hitching up his pants. "Guess I'll be heading back," he said. "I need to confirm identity—notify kin and all."

Patch excused himself and walked onto the floating dock leading to his plane. He opened the pilot-side door and gathered several objects. "So that's it?" he asked.

The other men nodded.

"If you need me, you know where to call."

The trooper waved in a fashion that was both salute and dismissal. "I suppose we got it all," he said, as though relating a summary of the facts.

Patch stopped. "What do you mean?" he asked.

"The stuff you brought over—her personal effects. You had everything in the cargo bin, right? There was nothing else?"

The ease by which Patch answered surprised him. He spoke without hesitation, as though the details of the woman's journey had always belonged to him. "You got it all," he said, and with the journal tucked under an arm, he walked to his pickup and didn't look back.

Patch wasn't bothered by his lie. He'd promised to deliver Kit Lerner's journal and it was a duty he intended to perform. More than that, the chance to understand the young woman's final deliberations was less a temptation than a necessity. He saw in her words a vicarious reckoning of what his daughter, Amanda, might have done if she'd only had the chance. And there's the rub, he told himself, maybe he'd agonized all winter because he'd never really healed from that earlier wound. Would the journal make sense of the whys and wherefores of dying and provide a salve?

On his way home he saw places linked to his memories of Amanda. Downtown Nikolai had changed since his arrival as a homesteader. In the beginning it had been no different than any other bush community—just a scattering of shacks amid endless stands of spruce. The only road, unreliable at best and impassable every spring, was a gravel strip leading to Moose Pass where the train made a stop.

Now the place boasted a movie theater, a bowling alley, two grocery stores, a couple of fast-food restaurants, and a traffic light. A paved road led to Anchorage a three-hour drive north.

In short Nikolai had become a town and, though it might not qualify as a metropolis, it did claim a noteworthy history.

Patch crossed the intersection leading to the town's most visible relics: Fort Nikolai (the log-wall edifice built by Russians) and the adjacent Orthodox Church. The chapel, with its blue onion domes and crosses, was still the site of weekly gatherings and religious rites. The fort was a combination museum and gift shop now. Both structures overlooked the river mouth across from where Patch lived. They were vestiges of an era when czars and Russian Orthodoxy ruled the land.

Patch remembered stories that Amanda had once told him. She'd returned from school one day, angry over wrongs committed by white men, and began a tirade with a single pointed observation. "Why does Captain Cook get credit for finding this place? Indians were here since Adam!"

She'd had the fire of discovery in her, sparked by classroom studies on Alaskan history. She complained about the Russian adventurers, who came to gather furs and continually promoted their main task, which was to keep the natives working.

"There were two things they did, Daddy," she said, disgust filling her pre-teen voice. "They invited the women and children to visit the fort. It was a big deal, so people went. But the Russians didn't let them leave. They used the kids like hostages. Can you believe it? Isn't that awful?"

For as long as Patch could remember, he'd processed information in terms of how it might affect him: If someone does shit to my family or me, they'll learn not to do it again. The idea of innocents being held against their will was disconcerting.

"What was the other thing they did, honey?"

She looked at him in an almost conspiratorial way, as if she'd known her father would abhor the deception. "They made the Indians convert to Christianity. Then the Russians told them something."

"What's that?"

"They said, 'If you don't help us—or, in other words, if you don't slaughter more otters, beavers, and other animals—you'll go straight to hell.'"

He remembered her other stories, too, about the natives in the area. The Athabaskan Indians and Aleuts had moved from traditional homelands to within daily commute of the fort. "It was squalor," she said, using a word that impressed him. "They got sick with measles and stuff like that. People died. Whole villages disappeared."

Patch saw the moral indignation in her eyes and it filled him with pride. He was astonished that anything so remarkable could have come from him. "Change the world," he told her. "When it's your turn to lead, change the world."

"Thank goodness things are different now," she said. "Back then, those poor Indians—they lost control of their lives. And that's the worst thing you can lose."

Patch considered her words and tried to assure himself that the world *had* changed. We've made progress, he thought. We have freedoms and technology, not to mention laws to protect us. Yet in his mind the advances couldn't redeem him from human inadequacy. We're all Indians, he decided, and none of us is in control.

Chapter 2

Some people say home is where the heart is, but
I believe home is a place in your heart.

- From Kit Lerner's Journal

Jesse Toyonek's life went topsy-turvy when his niece returned to the village. She'd been away at school, getting her head filled with strange notions, and came back like a whirlwind of opinions. It was her idea, for example, that Jesse get a job and make something of himself. But from the day he left for the Aleutians—a letter in his pocket promising him work—his only wish was to return home to the Killborn River.

If he'd been told he was on the moon, Jesse might have believed it. There were no tundra-covered valleys spilling out of mountain passes, no stands of timber. He saw only craggy hillsides, occasional tufts of grass, and the ocean surging around him. The co-workers with whom he shared a barracks could have been from another world, too. They were white kids on break from college, who talked of little else but sex and money. To Jesse—a thirty-five year-old virgin with no bank account in his name—their chatter amounted to nonsense. He'd never been among so many people, yet he'd never felt so lonely.

Then came a day worse than all the rest, a day bad enough to make him ache for the Dutch Harbor cannery where he butchered fish. He was hauling gillnet to a beach site across the bay when a fog came up. A few hours later he was still in the skiff, unsure of his location and out of gas. Throughout the day and the next night he drifted about in the tide, the fog so thick it soaked his black hair and formed droplets that rolled down his glasses. He rowed to stay headlong into the swells and bailed as water spilled over the bow.

Jesse wished for the wisdom of the old ones. In sealskin kayaks his people had once traveled the ocean and understood it in ways long since forgotten. From changes in water color, crosscurrents, and whirlpools, they could tell the location of land and bad weather beyond their sight. What would he give for that knowledge now?

He'd almost lost hope of ever seeing home again, when the fog turned to wisps and scattered in a rising wind. With a view to the horizon, however, a sense came to him that he was alone in a world without end. The water grew rough. His body hurt from exertion and cold. He almost wished for the fog's return, until he glanced over his shoulder and saw land in the distance. Jesse wondered how far it might be: one mile, or a hundred.

He stole another glimpse at the island and noticed spray rising off the shore, an indication that it was close. Even better, the wind and tide combined to push him toward it. In time he spotted a narrow beach pressed between steep bluffs. He aimed for the haulout and heaved with all his might across the chop. For an hour he worked the paddles, his back feeling like it might snap. The closer he approached, the more violent the sea became. White water threatened to swamp him, but he held his course.

When the hull finally scraped bottom, Jesse leaped overboard and wrestled the skiff forward. He came out of the water and fell, as limp as the seaweed surrounding him. His cheek struck rock and gravel before exhaustion raised a wall between his thoughts and everything outside his head. In seconds he was neither asleep nor fully conscious, but in a limbo between the two.

Time passed and Jesse became aware of movement, only to realize it was his own body shivering. He wanted rest, but knew he needed a fire. In agony he pushed himself to his knees, cleaned the salt off his glasses and scanned his surroundings. The tide was ebbing and the skiff was nearly out of the water. He stood to secure it and the effort to hoist the anchor overboard brought tears to his eyes.

Jesse took a seat in the back of the boat, his legs thigh-deep in seawater, and released the drain plug. As the water spilled, he checked a storage bin for anything useful and found a waterproof bag with blankets and a hatchet, matches and a flashlight inside. For the first time in what had seemed like days he smiled. Maybe I'll see my village again, he thought.

He compared the beauty of his home near Bristol Bay to the strange place upon which he'd landed. Except for the beach, the island was composed of right angles and black cliffs that reached to the sky. There were no trees, but Jesse saw a line of driftwood further up the haulout. He stepped out of the boat, intending to gather fuel for a fire, when he was startled by the sight of smoke. It rose from behind a steep hill to his right and he wondered if a cabin or campsite lay beyond it.

Across a stretch of surf-flattened rocks he stumbled to the bluff and began to climb. There was a ridge twenty feet up and he was halfway to it when he noticed something odd. The smoke continued to rise, but it vanished quickly and didn't leave a smell. Not until he reached the summit did he understand. What he'd thought was evidence of a fire was only steam hovering over a waterfall. And the queerest aspect of the scene was this: The water was hot.

It tumbled over a lip of rock and formed a shallow pool several steps down the summit. In his cupped hands Jesse caught a portion of the falling water and lifted it to his mouth. It was fresh and tea-flavored—hot, but not scalding. He lowered himself into the stream and the water crashed over him, soothing his aching muscles and warming the chill in his gut. Within minutes he was asleep.

###

Jesse awoke, dizzy with hunger, a share of his strength restored. He stepped out of the pool and raised his eyes toward the cry of seabirds. The thought of gull eggs made his mouth water and he looked to the cliff face for a way to the top. His view went from outcropping to ledge—from crease to crevasse—but in the end he rubbed the stubble on his chin and whispered.

"I could break a leg up there."

He turned and picked his way to shore. At the base of the bluff he found hairy crabs, snails, and seaweed. He cracked open a sea urchin and sucked out its creamy innards. Limpets and mussels clung to the rocks and he gorged on them. As his hunger abated, he began to think of the island as a magical place, like the setting in a child's fairy tale. It had saved him— even given him warmth and food. What other gifts might it provide?

He returned to the boat and dragged two driftwood logs together—enough fuel, he reckoned, to burn through the first few hours of twilight and signal his presence. Evening came and he could barely keep his eyes open and his legs moving. At the head of the beach, where the bluff began its straight-up rise, he found a cleft in the rock and dropped to his knees before it.

The opening seemed to lead into a warm and spacious cavern, but the interior was dark and smelled oddly like gunpowder. He crawled inside, drawing his survival gear behind him. With no other thought than the need for rest, he peeled off his wet clothes and wrapped himself in a blanket. Before his head touched rock, he was already dreaming of home.

###

The next morning the screeching of gulls startled Jesse awake. In the dark he put on his clothes and emerged from the cave with the sun overhead. He shaded his eyes to search the beach and saw a flock of seabirds fighting over a dead tomcod. Jesse chased the gulls away and salvaged the fish. He cooked it beside a newly kindled fire, when a mix of surprise and gratitude overwhelmed him.

Except for a few minor aches and scrapes, he felt like a new man. What's more, the fish seemed to have come as another gift, like the fresh water and warm shelter he'd received the previous day. He was happy to be alive, but his circumstances puzzled him. Who's doing this for me? he wondered. And why?

Jesse ate his fill and gathered more driftwood. He fed the fire to mark the beach and hoped to maintain the blaze by working and sleeping in shifts. Satisfied with his progress, he returned to the cave to rest, but as he slipped inside, sounds of his entry echoed and caused him to wonder what was hidden in the darkness. From his survival bag he fished out the flashlight and pointed it into the gloom.

What appeared on the far wall made his mouth open in shock. He saw drawings—dozens of them—like an ocean full of kayaks, whales, and other sea creatures. He panned slowly across the rock face, thinking: That's how it used to be—that's how my people once lived. He was lost in the glory of it, when the light fell upon a man sitting within a stone alcove. Jesse screamed and dropped the flashlight. He held his breath and listened for a response.

"Who are you?" he asked, but there was only silence.

Jesse's heart beat like a village drum and he wondered if his head had played tricks on him. He retrieved the flashlight and trained its beam again. The man was still there, sitting cross-legged and naked, not far from where Jesse had slept the night before. His eyes looked empty and his face was deeply wrinkled. Scattered about him were treasures: a kayak, ropes, spears, floats, and nets.

"Are these yours?" Jesse asked, but the man remained silent and unmoving. He didn't even breathe.

###

Early the following afternoon a plane circled overhead as if looking for a place to land. Jesse stood on the haulout and waved, but the plane left and was replaced by a Coast Guard cutter that appeared offshore the next morning. The ship lowered a motorized inflatable boat that two rescuers piloted to shore.

Jesse was almost sad to see them come. He'd enjoyed the company of his wrinkled and unmoving host, a being he'd begun to think of as the god of the island. At the time of the rescue Jesse was sitting outside the cave with the god and all his possessions spread out around them. Amazed by the craftsmanship, Jesse studied a bone-tipped spear and committed its design to memory. He looked up when one of the rescuers, a fellow with red hair and a thin moustache, drew near.

"Mr. Toyonek?" the man said.

Jesse nodded.

"We've been looking for you. Are you okay? Any injuries?"

"I'm good."

"What do you have there?" The rescuer knelt and pointed to the god of the island, whose head was resting in Jesse's lap.

"He saved me."

"Saved you?" The man laughed and moved closer. "It looks to be a mummy."

Jesse was stunned. How could the god of the island be a mommy, when he was clearly a man? Too flustered to correct his rescuer, he asked, "Are you going to take me home now?"

"Sure, but I'm wondering what to do with your friend." He turned to his colleague, who arrived carrying a medical bag. "Take a look at this."

"I'll be damned." The second man gazed at the items scattered before the cave mouth. "It's Aleut, isn't it?"

"Seems likely, but how old?"

"There's no metal in any of it. Even the fishhooks are made of bone. I'd say it predates the coming of the Russians. We can't leave it here, can we?"

"My thoughts, exactly."

Half an hour later Jesse was on the ship. The rescuers led him to the galley, where several uniformed people sat at a long table. They gathered around him, offered him hot coffee and asked how he'd survived the bad weather and days alone. Jesse tried to answer, but when the ship began to leave, he felt a pang of misgiving.

"Why are you taking the god of the island?" he asked. "This is his home. I know that much."

The galley quieted. Jesse looked from one crew member to another and saw confusion on their faces. A gray-haired man finally spoke. "Are you talking about what you found?" he asked. "Because it's quite a discovery. Folks at the university will want to study it."

"Why?"

The man shrugged. "It's in our nature, isn't it? Don't we all want to learn about our past?"

The words put new ideas in Jesse's head. Maybe, he decided, it wasn't an accident that he'd landed upon the island. The more he considered that possibility, the more it seemed right. But for what purpose had he been saved? Suddenly he imagined life as it once had been, the same life depicted on the walls of the cave where he'd slept. It was a simple existence with a clear purpose. Didn't the gray-haired man speak the truth, as if the words had been put in his mouth?

We must learn from our past.

Chapter 3

*Asking God to do this and that is like kicking the
ball into His court.*

- From Kit Lerner's Journal

Patch came through the door after his first flight of spring
and placed the journal onto his oak desk. For a dozen beats of
his heart he could only stare at it, finally understanding what
Emily had gone through—how she'd hungered to know the
particulars of their daughter's passing. He'd been wrong not to
tell her—he saw that now—and if he could relive the past, he
would try his best to relate each detail until Emily wrapped her
mind around it. Even so, if given another opportunity, Patch
knew he would only fail again. In Amanda's most noble act he
recognized his costliest failure. To speak of that day would be
like tending to a bullet wound: Sometimes it was best to leave
the cause of the damage stitched inside.

He looked out his apartment window to the parking lot. As usual winter had been deceptive in its tidiness, but now a month of dirt and debris was exposed to the sun. Trees had lost their frost, along with their luster. Dark puddles formed, only to freeze at night. New snow, it occurred to Patch, was like a pretense that feigned virtue, even as it masked a filthy soul.

Surrounded by evidence of his own pretenses and sins—the mounted animals, firearms, and antique steel traps hanging on the walls, the garage-sale furniture, and beer cans poking out of the trash—he couldn't help himself. He sat at his desk, let the journal open to a random page and began to read.

I cry when babies laugh. I get sick at the sight of crayons. Will I ever be forgiven? I can only hope it's possible.

A Prayer through an Open Window

Upon the night sky,
Lamplight scatters,
Like needles of itself,
Beginning a long journey
To touch thy face
A universe away.

And painfully now
Through darkness I see:
A long-drawn shudder
And glistening tears,

A more perfect light,
Weeping for me.

Patch stopped reading and contemplated Kit's words. He understood the need for forgiveness, but couldn't imagine who might grant it. Human beings, he'd come to decide, were little more than creatures in a maze, with obstacles placed in their way to satisfy an indifferent spectator's curiosity. What could better explain life's ironies and dilemmas—the passions meant only to be constrained, the physical and emotional needs impossible to satisfy?

He didn't want to revisit the past, but it was the very proof of what he believed. As thoughts of daughters and dying mingled in his head he was suddenly a fisherman again. He heard the explosion, knowing it wasn't a backfire. The *Citadel* shuddered, but didn't hesitate. It rose and fell through a fifteen-foot swell, when Amanda stumbled into the pilothouse.

"Fire, Daddy," she said between fits of coughing.

Patch saw that her blond hair and eyebrows were singed. "Are you okay?" he asked.

"The galley's on fire, Daddy. I tried to put it out, but there's smoke—a lot of it."

Alarmed, Patch told his twelve-year-old daughter to take the wheel. He left the pilothouse and bounded down the steps where a fire extinguisher clattered across the afterdeck. From the open galley door black smoke billowed. Patch poked his head inside and fumes stung his throat and lungs. A wave of nausea passed through him and he thought: Oh, God, it's in the insulation.

Patch ran to the wheel deck and set up the pump. He dragged the fire hose back and sprayed into the galley. Twenty minutes later the bilge motor was still idle and the boat listed. He hurried back to the pilothouse and worked the switch without success.

"Amanda," he said. "Hose off that fire. Keep the walls wet, you understand? Spray where you see smoke."

"Okay, Daddy."

With his heart in his throat, Patch watched Amanda leave and wondered if he should call her back. He likened her to a bright star, the point of light from which he gained his bearings. She was as delicate as a snowflake, but tenacious and irrepressible, like the salmon they chased over much of Cook Inlet. He vacillated between coddling and demanding too much from her, because she stood for all that was possible, despite the improbable nature of dreams.

At the crest of the next swell Patch spun the 38-foot vessel and heard the screws whine as they rose out of the water. He headed south across shipping lanes and picked up the radio to call for help. Only static came in reply, but he persisted until the receiver died and he shattered its plastic cover with a fist.

Patch had been in nastier water before, but never while abeam to it. He locked the wheel and hurried aft to get Amanda, hoping for a few minutes of forward progress. Together they stumbled away from the worst of the heat and fumes, when another explosion blew the hatch off its hinges behind them. The engines died and the *Citadel* put a shoulder to the swells and rolled. They slid across the wheel deck and slammed into the gunwale. Seawater spilled over the rail and drenched them before washing out the scuppers.

"Stay put while I get the raft," Patch said.

He wrestled a three-foot section of longline from his pocket, tied one end around his daughter's wrist and the other to the deck rail. He used a bowline, a knot she knew and could untie if necessary.

"We'll stay afloat for awhile. So don't free yourself unless the boat flips. You hear? Not unless it flips."

Amanda nodded and tried to speak, but Patch shushed her. On hands and knees he inched up the rocking deck and scrambled to the far side of the bulkhead. As he reached to unlash the survival gear, the ocean surged. It lifted the boat and launched him back. For a moment he saw clouds, then he bounced off the exposed hull and slammed into the water.

The cold was like a weight, crushing him. He kicked toward light, but a swell formed overhead and blackened his sky. His lungs ached as he fought the urge to breathe. In the instant before panic hit him the swell moved on. He broke through the surface, arms and legs flailing, and drew a desperate breath.

The *Citadel* was out of sight, but he forced his cramped limbs to move and whirled to locate it. He swam furiously down a wall of water, dove where it bottomed out and waited for the next swell to pass. Out of the following trough he rose only feet from the boat, but still a universe away. He began to sink, but a mooring rope appeared, trailing the deck. He didn't consider how it had gotten there—how a hatch could open and the massive rope uncoil and fall out—he only held to it and drew himself through a backwash. At the brink where panic became resignation, he found strength in thoughts of his daughter. Do it for Amanda, he told himself.

A wave washed over the gunwale and carried Patch to the rail. He hung there, a party to an uneasy truce with the sea. He coughed and his guts twisted. Time passed before he could draw a breath without pain.

"Honey," he yelled. "Are you all right?"

Patch rolled to the deck, surprised that Amanda wasn't by his side. Was she reluctant to loosen the cord that held her to the boat?

"Amanda?" He wiped the water from his face and turned to where he'd left her. "Oh, Jesus," he whispered and the sea roared. Where his daughter had once stood, only the longline remained, dangling from the rail.

It was a memory that had haunted him for eight years now, but despite the passage of time, he still struggled to buck up, employing a means of survival that Emily had never understood. It required he sling his feet off the sheets and walk out the door each morning before the cogwheels in his head meshed and spun. It was life in neutral, with motion possible only where gravity drew him.

Because living was intolerable otherwise.

He developed Kit's film and sequenced the prints to match them against events in her journal. There was only one picture of her, taken near water with a floatplane in view. She stood, dressed in layered clothing, with a pack and kayak at her feet.

Her golden hair fell in curls to her jaw. She struck a pose—one hand on a hip, the arm crooked, and her body leaning onto an upright paddle. The pilot, he assumed, had snapped the picture.

The next prints were of the river, of animals she'd seen, and a view from a high elevation. There was also a close-up of water that he'd first assumed was shot by mistake, but through the glare, he noticed spent salmon in their last desperate dash before death. Most of the remaining pictures were clear, but a few were blurred and left him wondering what she'd seen.

They awakened in Patch a desire to get away, which in turn caused him to wonder if his greatest loves were silence and danger as Emily had often claimed. He didn't think so. As a young man he'd planned his life and contemplated its mysteries while backpacking among sky-piercing mountains and babbling streams. His need for escape only heightened in the months after Amanda's passing, but he couldn't leave Emily alone in her grief. Instead, he stayed close to home, but took walks along the bluff to rage against his own limitations and bargain for a return of everything he'd lost. It was an exercise he curtailed when his wife asked to go with him and used the time to lament. He couldn't fix Emily's problem and she didn't see how silence—though perhaps not a thing to love—was at least a balm. There was this, too: He didn't want her to see what had become a ritual—a grown man shedding tears he couldn't wipe dry.

Beyond solitude, however, there was another, more subtle, aspect to wild places that Patch had missed. He'd once appreciated fishing for its precision: the dead reckoning based on compass points, duration, and speed, the validation he found in the sun's rising and dying, the measurable influence of currents and swells. Flying had added another layer of complexity to his days, not only in terms of vertical feet, but something more difficult to describe, a fullness like the infinity between zero and one.

In places unscathed by people he connected with an essence as honest as numbers. It told him that humans would always lose to nature, but in the process of losing, the rare and stirring flash of nobility defined a person. That's what Amanda had taught him and he aspired to be her equal. The idea gave him hope that there was a wild and free place, like the complex infinity between zero and one, reserved for her.

For that reason Patch was like a gawker to a burning house, captivated by what he recognized as Kit's search for redemption in a place as wild as any. Her story not only reminded him of his own need for forgiveness, but he heard his daughter's voice in its mix of confession and apology. At times the voice was demanding, too, repeating the journal's opening request: *When you find this, give it to my mom.*

While the story both horrified and intrigued Patch, he knew it would only devastate Kit's mother, but mindful of his promise, he copied the journal's pages for himself and flew to Anchorage with the original, refusing to see the act as an invasion of privacy. Kit, he reckoned, had invaded his thoughts as much as he'd been privy to hers.

The task turned out to be more difficult than he'd planned. Kit's address was near a downtown avenue where ladies in short skirts and parkas beckoned toward his rented Bronco. It was evening when, to no avail, he first knocked on Mrs.

Lerner's door. Several attempts later he was told by a neighbor that the tenant had moved.

"Nah, that's not true," the property manager told him the next morning. "We moved her."

"To where?" Patch asked.

The manager squinted hard. He sported a scraggly goatee and a dirty tee shirt with a picture of a dead rock star on the front. "Are you a relative?"

"No, but I've got something that belongs to her."

"Then you might as well take her other stuff, too. It's all here boxed and put away—what little there is."

Patch frowned. The last thing he wanted was more of another person's belongings. "I'm sure she'll be back to get them, but what I have she'll want right away."

An awkward silence ensued before the manager replied. "I suppose it doesn't matter if I tell you. The lady had a stroke awhile back. It happened right after her daughter left for school."

"Daughter? You're talking about Kit?"

"I believe that was her name."

Patch realized now why no one had reported Kit missing. Still, he wanted to know where the notion of community had gone and why neighbors didn't keep track of each other anymore. While memories of his Idaho upbringing weren't always happy, he at least remembered people taking care of people, no matter how misguided their reasons.

"Then you're mistaken," Patch said. "She never made it back to school."

He didn't state the logical conclusion—that the man's misunderstanding had contributed to Kit's death. If the fellow had known of her plans, he might have called authorities when she didn't return on schedule. If he'd done that, she might still be alive.

Patch traced the consequences of Mrs. Lerner's illness to an emergency visit to Providence Hospital. From there, she was taken to a rehab center, and finally to a long-term care facility just outside of Anchorage. Patch went to her final destination and found a nurse who seemed eager to help. He followed her down a brightly-lit hall and listened as she spoke of her patient's condition.

"Mrs. Lerner had an aneurysm," she said. "It burst and left her immobile."

Patch tracked the nurse's steps with his eyes. She was stocky and her brunette hair fell in tight ringlets. "She's okay now, though, right?" he asked.

The nurse turned her head briefly. "She's alive. And after what she's gone through, that's a miracle."

"Can she talk?"

"You'll see for yourself. She's not too communicative, but she'll understand what you say." The nurse stopped and spoke in a hush. "To tell you the truth I feel sorry for her—poor thing stuck here without a family. When she was first brought here, she kept saying, 'ki..ki..,' but we had no idea she was asking about her daughter. She'll appreciate your visit."

Patch looked down at the floor and said, "I wouldn't be too sure."

What he'd heard of Mrs. Lerner's condition didn't prepare Patch for what he saw. She lay motionless, sharing a room with two other elderly women. Her smooth skin, sharp nose, and delicate features suggested a faded beauty, but her face sagged on one side and allowed drool to seep from her lips. When she opened her eyes, Patch saw something that spoke of dread in them. He couldn't connect her to the woman Kit had described as something of a reformed hippy:

> *Once upon a time, Mom lived in a place where people shared everything they owned and believed in free love. But here's the thing: Free love gave her a baby and nobody owned up to being my father. So Mom started needing more from life. I guess that's when she found Jesus.*

The nurse patted Mrs. Lerner's hand and wiped spittle from her lips. "Pamela," she said. "This is Mr. Taggart. He has something you'll be interested in."

Mrs. Lerner jerked her head to the side and seemed to focus on a point that was belt high to her visitors.

"Ma'am," Patch said. "I've got something of yours." He stepped forward and pulled the journal from a paper bag. "It's something your daughter wrote while she was on her trip down the Killborn River."

Pamela Lerner shook in a way that unsettled Patch, in part because he'd hoped to learn more about Kit—to get answers to the many questions her journal raised—but that seemed unlikely now. He looked at the nurse and asked, "Is she okay?"

"She's fine. Go ahead."

Patch cleared his throat. "I was the pilot who found your girl. I should've brought this sooner, I know, but…well, I won't make excuses."

He watched the woman for signs of understanding and thought he saw a change in her expression. He'd seen it in animals he'd hunted. Anxiety—even terror—could be useful. It caused adrenaline to flow and gave strength to tired legs, but it could transform into panic and that marked the end.

The nurse put a hand on Patch's arm and said, "Maybe you can read to her."

"I don't think that's a good idea."

"You don't have to leave now, do you?"

"No, that's not it… " Patch couldn't bring himself to finish what he'd begun to say. He didn't want to discuss the contents of the journal.

The nurse smiled and turned to Mrs. Lerner. "It would do you good. Wouldn't it, Pamela?"

The woman continued to shake.

Patch stood rigid, chewing the inside of his lip. He wanted to be away from the room and its smell of something old and diseased. Kit's writings, he knew, would be painful to hear. Suddenly the woman in the next bed made a sound that began like a snore and ended with a bone-wrenching hack. The disturbance was like an alarm that jolted him.

"Maybe I could read a few parts from here and there," he said.

"Good." The nurse squeezed Patch's elbow. "I'll leave you two alone. If you need anything, just call out."

The nurse left and Patch took a chair next to the bed. He tried not to think of the woman lying there as an invalid. "I'll tell you what," he said. "I'll take a few minutes of your time and leave the diary. When you start feeling better, you can go through it yourself. It'll mean more to you then."

Patch opened the binder to its inside cover. He turned it and held it up. "Look here. Can you make it out? It says: 'When you find this, give it to my mom.'"

As the woman gazed at the writing, Patch considered her plight. He likened Mrs. Lerner to a genie in a bottle—intellect held captive and made subject to the whims of others. It was the ultimate lack of control and he could think of no hell worse. With that understanding, the hospital smells didn't bother him anymore and he no longer wished to leave. Rather than pity the woman, he saw her as a kindred spirit, or at least someone who comprehended his losses. Suddenly his purpose for being there went beyond a promise to deliver a journal. To this woman who'd lost so much, he hoped to be a friend.

"I can see that life has thrown you a curve," he said. "Good God, it's been mighty unkind, but remember one thing. Your daughter's last thoughts were of you."

Without waiting for a response, Patch read from an entry that Kit had written after her year at college.

Do you know how a cut can tingle and you
want to scratch it, until it starts bleeding again?
Well, that's what it was like coming...

49

Patch stopped abruptly and flipped through several more pages. He searched his mind for something to say, if only to buy time and find a safe passage in the journal. "I had a daughter once," he said. "So I know what it's like to have and lose a child. My little girl was like sunlight to me. I remember the night Amanda was born—how my wife woke me up a little after eleven and said it was time. She got up to take a shower and I watched a rerun of Hawaii 5-O, trying like the devil to keep my heart from leaping out of my chest."

Pamela Lerner licked her lips and her shaking seemed to diminish.

"We drove to the hospital and for thirteen hours I watched my wife go through labor. My God, what an ordeal! Amanda decided to greet the world face up, which caused some problems during the delivery, but she came out the sweetest child I'd ever seen."

He showed Mrs. Lerner the laminated photograph he kept in his wallet. It had been taken by one of the nurses, minutes after delivery. He pointed to Emily, who was resting on a bed, smiling despite her night of travail. She was blue-eyed and blond, slim and fair. He'd loved her then—still did, in fact—and would've traded places with her if he'd possessed the required plumbing, but love couldn't prevent pain. In fact, love only deepened it. That's what living had taught him.

"There's Amanda." he said, indicating the baby wrapped in a receiving blanket and nestled in the crook of her mother's arm. Only her face and still-damp hair showed. "Beautiful, isn't she?" he said. "Your Kit reminds me of her."

And there was Patch, too, leaning over the bed, only peering into the camera obliquely. He looked blurry eyed and depleted, as though he'd been the one to deliver. Patch recalled that day's sweep of emotion. While watching Emily in stirrups, he'd felt crushed by his inability to help and awed by her strange procreative power. Pride for his wife filled him, but it was the baby who stole his heart. He was enthralled, irrevocably and unconditionally. Amanda made him whisper words of undying love.

"I held that tiny thing—that perfect life full of possibilities—and pledged to always be there for her. For twelve years I kept the promise, but it wasn't enough. Sometimes, no matter how hard we try, it's not in our power to protect what matters most."

Patch looked back at the journal. "Oh, here's a good part."

> *When I was accepted to Berkeley, I thought: Not bad for a destitute gypsy. That's when I decided to learn something useful, something that would equip me to live the American dream, something practical like...philosophy (Ha!).*
>
> *I quickly discovered that to be at Berkeley is to be surrounded by people who question every premise, including the idea that there's a God who loves His creations. At first I was intimidated, but the more I learned, the more I realized that all the wisdom of the ages can't answer the most critical issues of life, or resolve away the need to act on faith. If we take numbers*

and logic as far as they lead, we arrive at canyons of uncertainty.

I see little difference between a belief in Einstein's theories and faith that God wills the sun to rise. Both require acceptance of something unseen. And though I've studied Einstein's theory of gravity, I can only profess faith in it, because its complexity is beyond my understanding. Since I can't see gravity, I can only presume it's the force behind the sun's appearance each morning.

What I know about God is just as imperfect, and so there's only one statement I can make with confidence: Faith has more to do with doubt than knowing the truth of anything. Admitting as much gives faith a place to sit beside human learning and allows us to accept what's true no matter where it's found. But here's the strange corollary to life's uncertainty: It makes belief essential! Does life have a purpose? If so, how do we actualize it? Answers to such questions are based upon speculation (a kind of faith) and must be considered by all thinking people—believers and non-believers alike.

That being said, how can I doubt God's existence, when I live in this beautiful land that still looks as if He put a finger to it and formed it out of chaos? It's the one thing that grounds me. I missed this place so much while away. So I came home for the summer filled with mixed emotions. I wanted to plant my feet in Alaskan soil, but there were things I didn't look forward to. The reminders..."

Patch stopped again and turned a few more pages. He felt himself sweat. There was silence, except for the rustling of the paper.

Mrs. Lerner stirred. "No," she said softly.

Patch looked up from the journal. "Did you say something?"

"No," Mrs. Lerner repeated, shaking her head.

Patch went to the door. He looked down both ends of the hall, but it was empty. "I don't understand," he said, returning to the room. "Is there something you want?"

The woman gasped with exertion. Her tongue searched the sagging corner of her mouth. "Read," she finally said.

"Read? Well, that's what I'm doing."

"No…read…"

Patch waited.

"…all."

"Read all of it? Read it from the beginning?"

The woman relaxed. "Yes."

"I don't think so. Some of it won't be easy to hear—especially in your condition. Maybe when you're feeling better, you can read it then, but…."

Mrs. Lerner closed her eyes and whispered, but her voice seemed to bounce off the walls. "Please."

Patch sat down slowly and stared at the journal. To relieve Emily's sorrow he'd done all he could—everything but open his heart to her and detail what had happened to their daughter. So how could he read the journal to Kit's mother? On the other hand, circumstances were different here. Amanda wasn't the topic of discussion and Emily wasn't in the room. Maybe he was detached enough from Mrs. Lerner's loss to offer some amount of comfort and earn a partial redemption from his other failures.

"All right then," he said, unable to deny her. "I'll do it. But when you can't hear anymore, you'll have to speak up."

June 3, 1978

I think I'm pregnant.

Patch cleared his throat and saw that Mrs. Lerner had begun to cry. "She never told you?" he asked, reaching to take her hand. "I told you this wasn't a good idea."

"Okay. Go on."

June 4, 1978

I was hoping to run away with Cooper. But he handed me a check instead and told me where to go with it. At least he didn't do like some guys and drop me like a hot potato.

June 7, 1978

The counselor was an older lady, who reminded me of Grandma. She said sometimes a girl's body only thinks it's pregnant and so she ordered a blood test for me.

June 8, 1978

The counselor called. Bad news.

June 15, 1978

Cooper is gone to the Slope, so there's nobody to talk to. I'm supposed to take the bus to the clinic tomorrow. Should I go?

June 16, 1978

A nurse gave me a shot and said it would make the fetus start to come. After it was all over, my boobs started to swell and hurt. The doctor said it was nothing to worry about, that I was only making milk. A couple of hours later I walked out the door, just like nothing had ever happened.

June 26, 1978

Cooper is back and I asked him the thing that's bothered me since leaving the hospital. If the baby wasn't meant to live, why did I make milk for it? He just sat there and didn't answer.

June 27, 1978

How can I ever be forgiven?

Chapter 4

When God told Adam to replenish the earth, wasn't He telling us to be kind to nature?

- From Kit Lerner's Journal

Jesse Toyonek returned to Kaknu before the end of the salmon run. He hunted caribou in the fall and watched winter settle. All the while he thought of his time in the Aleutians, believing it had marked a change for him, as if he'd been chosen for a great work. But what was he supposed to do?

He stepped out of the Marina House, the red barn-like building that was a combination general store and machine shop on the northern shore of Killborn Lake. As the only source of gasoline and groceries in the village, it bustled in the summer with small boats, floatplanes, and people buying supplies. But the salmon weren't running yet, so the Marina House stood mute, surrounded by dirty snow.

A gravel road hugged the shoreline and Jesse walked it, carrying a small box of canned food and cereal he'd picked up. The school stood on his left, incongruous to the weathered stick houses and yards full of rusted oil barrels. Further down the path a wooden shed smelled of old smoke and salmon drippings. He passed it and entered a metal building that served as both tribal police headquarters and post office.

Jesse asked for the day's mail and received a decorative postcard in return. He held it up to the light and was surprised to see a picture of the god of the island and his ancient treasures. At the bottom of the card an inscription read: From the University of Alaska Anthropology Collection. Jesse turned the postcard over and studied the handwritten message there.

> *You'll want to see this, Mr. Toyonek. We've learned a lot, thanks to you. Won't you spend a day with us?*

Jesse couldn't believe it. He was going to see his old friend again.

His niece, Belle, arranged the flight that whisked him away from home for only the second time in his life. He flew east beyond tundra-covered plains and a turquoise lake that seemed to stretch forever. Later the plane bobbed and weaved through a mountain range, until he thought he might get sick. Then the motion diminished and he was suddenly over a slate-gray sea. Land appeared in the distance, as did a great many buildings.

At the university, nearly four-hundred miles from his village, he received a celebrity's welcome. Young people led him into a large room, where he passed glass-encased rows of willow baskets, oil lamps, and bone tools. At the end of a long aisle they pointed him toward an interior window and an exhibit where the god of the island sat with a breechcloth covering his private parts. The display, Jesse noted, was made to resemble the cave in which he'd slept not so long ago. A plaque read, "Toyonek Man" and included information about the discovery. Jesse was happy to see his old friend again, but all he could think of was the sadness in the hollow eyes that stared off into a distant place.

"I don't think he likes it here," he said.

On the glass he saw the reflection of the people gathered around him. Their smiles disappeared and one of them—an older man whom the others called Professor—patted Jesse on the back. "I know how you feel," he said, "but we'll return him to the island in a few days. That's why we asked you here—so you could have a last look."

Jesse nodded. "And what will you do with his things?"

"We'll keep them. It's important that folks see how clever the Aleuts were."

"But how will he fish, or hunt?"

The professor shrugged. "He won't need that now, will he?"

Jesse wondered if that was reason enough to take someone's belongings. He asked for time alone with his friend and waited for the others to leave. Through the display window he gazed at the god of the island and remembered their days together. He remembered the smell of the cave and its warmth.

"Tell me what I'm supposed to do," he said.

The request had popped into Jesse's head, like a sudden bit of inspiration. If he *had* been selected to a new work, maybe the god of the island could explain it to him. He waited for a response—and waited and waited some more—but an answer never came, so he wished his friend a safe journey home and walked away to find the others.

When it was time to leave, the professor drove Jesse to a small lake on the outskirts of Anchorage and waved goodbye. There, beside a floatplane, stood the man he knew as Patch Taggart.

"Ready for home?" the man asked.

Jesse nodded. With any other pilot he might have sat without speaking, but Patch put him at ease. Sure, the man flew rich folks into the woods, but he was nothing like them. He didn't shout when a whisper would do, or brag on himself, or seek attention. In fact he was just about as sad and quiet as any Indian. So as they traveled to Kaknu Jesse talked about his days in the Aleutians and was surprised by the man's response.

"That explains a lot."

"A lot of what?"

"Something your niece once told me."

Jesse didn't care to inquire further. He knew Belle had little else but bad things to say about the god of the island. Besides, he was far more interested in another—more personal—question, one Jesse wouldn't have trusted with just anyone.

"What do white people do with their gods?"

Funny thing, Jesse thought, but he didn't know what to make of the answer. Patch said, as if reciting a humorous joke: "They draweth nigh with their mouth and honoureth with their lips, but their heart is far from me."

The answer took Jesse off guard and put another question in his head that demanded his attention and kept him quiet for the rest of the flight home: If white men's hearts were far from their gods, is that why they tramped through the woods, destroying the land and taking the fish and game Indians needed to live? If so, it seemed to him that returning to the simple life of the old ones was what he and the rest of the world must do. Maybe, he thought, that's what the god of the island had been trying to tell him all along.

###

When Jesse noticed an opening beneath the roots of a dead cottonwood tree, he knew something had taken residence there. He approached the tree, dropped to his belly and stuck his head beneath the exposed roots. The dirt at the lip of the hole consisted of sand and yellow loam that dusted the surrounding snow. Jesse couldn't see much inside, but he detected the faint smell of dead salmon and something musty that told him all he needed to know.

He backed away and quickly retraced the steps to his idling snowmobile. Spring and its meager daylight gave him a sense of urgency. He hurried home, burst through the door and saw his niece's son, eight-year old Martin, sitting on the couch with a book in his lap. The boy was squat and stocky, with red cheeks and the restlessness of a wolverine.

"Let's go," Jesse said. "I got something to show you."

Before the boy could put his book away, Belle stepped out of the kitchen with her jaws clenched. Her hair shone like obsidian and fell in a loose braid. Irritation was evident in her dark penetrating features.

"Leave him be," she said. "Martin's doing school work."

"Can he finish later? We won't be long."

Martin's eyes pleaded his uncle's case. "Is it okay, Mom? I'm almost done."

Belle sighed. "Okay, but you better be back before dinner."

Jesse quickly strode to his bedroom and grasped a rifle and a pair of wire cutters. He told the boy to fetch a flashlight and they sneaked out the front door, hiding the objects from Belle's view.

"Where are we going?" Martin asked, as they hopped onto the snowmobile.

"You'll see."

They rode away from the village, weaving a path through the trees and hilly terrain. They didn't speak over the whine of the engine, but only gazed ahead at the packed trail. Several miles later, Jesse stopped at the base of a slope and killed the engine. Martin dismounted, seemingly eager for an adventure, but Jesse only turned in his seat.

"We have to be careful," he said. "Don't move fast, or speak too loud. And don't do anything to offend the bear."

"A bear? Is that what we came for? You can see them at the dump all summer."

"This one's asleep."

"Are we going to shoot him?"

"No need for that."

"Okay," Martin said with a shrug. "But what do you mean, don't 'offend' the bear?"

Jesse cleaned his fogged glasses. Here was a chance to share the wisdom of his people and teach secrets handed down since *Dotsuna*, the raven, created the world. "Don't brag on yourself, or act too big for your britches. If you do, the bear will tell his friends and they'll lose respect for you. Most of all be polite and thank him."

Jesse cracked open the chamber of his rifle and checked it for a shell. He remembered the winter hunts of his youth, when one of the brave men of the village would crawl into a known bear den and sling a noose around the hibernating animal inside. Once the bear was drawn out—still sleepy and blinking from the brightness of the sun—the hunters would dispatch and butcher it. Jesse tried to recall the rituals associated with such hunts. Certain parts of the animal, for instance, were to be eaten only by men, away from the village, but there was so much more he couldn't remember.

He led Martin to the cottonwood tree and knelt before the hole. Using the flashlight, he peered inside. The cavity sloped downward and the distance between floor and ceiling diminished gradually. Several feet away, against the far edge of the hollow, a young black bear rested with its back to the crevasse. Its breathing was barely perceptible. A ridge of soil and leaf mold was built up around it. Jesse crawled inside and, in a whisper, called Martin into the lip of the opening.

The boy squeezed over Jesse's legs, which were dangling outside the hole.

"Far enough," Jesse said.

Martin studied the animal from a distance. "That's a bear, all right," he said, "but not a very big one."

Jesse scowled over his shoulder. "What did I tell you?"

"Oh, yeah." The boy's voice softened. "I bet he's big for his age, though. And he has real pretty fur."

"That's right. He's a handsome animal." Jesse smiled. He was pleased that Martin was learning truths not taught out of schoolbooks, truths that the god of the island had certainly known. "And he's a powerful bear. You can see that. Just look at his muscles."

Jesse reached into one of his back pockets and pulled out the wire cutters. After telling Martin to stay put, he wormed his way to one of the bear's hind limbs and laid the flashlight beside it. He poked a paw and felt no resistance. Separating two of the toes, he raised the clippers and opened the jaws against the base of a claw. Jesse squeezed, but the cutter blades slipped over the bone-like surface. He tried again and felt the tool bite. The claw fell and a drop of blood emerged.

"Why did you do that?" Martin asked.

"We'll keep it for good luck. It'll grow back before long."

He repeated the procedure with another claw and the bear flinched. A moment of tension followed as they waited for the animal to settle. It eventually resumed its slow, almost impalpable, breathing.

Jesse picked up the claws. "We should go," he whispered. "You can get away with a few things, but you can't change nature. Remember that."

"Okay, but can I show my friends what we got?"

"Let's not worry about that now."

Suddenly the bear raised its long face toward them. Jesse went rigid, but he managed to grab the rifle. He expected the animal to rise and voice displeasure, but it remained quiet and squinted as if trying to focus its eyes. Jesse moved the flashlight so it wouldn't shine too directly at the bear.

"Go," he said to Martin, but the boy didn't move.

Jesse wondered if the bear could be convinced it was only dreaming. "Brother," he said. "In the summer you ate many salmon. The other creatures ran when you came, but it's time to sleep now. We'll leave and let you rest." Jesse handed the flashlight to Martin and nudged him toward the opening.

"Sorry we woke you," the boy said in a whisper. "And thanks for the toenails."

"Go now."

Martin backed outside carrying their source of light and Jesse was left in the dark. Before the chamber went black, he saw the bear rest its head and curl back into a ball. It moaned, but seemingly out of annoyance rather than anger. Jesse was no longer afraid, but exhilarated. He could hear the animal as it tried to get comfortable, its need for sleep stronger than its instinct to attack. He'd convinced it of his good intentions and it had listened.

"Don't think badly of the boy," he said. "Martin is young, but he'll be a good partner to you. I know that much."

Jesse backed out of the hole and stood, swatting the dirt off his pants and parka. He turned his attention to Martin and cleaned him off, too.

"That was neat," the boy said. "Can I see what the nice bear gave us?"

Jesse held out his open hand. The claws were the size of a child's curled finger and black, like the coal they sometimes picked up on the beach. "We shouldn't tell your parents about this," he said, patting Martin's head.

"Why?"

"Because they'll never accept the old ways." And with that Jesse spoke of events that Belle had warned him never to repeat. He told Martin about the god of the island and the many miracles Jesse had experienced while away in the Aleutians. They talked of respect for the woods and how his people once lived with simple tools fashioned from nature's gifts. The stories, he reckoned, were as important as anything the boy would learn from books or school lessons, and he resolved to share everything he knew.

Chapter 5

In the same way Cantor proved the existence of higher order infinities, it stands to reason that there is more than one kind of eternity.

- From Kit Lerner's Journal

Though he couldn't accept the premise that God lived and loved His children, Patch found Kit's words strangely compelling. One particular passage—written the summer before she left for college—further appealed to his need for solitude and renewal.

I'm looking for a place as perfect as Eden, where God can come and not be defiled. Maybe there He'll speak without reservation and explain His plans for me. Nothing would keep me from it. I

would mark my arrival as a new birth and
become the better angel inside of me. Where
might I find such a place?

Patch read the passage again and again, at once ridiculing it, but feeling its quixotic idealism take root in his head. Was there a place where he could be tested and uncover what remained undefiled in him? Might he dispel the ghosts in his mind by getting away? Kit, he decided, had understood a man's need to be alone to think—not like Emily, who after Amanda's passing sought the company of friends and venues to express her grief—but he saw no role for God in such matters. Why seek spiritual gifts among sinners huddled in dark cathedrals, when the holy grandeur of mountains, river valleys and oceans beckoned?

Patch recalled the last religious rite of passage he'd attended. Amanda's funeral had taken place the year of the nation's bicentennial, a week after he was saved from his crippled boat. He remembered driving to the mortuary with Emily, past patriotic banners hanging from streetlights along Nikolai's Main Street—some with the message, "Land of the Free," the others, "Happy Birthday!"

That's when he first challenged the cause for celebration: Can a government make men free? Of course not, he decided, it could no more liberate a man than keep him from having bad dreams.

After the memorial service they left to bury an empty coffin in a corner of Nikolai's only cemetery. Cook Inlet was vast and ravenous, devouring as fully as it acted without conscience. The cursory attempt to find Amanda's body had ended unsuccessfully. Patch understood the need for a ceremony, but he was disturbed by the imitation burial.

"Why are we doing this?" he asked, trying to understand the symbolism. If the box didn't house Amanda's body, would it forever imprison her soul?

Emily took him by an arm and led him over a muddy path, accompanied by a group of mourners and a clergyman Patch had never met. He watched her tuck a strand of blond hair behind an ear. She was as pretty as an heirloom china doll and just as fragile and rare, a gift to be protected, but he had no idea how to shelter her from the cosmic joke at play in their lives.

They came to a cleared section of the bluff, where waves could be heard crashing onto the beach below. A mist hung in the air and hid their view of the sea, but its fecund scent was a reminder of life's ebb and flow. Emily pulled her wool blazer around her throat.

"I need this place to visit," she said, "a place to bring flowers and pay my respects. I want to think of Amanda as being at rest somewhere and not drifting about in the tide."

They stood before the open grave, Patch in a blue suit he hadn't worn in a decade. Amanda, he thought, had never been a girl to seek rest. He found comfort in the knowledge that she'd loved the ocean. So what if her greatest passion had led to her undoing? The same could be said of more than a few folks, saints being as susceptible as sinners.

While Emily hoped their daughter was loved by a being more powerful than a human could reason, the idea of heaven made Patch shiver. Why, he wondered, would Amanda—or anyone—seek eternal rest? Death, without Jesus, got you there, too. And why must she sing praises to God all day? Did the Almighty have a self-esteem problem? As for Patch, he chose to think of Amanda as free to be where and when she wished, a girl with no constraints to her being. To aspire for anything less would have left him with no aspiration, at all.

Of course, it was a wish he held for Kit, too. At the very least he hoped she was finally liberated from her oppressive guilt. If so, there was hope for him, as well. He knew with painful clarity, that faith wasn't requisite to feelings of remorse. Since Kit wasn't the first woman he'd left behind, he had plenty of wrongs from which to be redeemed.

He began to make regular trips to Anchorage, where he called on Mrs. Lerner and visited places mentioned in the journal. By all appearances Kit had preferred solitude, like a drive along Turnagin Arm. Her writings mentioned associates only in passing. Aside from her activities with a math club, she said nothing about school. In fact she seemed to have lived in her own head, avoiding people and other distractions, but there were exceptions to the rule. Desperate to know more about her, Patch attended a service at her church and stayed past its conclusion to seek a private chat with the minister. They sat in a windowless office, where a painting of Jesus smiled over a shelf of books and the reverend's balding head.

"I can't tell you much," the man said. He was large, with a neck that bulged over the top of his collar. "Kit would come in late and sit in the back. Usually she was gone before the sermon was over."

"But you must have talked to her—in passing, at least."

"Sure, newsy stuff about school and things like that. She wasn't an easy girl to talk to—kind of quiet. She used to attend our youth activities, but stopped without explanation. That was four or five years ago. We kept inviting her, but she was busy. At least that's what she said."

Suddenly Patch understood the depth of Kit's despair. Five years ago she'd been fifteen and pregnant. He stared at the minister, believing the man to be honorable, but wanting to shout at him all the same: Do you have any idea what was taken from her? How she lost more than a burgeoning life, but something more intimately connected to her? Have you any idea how hopelessly Kit sought absolution?

"Still, you saw her now and then, didn't you?" he asked.

The man nodded. "It was like she couldn't stay away, but I got the sense she only tolerated us. Kit would visit in fifteen-minute snippets and at the oddest of times, too. She'd find a corner and pray up a storm. If the doors were locked, she would sit on the front steps. I thought the girl might need counseling. Then I found out she was some kind of numbers genius—accepted to a very good school. I don't remember which."

"Berkeley."

"Ah, that's right. Well, it seems you know more about her than I do."

"I doubt that. Can you tell me what she was like?

"I told you, she was a quirky girl—very idealistic. The few times we talked in earnest, she was pushing some agenda or another."

Patch sat up straight. This was new information to him. "An agenda," he said. "Like what, for instance?"

"Oh, let's see. Once it was a tutoring program for kids in a half-way house. We tried to make a go of it, but things went missing here at the church and there was some property damage, too, so we shut the program down. Kit was upset, but what could I do? I have a flock to watch over. Otherwise, the girl kept to herself. I wish I could say more. It's sad, really, what happened to her."

Sad? It was a travesty, Patch thought, one that might have been prevented if someone had paid attention. Then a second idea, carrying the impact of a reprimand, occurred to him: The same could be said about Amanda.

"Did Kit have any friends?" he asked.

"I met her mother once—a real pistol—and they seemed to be close. Other than that, I don't know. Have you talked to Pamela? I think that was the mother's name."

The conversation led Patch to a startling possibility: that by his possession of the young woman's journal, he knew most of what was knowable about her. It was a notion that bothered him and he wondered if anyone had truly loved and honored Kit. In his mind devotion wasn't possible—not without full knowledge of her sorrow.

"Is there anyone else who might know more?"

The reverend put his fingertips together and settled back into his chair. "There's a member of our congregation, a fellow named Cooper. He used to give Kit rides to church—that was before she could drive herself. I think he lives in the same complex as the girl did."

"Cooper?" Patch wondered where he'd heard that name before and then he remembered: It was the fellow who'd started Kit on her journey by getting her pregnant. If there was a villain in the story, it would be him. "He's a member of your congregation?" Patch asked.

"That's right. It was a nice gesture on his part—driving Kit to church until she could get her own license. Few people would have been so helpful."

"He sounds like a real gem. I suppose your church is full of good folks like that."

The reverend's eyes narrowed, as if he was trying to make sense of the comment. From somewhere a clock ticked off the passing seconds, when suddenly the man sat forward and frowned. "I have to ask," he said. "Why are you so interested in Kit, anyway?"

"Like I told you, I found her body."

"I understand that, but you didn't end her life, did you? Seems to me you're a bit obsessed about the girl and that worries me. You have to find a way to forget. She was a mixed up kid who thought too deeply. What happened to her was inevitable—lost souls wander—and think of it this way, if you hadn't been so observant and seen her on your flight last year, you wouldn't even be here, right?"

Patch considered the reverend's comment. "No, I probably wouldn't, but there'd still be a reason for a loving God to grieve."

"So let God do His business. The way I see it, we take care of ourselves first and then the people we love. When that's taken care of, we extend our spheres of influence and help where we can. In Kit's case, she was never in your control. So you have to believe that God has taken care of her and will continue to do so. Have faith in that and take comfort in it. Does that make sense?"

"Sure," Patch said, but his thoughts were contrary to his claim. The only part that rang true was that he'd had no control over Kit's circumstances. And that was because he wielded no control at all.

When evening fell, Patch returned to the apartment building where Kit had lived and searched the mailboxes for a name. He found what he was looking for and knocked on the corresponding door. A man's voice sounded from inside.

"Who is it?"

"I've got your check," Patch said.

The door opened and a man stood in the entryway. He was nothing like Patch had imagined: instead, pot-gutted and burly, with a receding hairline. The smell of beer wafted from inside. That much was consistent.

"Are you Cooper?"

"Yeah," the man said. "Did you mention a check?"

"I did. Check this out. It's from Kit Lerner."

Patch stepped forward, clenched his fist and struck the man squarely on the jaw. Cooper tumbled back and fell onto a coffee table. "What the hell?" he said and put a hand to his lips. Blood spilled down his chin and he winced. "Who are you?"

"Never mind that." Patch held up a page from Kit's journal, an entry she'd written after years of introspection, just days before she left for the bush. "You deserve a lot more than what I just gave you, but I'll leave this behind and let you consider what you did."

Patch dropped the paper and saw recognition on the man's face as he scanned it.

*I was fifteen and that wasn't a secret, so he told
me to keep what we'd done quiet—that we'd shared,
in his words, a special gift.*

That Special Gift

*Head against headboard,
Trying to ease his entry,
He whispering words,
Not out of affection,
But from a sudden urgency.*

*And I wonder:
Should romance be company
To the smell of sweat,
Cigarette-stained fingers,
And stale beer?*

Patch watched for the man's reaction, remembering that he'd come on a whim, only hoping to learn more about Kit, but by striking Cooper, he'd certainly lost that opportunity. Damning his own impulsiveness, he started to leave.

"Wait," Cooper said. "Tell me where you got this."

Patch stopped at the door. He had no intention of getting chummy, but thought he could impress upon Cooper the cost of getting a young girl pregnant. "It's from Kit's diary," he whispered.

"Diary? I didn't know she kept one. Listen, I'm a damn fool—I know that—but what do you plan on doing with this?"

The question nudged Patch in an unexpected direction to consider what the police might say about Kit's journal. He could report Cooper to authorities—an idea that appealed to Patch's desire for justice—but would any judgment compensate for what had happened? No, there was no possibility of justice for Kit, but maybe he could accomplish the purpose of his visit.

"I hope this gnaws at you the rest of your life," Patch said, "but Kit's mother is the only other person who knows what you did and she's in no condition to press charges. Your secret is safe as long as you're not a predator."

Cooper seemed to relax. "I figured this was one of the poems Kit used to write and bury," he said. "I've fretted about what might show up someday."

"Buried poems?"

"That's right. Kit used to leave them in the strangest of places. She said they were offerings."

"Where?" Patch asked.

"You know that trail overlooking Bird Creek? Mostly there, but other than that, I have no idea."

Patch nodded. He knew of the place and resolved to climb the trail, hoping to catch another glimpse into the woman's life and thoughts.

"What's your connection to Kit?" Cooper asked.

"No connection at all. Unless you count how I found her dead in a tent."

The man's eyebrows furrowed. "Dead? How?"

"She could've died a dozen different ways, but it was cold and starvation that got her. I figure you're to blame."

Cooper's shoulders sagged and the pain on his face was disarming. He looked as if he might cry, which embarrassed Patch, even caused him some regret. He thought it was long past time to go, but decided to apologize first. "I hadn't planned on hitting you," he said. "It just happened."

"What *had* you intended?"

Patch shrugged. "I wanted to ask about Kit."

"Then we're alike on that account. You might as well sit."

Patch took a place on the sofa and Cooper fished a handkerchief from his back pocket and wiped the blood off his chin. For a minute neither man spoke, but sat as if poured from concrete. The sound of traffic filtered through the walls.

"What can you tell me about her?" Patch asked.

The man took a long time to answer—so long that Patch wondered if he'd heard the question. Finally Cooper turned and said, "Are you a religious man?"

"What does that have to do with Kit?"

"Nothing, I'm just wondering how you'll take this."

Patch nodded and said, "I was raised to believe in God. It never took."

"Okay then." Cooper stared at the poem in his lap and shook his head. "Kit was damn-near perfect," he said. "In fact, the worst I can say about her is she was God-loving fanatical. After she got in trouble—"

"Got in trouble? You say that as if you played no part."

The man's eyes fell. "You're right. I'm not proud of what I did, but my point is that Kit changed afterward. It wasn't enough for her to be a church-goer anymore. She was always trying to prove her worth—always working out her salvation."

"How so?" Patch asked.

"I could tell you all kinds of shit, but here's a story for you. When I got back from the North Slope, I found out she'd adopted a dog—a three-legged mutt. It was against the rules of the complex here, but she got away with it. The dog was quiet enough and when people heard its story, they didn't complain."

"The dog had a story?"

"Cancer. The mutt had developed a tumor in its hip and the owners were going to put it down. Kit took the dog off their hands and arranged to have its leg amputated—paid for it herself, along with a chemo treatment."

"And the dog lived?"

"For only six more months, but Kit said it was worth the trouble and that she'd do it again. See my point? The girl was so intent to help and do no harm—to be like Jesus Himself—she opened herself up to all kinds of misery."

Patch had heard people blame the devil for their problems, but this was something new. "God made her vulnerable?"

"In a way, yes."

The more Patch thought of the assertion, the more it concurred with his worldview. "Can you help me understand something?" he said. "There's a strange entry in Kit's journal, one she wrote at her final camp. She apparently buried something—a symbol of her sin, she called it. Would you know anything about that?"

"A symbol of her sin? No, but that's exactly how she talked—saying one thing to mean another. It's just a figure of speech, I'm sure."

"I don't think so. Her diary is pretty clear. She says: 'In a place where the river cuts into the bank I hid the reminders of my sin. I won't return to it ever again.'"

"You memorized her words?"

Patch nodded, but he didn't recite the passage that followed—a phrase he deemed even more significant—which in combination with Kit's talk of solitude had formed the nucleus of a plan developing in his head.

I finally feel as if I've been redeemed.

"I can't help you," Cooper said. "Kit could be a strange one—that's for sure. She's probably just talking about another poem."

No, Patch thought, that can't be, not if she'd been writing and hiding them all along. He stood and walked to the door, suddenly believing it was possible to know too much. He wondered if he'd sought flaws in Kit, to uncover a cosmic justice in her passing. There was little need for another example of the good dying young. "I've overstayed my welcome," he said.

"You can't go. I got questions, too."

"Maybe that's our penance," Patch said, but even as he stepped into the night he knew his search for answers had only begun.

Patch found it before he had a chance to catch his breath. At first he thought it was a piece of garbage, but the baggie contained a folded poem written in Kit's distinctive hand. It was buried with a corner exposed, beside a boulder that was marked with a palm-sized cross. The crag overlooked Turnagin Arm and farther out the rugged Kenai Mountains. Patch could see the tide racing through the riddled dunes of the mudflats below him. It had taken him more than an hour to walk the two miles of steep trail, but he was grateful he'd made the effort.

At the summit he sat on an exposed rock and worked gingerly to unfold the paper. Though the print was blurred from moisture, it was still legible and he read the words several times.

Driving through a blizzard
At top speed,
Darkness settling,
Headlights on bright.
The view out the windshield:
Mesmerizing.

That's how I imagine it.

We are then weightless souls
Whisked away at light's speed,
Finally seeing what had been there all along,
Hidden behind a façade:
Time is but another location.

Then all the pieces fit,
And we're privy to both past and future—
Including the narrow corridors of mortality—
Suddenly earning full knowledge,
Rendering us unable to suppress the notion:
"Aha!"

To that future self, I speak:
Don't judge me as I do now,
With a stern eye that belabors each point,
Recollecting the infinite number
And irreconcilable costs of my shortcomings.

Let's agree, instead:
Yes, I wield unrighteous dominion
And my faults are limitless,
But somewhere beyond time,
Against all odds and expectations,
I am you.

For an hour Patch searched for other messages, but finding none, he decided it was time to go. Along the downhill trail and with the spectacular view of an untouched land before him, Kit's words reached him in a way that he couldn't fault or ridicule. Had she become the weightless soul of her speculation? If so, Patch hoped she could share with him the hard-earned wisdom of someone privy to both past and future.

###

The journal mentioned a sporting goods store near the intersection of Northern Lights and the Old Seward Highway. Patch located the place and found it filled with the kind of equipment he razzed clients for bringing. Everything was too pretty, he thought, the result of some marketing guru's scheme to turn a hike into a reason to shop. Still, as he studied the merchandise displays and compared their prices against meticulous notes Kit had kept, the idea of a getaway muscled its way into his consciousness and took up space.

While he stood in front of a boot rack, a young woman dressed in khaki shorts and a matching cotton tee shirt approached. Her dark hair was tied up in back, with flyaway strands at the base of the bun. She wore a perfume he didn't recognize. A tag on her shirt read: Maggie.

"Can I help you?" she asked.

Patch wondered if the young woman had ever waited on Kit. If so, might she remember the occasion? "I'm just looking," he said.

"Let me know if I can help."

She was about to walk away, but Patch touched her lightly on the arm. "You might tell me about these."

The boot in his hand was the same brand Kit had worn. While he held it upside down and studied the grooved sole, Maggie summarized its attributes: It was light, constructed of man-made materials, and comfortable—perfect for an extended trip. "But if you're planning to be out in cold weather," she added, "you'll do better with something heavier."

"I'll take it." By speaking those words Patch settled a matter he'd only begun to consider. He felt a curious exhilaration, as if he'd come upon a familiar trail after being lost.

"Sure, I'll find your size in back."

The boot fit, but Patch wasn't ready to check out. He quizzed Maggie about fleece pants and the jackets hanging on their racks. He examined socks and caps, mittens and lightweight packs. He spent half an hour considering the finer aspects of kayak construction and decided to buy everything the young woman recommended.

"You bought a lot," she said. "Especially for someone who was only looking."

"I guess you sold me."

As Patch waited at the checkout counter he considered what he'd accomplished. At first he'd known only this: that by his presence in the store he'd felt a strange affinity to Kit, as if he could see the world through her eyes. The effect was like adding another line to a connect-the-dots puzzle. An image gained clarity in his head, offering a hint of what a person might do to dispel shame and gain pardon.

Suddenly Patch realized he'd done a surprising thing. In the time it took to buy a pair of boots, he committed himself to do what he'd only wished he could after Amanda died. If not clear in his mind, he at least had direction. In solitude on the Killborn River he would mourn his losses and offer his unplumbed sorrow as penance. The vision of it conformed to his sense of a man's duty: If he couldn't commune with whatever dictated the vagaries of life, he would at least negotiate with it and seek the return of a clear conscience. But as unlikely and meager as these efforts might be, it was all he could think to do. Gutting it out had only led him to more sorrow. Peace of mind, he hoped, would come by tracing Kit's footsteps and burying the reminders of his own sins along the way.

Maggie carried out a portion of the equipment and helped tie the kayak onto the roof of Patch's vehicle. For the entire time she chatted spiritedly, asking where he was going and what he was planning to do. Patch kept his answers short and cryptic—I'll be checking out a place or two and I'm hoping to catch a trophy. She smiled in a way that caused him to take a long look at her.

"Thanks for your help," he said, suddenly liking what he saw.

"No problem. But I hope you didn't buy all this just to get my attention."

"Excuse me?"

"Maybe I read you wrong, but it seemed like you wanted to ask me something."

Though he sensed a guarded purpose in Maggie's comment, Patch knew she was right. From the moment he'd walked into the store the spirit of something familiar touched him. Kit had spent hours there. Maybe a part of her still inhabited the place. He hoped Maggie could tell him about her.

"Actually," Patch said. "There is something I would like to talk to you about."

"Good. Why don't we get together around seven? There's a steakhouse where the road crosses Spenard. Do you know it?"

That evening Patch walked into the restaurant and saw Maggie wave from a booth next to one of the front windows. She stood, wearing a short skirt and tank top. He took note of her long muscular legs and graceful neck. Her hair was drawn out of its bun and fell over her left shoulder in a French braid.

She asked for a porterhouse steak, which surprised Patch. "I thought all you young people were vegetarians," he said, before ordering the king crab plate.

Maggie shook her head, saying her old man was a rancher from eastern Oregon and that beef was in her blood. "Our herd is known all over the state. But that's mostly on account of Dad's Hereford bulls."

"Prizes, are they?"

"Sure, and just about the horniest animals to walk the earth—no pun intended."

Patch laughed, beginning to feel a bond to her. She'd lived on a farm, in a region similar to the valley where he grew up. Patch asked about her life and Maggie answered candidly. She attended the University of Alaska, studied psychology and got grades that qualified her for academic probation. Her two roommates were hockey players on the university team and she'd recently dumped a boyfriend who left for Kodiak to fish for shrimp.

"What else do you want to know?" she said as their food arrived. "You've asked everything about me but my favorite color and turn-ons."

"What's your favorite color?"

Patch was getting titillated just sitting across from her. He'd never heard a woman talk the way she did—with a seductive lilt and words full of double entendres. Sometimes she came to a punch line or an important detail in a story and reached out to touch his hand. The contact alone was enough to make him quiver, but each time she bent toward him the neckline of her shirt fell and allowed him a glimpse of her black tube-top bra and a hint of cleavage. Patch wondered if she was making a pass, or if all young people teased in the same way.

"There's something I wanted to ask you," he said, trying to keep the conversation safe and honorable.

"Go ahead. I hope it involves whips and handcuffs."

Patch chuckled nervously. He took a photograph from his shirt pocket and placed it on the table. It was the picture of Kit standing on the shore of Upper Killborn Lake. "Do you know this woman?"

"I can't place her. She looks familiar, though."

"She was a customer at your store."

Maggie's eyes showed sudden recognition. "Now that you mention it, I do remember her. She bought a ton of stuff—said she was going on a long trip. Why do you ask? Is she a runaway girlfriend or something?"

"Never met the lady, but she buried something on her trip and I hope to find it."

"Buried something? Like treasure?"

"No, nothing like that, but can you tell me anything more about her?"

Maggie rocked her head from side to side. "Well," she said. "What I do remember is that she was always jotting things down in a binder—prices and such. It seemed strange. We thought she might be a spy. Then she bought all that equipment. When I asked where she was going, her answer was a bit goofy. It was about someone named John and baptism and a place with lots of water."

Patch sat up straight. The reference brought to his mind an obscure passage in the Bible:

> *And John also was baptizing in Aenon near to*
> *Salim, because there was much water there.*

He knew the scripture, because his father used to quote it, supporting the Mormon requirement of baptism by immersion (why else would John need a lot of water?). Yet to Kit the reference had most likely held a different meaning. Did the Killborn River—a place with much water—represent her chance for redemption? An opportunity to be cleansed of her failings?

"Hey," Maggie said, interrupting his thoughts. "Is that why you wanted to see me? To ask about her?"

"Yes. Why?"

"I was hoping to get lucky, that's all."

The look on her face—the combination of youthful optimism mixed with something feral—made Patch lose his breath. "Get lucky?" he said. "I could be your dad."

"I like older men. Besides, you keep yourself in shape. I can see that."

Patch wanted to take her by the hand and lead her to his room at the Golden Lion where he'd been staying the last few days. He wanted to undress her slowly, run his hands over the soft curves of her body and press his lips to hers. The thought made his head spin.

"Believe me," he said. "You're a hell of a temptation and I'll probably kick myself later for this, but what you're suggesting—it wouldn't be right. I had a daughter once."

"Had?"

"Amanda died when she was twelve."

"Then you didn't see her with hormones kicking in. Listen, you don't have to be interested, but don't let the reason be our age difference. I'm fine with that."

Patch considered various reasons to pay the bill and drive off alone. For one, he'd only had one woman in his life and she divorced him over a year ago. That meant he'd be rusty, but sex didn't require a refresher course, did it? More importantly, his lack of practice had been intentional, a way to avoid getting hurt or hurting someone again. On the other hand, a little recreation never bothered anyone. It was another issue, though, that troubled Patch the most: Did he want to be a man like Cooper, preying on the innocence and curiosity of youth? To this he reminded himself: Maggie wasn't fourteen and she could probably teach him a thing or two.

"We shouldn't," Patch said, but he saw her sitting there, fresh and pretty, and decided to keep his options open. He hoped to make the right decision later, but knew it was a risky strategy. "There's no reason why we can't buy a single-malt whiskey and watch some TV back in my room."

From then the evening lost its focus, like a drive through fog. Patch got a general sense of it, but lost track of the specific bumps and turns. Sex, he decided, had become a high-stakes game of Twister. Maggie's choked utterances—touch me there, try it like this, let me move here—were distracting and more than a little intimidating. Straddled over him, she finally shuddered and fell to his chest, and it came to Patch as a great relief.

He finished with a fury that was as frightening as it was carnal. Later as he tried to sleep with a taut body twitching in unexpected ways next to him—after that inexplicable moment when his passion transformed from the most to the least urgent aspect of his life—he heard Emily's voice cry out of his half dreams. Awake to the smell of sex and the warmth of unfamiliar flesh, Patch wondered if he'd traded a moment of pleasure for another variety of guilt to last a lifetime. Remorse, he decided, was the thing he knew most intimately and that fact led him to a startling conclusion: Baptism wasn't such a bad idea.

Chapter 6

Good people aren't tempted by evil, but sometimes they have to choose the lesser of evils.

- From Kit Lerner's Journal

Winter rallied with a dry cover of snow and a bone-splitting cold. The deep lake at Kaknu's southern border remained open. It gave rise to an icy fog that floated ghost-like over the water and painted the spruce and leafless birches along the hillside with frost. Half-hidden among the trees a dozen clapboard homes lie scattered. Their chimney smoke hovered along the hillside as if frozen in space.

While the temperature dropped outside, Jesse sat at dinner with his niece and her family. Heat from a wood-burning stove filled the room and the smell of spruce gum was heavy in the air. From where Jesse sat he could touch the kitchen counter behind him, or step into the living room in four easy paces. Simulated-wood paneling and family pictures covered the walls.

Jesse tried to appear attentive while his niece spoke. He was used to her long-winded speeches. They usually began when he mentioned the god of the island or the lives of the ancient ones, but this time her arguments seemed to be heading somewhere. That made him nervous.

"Sure," she said. "It's fine to appreciate the past, but you can't step back into time without jeopardizing your future. You'll let the twentieth century pass you by!"

Jesse paled under Belle's gaze. She spoke from across the Formica dinner table, saying her status in the village would be tarnished if their household became the subject of jokes. "You need a job," she added. "It'll do you good."

As president of Tuekhna Corp, Belle was in a position to give him work. Tuekhna was one of the state-sponsored corporations organized after native land claims were settled a decade earlier. It owned stretches of Bristol Bay watershed and received income from mining and timber contracts. It invested in mutual funds and fish processing plants. Most of the paid positions in the village were managed by the company.

"We have a job opening," Belle said. "Once you make a few dollars, you'll see how the system works."

Jesse remembered his month working as a cannery worker in Dutch Harbor and frowned. "I made money before," he said. "I didn't like it."

Belle's husband, Clarence, cleared his throat. He was a tall, barrel-chested man, with a beaked nose and pockmarked face. People thought of him as a town Indian, not only because he

91

was from Fairbanks, but also for his highbrow job as the school principal. He was an "apple"—a white man in a red body—but the parents in the village still considered him a role model for their children.

"What kind of job are you talking about?" Clarence asked.

"Hang on, I'm getting to it."

Their son, Martin, pushed his bowl of stew away. "If Uncle has to work," he said, "who'll take care of me when I come home from school?"

Jesse looked at Belle, the same question having occurred to him. He loved the boy and spoiled him with undivided attention. The dreams he had for his people found fertile ground in Martin, who was Jesse's main reason for not living alone in his fish camp.

"Don't worry," Belle said. "He'll be up early and done with work before you get home."

"Not that," Clarence whispered.

Belle quieted her husband with a stern look. "It's an important and necessary position."

"What are you saying?" Jesse asked.

"It's like this," she said. "We need a new honey truck driver."

Jesse felt his heart sink into his stomach. Even if he was interested in work for wages, he wouldn't choose to drive the honey truck. In his mind it stood for everything wrong with how his people had changed, their actions showing little reverence for nature. Yet what more could he expect from them? They no longer followed the caribou, or set up fish camps on distant waterways. The culture of their fathers had been lost, replaced by the honey pot.

In Kaknu, he reminded himself, there were few toilets or outhouses, so people got along by using buckets. Each morning they set their containers outside to be picked up and dumped. The driver took the contents to a place outside of town called the honey pot. It was an open pool of sewage, its stench an evil presence.

"I'd like you to take the job," Belle said.

Clarence frowned. "You don't want your uncle doing that."

"Why not? It might lead to something better."

Jesse remained silent and wondered where he might go after honey truck driver—school janitor, maybe? Though his yearning was a colorless thing, he knew that a job wouldn't take him where he wanted to go. Still, Jesse had already decided to do as his niece asked. Nothing could stand in the way of her notions of progress.

A decade earlier—as new graduates of the University of Alaska in Anchorage—Belle and Clarence had gotten hitched and left for fortunes elsewhere. In Seattle Clarence entered a master's degree program and the two former bush bumpkins hobnobbed with artists and smart people. They learned a lot about the world, but missed Alaska and the association of Indian friends. Two years later, when Clarence was offered a teaching position in Kaknu, they jumped at the chance to return to Belle's childhood home.

Though they seemed excited to be among their people again, six years of city life had caused them to forget the inconvenience of living in the bush. It was autumn, so getting their home wired and plumbed before freeze up wasn't possible, but they figured an outhouse was a good place to start. Within a grove of spruce trees behind their house Clarence dug a deep hole and built a two-seat facility over it.

Winter came and Belle went out to use the privy. An hour later she hadn't returned and Clarence was worried. He went outside calling for her and heard a whimper from within the outhouse. Belle, he soon learned, was still inside, crying and shivering from the cold. She couldn't get off the seat. Her rear end was frozen to it.

Clarence got a crowbar and pried the top off the toilet. He carried the weight of the plywood, while Belle—her jeans still around her ankles—walked on hands and knees across the snow into the house. It was an image that horrified Jesse, who thought they were involved in a strange bit of sex play, but after averting his eyes and learning what had happened, he did his best not to chuckle.

Once the connection between Belle's rump and the seat thawed, Clarence pulled off the plywood cover and exposed a frostbite ring that was sore for weeks. Needless to say, they saw the wisdom in using buckets, but they planned more earnestly to bring running water and a toilet to their home. By the following August a construction crew from Dillingham had installed a generator, dug a cesspool and otherwise completed the home's transformation.

It was obvious to Jesse that arguing with his niece was futile. Anyone who could bring hot running water to the bush might demand and accomplish anything. It caused Jesse to consider a notion that had left random tracks through his head since his time in the Aleutians. Belle no longer needed the honey pot, but did progress lead to improvement? It seemed obvious to him that every modern advance his people took caused their hearts to step backward. How many of them could weave baskets out of willow? None, he decided, ticking off the names and faces of the women in Kaknu. Tupperware satisfied that need now. How might Velcro further impair their lives?

From Killborn Lake's outlet the river flowed less than five miles to the ocean. Off the coast, where the water emptied into Bristol Bay, humpbacked whales passed northbound in the spring and southbound in the fall. From time to time a whale beached itself there and gave the villagers a cause for celebration. The people rejoiced, not only for the meat, but also for the muktuk, the thick blubber that was a favorite food.

A week before Jesse was to begin driving the honey truck a young whale became lost early in its migration. Separated from its mother, the animal weakened and stranded itself, providing a gift to the village.

Two men on snowmobiles discovered the animal and notified their friends. Jesse, who normally would have helped with the butchering, was already in bed knowing that an early first day of work awaited him. A party of men and women from Kaknu labored through the night, using gas lanterns for light and drawing warmth from a bonfire. They took care to peel and carve the muktuk from the carcass and, in the wee hours of that morning, the blubber was parceled out into clean plastic containers and left in front of each home.

Later, with the fog thick off the water and the sun yet to rise, Jesse made his rounds to gather the honey buckets and mistook the whale blubber for human waste. The error was understandable, since he couldn't look into the receptacles for fear of getting sick. Yet as he lifted another full container, Jesse whistled in astonishment at people's capacity for defecation.

"What do they do," he whispered, "hold it for a week?"

He wasn't aware of the blunder until Rodney Baktuit showed up at Belle's house later that morning. The man's sparse mustache seemed to stand on end with his fury. He dropped a plastic bag full of feces-covered muktuk and yelled, "Can't you tell the difference between crap and candy?"

Jesse looked into the bag and the stink hit him in the face. Minutes earlier, he'd finally stopped gagging over the memory of his labor. He jerked his head away and grimaced, not only from the smell, but the reminder of the work he must perform again the next day.

"I can't dump it now," he said. "It's supposed to be in a bucket. Just leave it outside your house and I'll take care of it tomorrow."

The veins in Rodney's neck seemed ready to burst as he held the bag open. "Look in there. I found this in the honey pot. You threw away our muktuk."

"Muktuk?" In the daylight Jesse could better distinguish the various components in the bag, but all he could think of was the strength of will (not to mention the ironclad stomach) required to fish an object out of the open sewer. "You got this yourself? That must have been a chore."

"What are you going to do about it?"

Jesse shrugged. Hadn't he done his duty by dumping the containers set outside the village homes? What else did Rodney expect? "I did my job," he said. "Do you want me to wash it off now?"

Rodney shook his head. He turned and left the bag on the porch, muttering to himself as he followed a footpath through the trees.

Belle returned in the early afternoon and asked Jesse if he'd brought his work home. By the tone in her voice he knew she was talking about the bag outside. He described his encounter with Rodney and spent the next two hours watching her roll her eyes and chew her bottom lip. While preparing dinner she didn't speak, but raised a clamor nonetheless. The frying pan landed with force on the stove. Plates and silverware clattered onto the table. The noise seemed to frighten Martin, who sat in the living room, reading a primer from school.

"Jesse," Belle finally said. "This was not your finest hour. I'll try to protect you, but people will be pissed. And it couldn't have come at a worse time. I may need to terminate you. It depends on what happens at the association meeting."

Jesse was afraid to ask what she meant by termination, but hoped it wouldn't involve a firearm. On second thought, he told himself, if it meant he could stop gathering buckets, termination might be the way to go.

###

Kaknu's center—socially as well as physically—was its school, the place where people met for traditional potlatch and other gatherings. The state had spared no expense in its construction. It was a two-story, squared-log building standing at the edge of Killborn Lake. Its large picture windows faced the water, giving it the look of an upscale resort.

Two days after Jesse had taken over as the honey truck driver, Belle officiated in a Tuekhna Corp meeting held at the school. Natives from Kaknu and other neighboring bush locations gathered, as they did twice a year, to hear a summary of the company's financial results. Of most concern was the value of the next dividend. The payment was a vital part of the people's income—large enough, at times, to purchase a snowmobile or skiff.

As important as these matters were, the meeting was equally necessary as a chance to mingle and share news. Young children entered the gymnasium with necks bent and eyes studying the crossbeams and ceiling lights. They passed the drinking fountain and their faces brightened at the arc of water that sprang from it. To harness the water, their smiles seemed to say, was like controlling the river, and if the village could control the river, anything might be possible.

The people began to assemble early Saturday morning and the sounds of tribal drums and folk songs echoed over the lake. The elders, dressed in fur parkas and mukluks, performed traditional dances. Down a locker-lined hallway a teenage girl strummed her guitar while a group of her friends sang Beatles' tunes. The tables were set with traditional fare: moose jerky and hotdogs, stink fish and chili, seal oil and macaroni.

The program started early in the afternoon with nearly 400 people sitting cross-legged on the floor. Jesse was disheartened over his whale blubber mistake and needed Martin's encouragement to attend. Together they sat near the center of the gym, not far from the front, commenting on events of the day.

Belle called the meeting to order by first introducing the school basketball team. As she displayed their new uniforms, her husband spoke of Tuekhna Corp's sponsorship of the local athletic program. Clarence, who had coached the Kaknu Cohoes for three winning seasons, spoke confidently of further victories and championships.

Excitement mounted as the team members returned to their seats and Belle announced a surprise. She gestured toward an entryway and five white men in formal attire walked into the gym. Two of them held trumpets, one a French horn, and another a trombone. The last to enter was a longhaired man with wire-frame glasses who carried a tuba. Three helpers from the village set up folding chairs and music stands. Martin giggled at the unusual procession and Jesse put an arm around the boy.

Belle introduced the musicians as students from the University of Alaska, and then she added without fanfare: "They've come to perform a few numbers."

As the men played, Jesse listened with interest. One piece in particular appealed to him. It had started out like a sad cry, the separate parts joining like the weave in a drab shirt. Then unexpectedly the sound changed. He couldn't say it had turned into something joyful, but neither was it sad anymore. Jesse realized it signaled a decision, a promise to endure despite difficulty.

The music gave him hope. Ever since the muktuk incident, people had avoided him and Rodney's words: "Can't you tell the difference between crap and candy?" stung in his memory. Likewise, Belle appeared edgy and anxious, especially as time for her Tuekhna report approached. Jesse wondered how she would deal with the subject of his stupidity once it came up. As for him, he resolved to hold his head high, no matter the result of the discussion.

After a half-hour of play the musicians left to take a short break and the villagers stood to exercise their legs. While the crowd mingled, Jesse saw two men standing near the tuba. No one seemed to notice as they melted into the crowd with silly grins on their faces.

The musicians returned for another set and settled into their chairs. One of the trumpet players counted time and the crowd quieted. The composition that followed was powerful and grand, but Jesse could tell something was wrong. It lacked the deep drum-like sound he'd heard in the earlier pieces and the trombonist was glancing strangely at the tuba player.

The only noise the longhaired man could coax from his instrument was a strange vibration and a throaty groan, like the mating call of a bull moose. The tuba player stopped and adjusted his valves. He started to play again and the moose-grunt continued. Only one thing to do, he seemed to think— blow hard. He took a full breath and reached for the sky. At first the vibration resumed, but suddenly there was a pop like an inner ear clearing at a high altitude and a burst of tuba sound emerged.

Yet something still wasn't right. There was a muted quality to the playing and Jesse saw something rise up from inside the tuba bell. A few people pointed. Others were holding their hands to their faces. Belle mouthed the words: Oh my.

Before long people weren't pointing so much as holding their stomachs and laughing. When the music reached its full-bore finale, the room exploded with cheers and applause. While the other musicians bowed from where they sat, the tuba player ignored the ovation. He rested his horn in his lap and reached into the bell, but the object spilled before he could grab it. A breeze from a heating vent blew the article away and a dozen boys chased it.

"What's that?" Martin asked, his eyes sparkling.

Jesse wasn't an expert (though he'd purchased a few and studied them thoroughly—even put one on once) but he guessed it was a Trojan brand, one of the perfumed kind with a receptacle at the end and ribs to heighten sensitivity. It was blown up to look like a giant erection, but it was crooked.

"Ask your dad," he said.

Amid the confusion an old man in the audience yelled, "Is that what they call safe sax?" and everybody laughed. Only a few weeks earlier, people from the Department of Health had called on the village to explain the consequences of a new disease and the precautions one should take to avoid it.

Belle hollered, "Aren't they great?" and another enthusiastic round of applause followed. Jesse looked at his niece's smiling face and realized what she was doing. The music and discussion about basketball had fulfilled a purpose. Belle was giving everyone a good time—distracting them, he figured—so she wouldn't have to terminate her uncle.

###

After the musicians finished their performance, Clarence rolled a slide projector to the front of the gymnasium and set up a movie screen. Belle stood again and a hush came over the gathering. She wore blue jeans, a corduroy jacket, and a green felt shirt. Her hair was out of its braid and fell over her shoulders. When she opened her mouth to speak, Jesse saw a twitch in her dark eyes that he'd never seen before. It made him wonder if something other than the lost whale blubber was bothering her.

Only a few days earlier she'd gone to Dillingham and returned the same evening to have a whispered conversation with Clarence. Jesse tried to recall their discussion and remembered Belle saying there'd been a problem in a fund. It was the result, she said, of unwise investments in something called IO strips. A lot of money had been lost.

"Just like that?" Clarence asked. "Into thin air?"

There was anger in Belle's reply. "Corbin says it's the nature of the marketplace, but that's not what he told me a year ago when he recommended the fund."

"I could never trust the guy."

"Me either, at least not now."

Belle said her financial adviser, Corbin, had received a kickback from the fund when Tuekhna made its investment.

"Can you believe it? I'm paying him a consulting fee and he's making recommendations that earn him a commission, too. I terminated the bozo."

Jesse shivered, remembering that Belle had made a similar comment to him: "I may have to terminate you." He wondered if Corbin's advice was as bad as throwing muktuk into the honey pot. It must be, Jesse thought, to get his niece so riled.

From the front of the arena Belle asked if everyone had enjoyed the day's entertainment and warm cheers filled the gym. She reminded the people that Tuekhna meant "paradise" in the language of their fathers. "It's my intention," she said, "to bring a bit of heaven here. I've tried to do it, in part, by bringing us together with festive events that remind us of our heritage."

People nodded, but Jesse could see she was preparing them for what came next. She had reason to be careful. Her position at Tuekhna was an elected office. Three years earlier she'd won her first two-year term by a narrow margin, then she survived a second—even closer—contest a year ago. Belle had argued that she was the only person in the village capable of guiding it into a modern age. The implication was clear: Education was a requirement for leadership and she was the tribe's only college graduate besides Clarence. What would people think if they knew Corbin had duped her?

"While I have some bad news about the next dividend," she said. "I'm happy to say we have a secure base upon which to build the corporation."

An atmosphere of concern descended upon the gathering. Jesse heard someone whisper, "Bad news? What does she mean?" There was another twitch in Belle's eyes and her forehead wrinkled as the mood of the crowd changed.

"I'm going to sleep," Martin said, and the boy laid his head in Jesse's lap.

"Don't you want to hear your mom speak?"

"No, I get plenty of that at home."

Belle asked Clarence to turn on the slide projector and a graph appeared on the screen. It showed historical revenues for one of Tuekhna's businesses.

"We've had good results with our timber contracts," she said. "Based upon an impact study, we auctioned timbering rights to another 25,000 acres north of Tikchik Lake."

There was a click and another chart appeared on the screen. Belle talked about the discovery of copper deposits southwest of Point Alsworth and said she was negotiating terms with the Westco Corporation to allow mining there. She continued by discussing the financial results of Tuekhna's fishery assets. Receipts were down, she said, as a result of the cheaper Yen and a glut of European pen-raised salmon.

"Now for the bad news." Belle paused and swallowed hard. "We had a loss in one of our funds—the result of a flattened yield curve and the manager's purchase of interest-only strips."

Jesse figured there wasn't a soul in the place who understood the explanation—he certainly couldn't make heads or tails of it—but Belle seemed to count on that. When unsure of herself, she spoke more loudly or used bigger words. People in the village rarely questioned her. They appeared to take comfort in her grasp of the issues.

"As a result," she said, "the dividend will be reduced by fifty percent."

People groaned. Jesse knew that most of his neighbors were counting on a larger sum. Many had earmarked their dividends for new outboard motors or hunting rifles. The frustration mounted and found its center in an angry voice that sounded from the back. Jesse turned and saw Rodney Baktuit getting to his feet.

"Damn it," he said. "This is one more screw up. Just like your driver with the muktuk."

The murmuring grew, but Belle raised her arms and quieted the crowd. "I've accomplished a lot for the village," she said. "The dividend has doubled in three years. I'm only human, but I recognize and fix my mistakes. The fund has been liquidated and the proceeds reinvested."

"What about our muktuk?" Rodney said.

"Do you want me to go out and kill a whale?"

The audience laughed.

"I can't save what's already been dumped," Belle added, "but I won't allow any more to be wasted."

"How will you do that?"

Belle hesitated. She glanced at Clarence, and then she searched the crowd. For an instant her gaze fell upon Jesse and he could tell there was a struggle going on inside of her. Belle's greatest source of joy seemed to be her work at Tuekhna, but she would put aside her plans for the corporation to protect him. Isn't that what she'd promised? The thought warmed Jesse and he wiped his face with the back of his sleeve.

Belle looked away and her answer caused the crowd to quiet. "I'll get another driver."

When Jesse realized he wouldn't have to work anymore, an odd mix of feelings came over him. He was happy not to be dumping buckets, but an idea sneaked into his head and stirred up trouble there. I'm not good enough to pack shit, he thought. Am I good for anything at all? His face turned hot and he wondered if the village had any use for him.

"What's happening?" Martin asked, waking and sitting up.

"Nothing," Jesse replied. "Your mom just said I can have breakfast with you. That's all."

Chapter 7

I used to think freedom came from the DMV, something we called a driver's license. Then I received mine and Mom set down rules for using the blue Dodge Coronet parked outside. When she said I had to help with the upkeep, I realized a license hadn't made me free at all. Freedom, I decided, was a full tank of gas!

- From Kit Lerner's Journal

Kit had described the first day of her trip as glorious, with only a hint of early morning frost. She even wrote a poem—a haiku, she called it—to describe the scene.

The lake lies placid,
Dimpled with tender kisses:

Trout rising for flies.

A year later, when Patch stepped from the passenger door of his Piper Cub, the sky drooped like a gray canopy. With one arm extended for balance he unfastened his kayak, let it fall to the water and kicked it toward shore.

From inside the plane the pilot handed out a small pack and a larger waterproof bag. "She'll get sloppy today," the young man said.

Patch looked at the sky and felt the first drop of mist weeping from it. He grabbed his gear, traversed the length of the pontoon and leaped to shore. He set his provisions down on an outcropping of rock before turning and pushing the plane into deeper water. The engine coughed and roared. The propeller whirled.

"If God had meant man to fly," he whispered as the plane rotated in search of a straight line to the sky. Patch raised a hand in farewell and watched the Piper Cub accelerate and skip across the surface of the lake before rising.

By most measures Patch ran a successful air taxi business. In addition to his Cessna, he owned two Piper Cubs and a de Havilland Beaver. He employed two full-time pilots and they specialized in flying hunters and sport fishermen into the Bristol Bay watershed.

In prior years he would stay weeks at a time in a spartan cabin on the northern shore of Killborn Lake near the village of Kaknu. From there he could reach Dillingham on the Bristol Bay coast, Anchorage and Nikolai the opposite way across Cook Inlet, and dozens of other places. The region was full of his favorite haunts and their names tumbled singsong in his head: the Naknek and Nushagak Rivers, Tikchik and Illiamna Lakes, Stuyahok and Katmai. He'd seen all of it, but for the first time he asked himself: Is this what it's like to be left behind?

The previous evening he'd visited Mrs. Lerner and announced his plan: He would mark the anniversary of Kit's departure by setting off to complete her intended journey. Wide-eyed and trembling, the woman asked, "Why?"

Though he'd heard the question before and answered in ways ranging from flippant (just chasing my *dreams*) to philosophical (just *chasing* my dreams), for the first time he replied honestly. "I'm looking for answers."

"About Kit?"

"In a way, we were searching for the same thing."

"What's that?"

Patch shrugged. "Best I can say is it has something to do with forgiveness."

"Nonsense," the woman said, looking away.

"You're right. It may not make sense, but it's a fact. Maybe once I'm out there, I'll clear my head and finally make my way to forgetting all the mistakes I've made. But there's something else, too. I want to find whatever it was Kit left behind."

"Nothing there."

"No, I don't believe that. I think your daughter buried something meaningful to her. And it may have meaning for me, too, once I find it."

Mrs. Lerner glared. "Run away," she said. "That's all."

"Yes, ma'am, you're probably right, but even that won't change my mind."

109

On the lakeshore, Patch thought of their conversation and realized he'd accomplished a leap in logic. He was open to hearing the voice of something Godlike on his journey—he would even stop and listen should it happen—but if there was no creator and master judge, who else might grant him pardon? The best a fellow could do was forgive himself, which might not be possible without some amount of forgetting. Forgiving and forgetting: Were they two sides of the same coin? That, he mused, might explain the allure of liquor and other escapes from reality.

"But like I said," Patch muttered. "Even the truth won't change what I'm doing."

With that he pulled his raingear from the bag, put on his jacket and stowed the remainder of his equipment into the kayak. After slipping into its apron, he squeezed himself into the craft and adjusted the waterproofing around him. Before paddling away, he thought to consecrate his efforts by reciting a poem he'd memorized—a composition that Kit had written before her departure.

> *Drawing its wonder encapsulated*
> *As from an apothecary's jar,*
> *The Word stretched me beyond horizons*
> *To give me a sense of God.*
>
> *For what of Godliness*
> *Less it be unfettered, unchained,*
> *Free of horizons constraining mortal men?*

Its good news changed this mortal's course,
(Having swallowed, but being swallowed in return)
And hearing Him, who was more than philosopher, say,
"Know the truth," I have searched.

But the search continues,
For somewhere, unbound and never resting,
The father to my soul urges onward,
To walk the path free of mortal constraints,
To be like Him,
Unfettered and unchained.

Patch shoved off, shook the lethargy from his limbs and began to paddle. He found the lake's outlet and eased himself into the current of the Killborn River. Stunted spruce trees bowed at his passing. The hiss of moving water filled his ears and a soft drizzle settled from the sky. He looked into the river and saw salmon there—not the kind that men who were otherwise tied to their desks paid money to catch. These were spent fish, the color of blood and scarred from battles with seals and bears and rocks and fish wheels.

He loved them, but even in this regard he could not say the word. They were the few who would likely beat the odds, to travel through the upper lake and into one of the tiny creeks that fed it. These salmon were survivors and the river required their seed. While taking strength from their example, a thought came to him: What would be better than to accomplish the goal of a lifetime and pass away without need to make amends?

As to his own life Patch couldn't shake a sense that he'd made errors demanding restitution. In a way that often struck him as perverse, he didn't consider Amanda's death to be the greatest of his mistakes. The accident took what he'd cherished most, but not without a fight in bad weather. Patch's divorce, on the other hand, was clearly his fault. Not Emily—not even fate—shared blame.

At one time they'd lived in a cedar A-frame home that Patch had built on the Nikolai River. From its ground floor den he once assigned flights and issued payroll checks, but just as often he would stand at the sliding glass door and watch Emily raise a hoe to the quarter-acre plot she'd cleared and filled with topsoil. The garden had started out as a whim, a project to occupy her time. She'd claimed no prior experience with the organic reach of life to light and took it on with a passion, as if it were a magical thing.

"It's a wonder," she told Patch the year after Amanda passed. "How'd you ever leave a farm?"

Patch considered the Idaho spread his parents owned: 700 acres of barley, cattle, and a family garden at the foot of the Grand Tetons. He'd loved it once, but he could never go back to its narrow-mindedness and sanctimony. Thinking less of the farm than his own upbringing, he said, "Compared to natural cover, that garden was just a scar on the ground."

Emily wilted then, like a flower touched by frost. He hadn't considered—not until much later—how his words could be mistaken as a reference to her quarter-acre. Yet she held true to her plans. As the garden took shape, dominated by sweet peas, rhubarb, and cabbage, Patch came to recognize a purpose in her effort. While Emily toiled, he marveled at her impulse to nurture. A part of him wanted to be the recipient of her care, but he couldn't speak of the need without fear of where the words might take him. In fact, he couldn't say much at all.

He remembered one day in particular, the summer prior to their divorce. Emily was working in the garden, when a squirrel entered to forage among her strawberries. She noticed the intrusion and shouted at the rodent, but it only turned to face her, stiff-legged and quivering as if issuing a dare.

What else could Emily do? She gave chase in a way that seemed all flopping rubber boots and flying mud, but five steps into her pursuit gravity and wet ground took command. Her feet came out from under her and she fell to her rear, where she remained, rubbing her lower back.

At the same time the squirrel escaped to a nearby birch tree and chirped a reprimand from one of the limbs. Emily grasped a clod of dirt, took aim and heaved, but the intended weapon crumbled in her hand and fell in a shower.

"Be quiet, you thief," she said.

Patch watched the dispute, when a promise he made came to mind. He'd agreed to build a fence to protect the garden from foraging moose, but he'd done nothing to fulfill the pledge. Now he had a squirrel to worry about, too. Emily's desire to nurture, he decided, had certain liabilities attached to it.

He went to the sliding glass door and opened it. "Are you okay?" he asked.

Emily turned her head, a look of surprise and a smudge of dirt on her face. She stood and tried to wipe the mud off the seat of her pants. "How much did you see?"

"Enough."

"Then you know I need a fence."

Patch stepped outside to help her and tried to view the situation logically. "Baby," he said, "that won't keep the squirrels out."

In their younger days he might have patted her on the backside and told her she was "good crew." That was enough to keep her beaming, but he couldn't do it anymore—not without a crack in his voice. After a moment of consideration he scolded himself for not volunteering more of what was in his heart: that his greatest wish was to have the world conform to her will, to prevent it from disappointing her again. Yet to make such a confession was to admit destiny wasn't in his hands.

He could almost grasp his culpability—that his reticence left Emily with few options but to lavish attention on plants born from envelopes—but he couldn't change. His grief and nature were set, like commandments etched into brittle stone. He could easier grow horns than change that.

Several hours after the start of his journey the fog lifted and Patch saw the promontory Kit had chosen for her first camp. Her description was so precise that he recognized it straight away. She'd called it a hill, but her description suggested something more imposing.

It appears out of nowhere, the lower back of a
spine of sharp ridges that stand in the way of the
river's meandering path.

The water slowed and gathered in a pool where the river took an oxbow course and left a gravel bar along one bank. Patch stopped and dragged the kayak out of the water and hid it behind trees within a bog. Studying the mountainside, he marveled that a young woman—barely a spot of dust to its bulk—could ever scale it. Somewhere on the summit, overlooking the vista from its lofty height, she'd selected rocks and built an altar. He wondered what the reference meant and reviewed the passage again in his mind.

Reached the peak and felt God's presence. He
lives here—that's what the land said to me. So I
raised an altar of rock and offered a portion of
my bounty. And then He talked. He told me there
was a purpose for my life—a specific plan—and
over the next few days, He would show it to me.

As Patch walked up the mountain, his pace regular and undeviating, he mulled over her words and wondered what manner of God could allow a young woman to die in such lonesome circumstances. What class of being would, despite His omnipotence, leave hell unbound on earth?

Was Kit—as his parents might have claimed—too good for the world and called back to a better place? No, a voyeur to her innermost thoughts, Patch knew her foibles as well as anyone.

As a fifteen-year old, she'd had an abortion, an act kept secret and paid for by the roustabout who'd satisfied her curiosity about sex. Wasn't that a sin? If so, would God pluck her off the earth only to damn her soul? All the questions made his head hurt and his breath come faster. He pushed them from his mind, knowing he'd sought other answers and found little to satisfy him.

Patch remembered a time early in his life as a church-going boy. Typical of Mormon males, he'd progressed through various rites of passage, having first been ordained a deacon at the age of twelve, teacher at fourteen, and priest at sixteen. He recalled the Bishop's interviews, the purpose of which had been to keep him on the straight and narrow road.

Do you obey the Word of Wisdom, Patch?

The reference was to the Mormon health law that prohibited use of tobacco, alcohol, coffee, and tea. It was a requirement Patch had observed until after Amanda's death, when his eyes opened to the medicinal purposes of a beer and whiskey chaser.

Do you keep yourself chaste?

Sometimes the Bishop enumerated ways that a hormone-crazed boy might defile himself. The methods ranged from self-manipulation and the touching of a girl's private areas, to varieties of sexual intercourse. Each description ended with a query: Have you ever done that? The questions not only mortified Patch, but filled him with thoughts that had never occurred to him before.

In spite of that, it was another question that caused him the most dread. *Are you preparing to go on a mission?*

Nineteen-year old men were expected to spend two years and their own money to preach the gospel in an area of the church's choosing. Patch felt he had reason to avoid the work, but the Bishop encouraged him to pray about the decision before committing one way or the other.

Patch had no problem with the request, but he had more pressing concerns than the question of a mission's value. He'd come to doubt the existence of truth—at least a truth accessible to human minds. Religion confounded him with its tortured apologetic logic, but he treasured numbers and physical laws for their honesty and lack of ambiguity. He guessed he might make sense of life if given a better view of the universe and its other dimensions. Until then the Mormon Church's claim that it was the only true faith could mean little to him.

He was reluctant to share such a skeptical view, knowing the arguments meant to counter it: "Satan has deceived you," and, "You're not exercising faith." The replies were unassailable, not because they held moral weight, but because they could be used in combination with claims considered self-evident. *The church is true. God speaks through His prophet.* How could anyone argue with that? Religious beliefs, Patch decided, were like a child's concept of Santa Claus: little understood, but even less questioned. Doubt itself had gained status as a sin.

The summer after he graduated from high school, Patch told his mother how he felt. In response, Alma's face went blank and then soured. "How can you do this to your father and me?" she said.

"This has nothing to do with you," Patch answered. "I just don't believe like you."

Alma was a big-hipped woman, who curled her sandy blonde hair and plied it high. She dictated morality like an oracle, teaching her family that church came first, respectability a close second, and hard work was all that was left. Concerning Patch's decision, she was grim with indignation.

"You need to pray and the Lord will take your disbelief away. 'Ask and it shall be given you.' That's a promise you can bank on."

"I've tried, but it doesn't work for me."

"Then you've got one more thing to do. Go on a mission and the truth will come."

Patch shook his head. He'd seen how the admonition to accept on faith was like a wedge to separate people from useful inquiry. Mormons in particular were susceptible, since they believed in a living prophet to whom God revealed His will. Patch understood how logic led to intellectual canyons into which a leap of faith was necessary. But he couldn't accept the way some people couched the leap in terms of truth, even if it resulted in an ignorant bliss.

"I don't believe I could worship a God that would demand that from me," Patch said.

Alma's mouth fell open. "Don't say that—not about the source of your blessings."

"Would you rather I lied about how I felt?" Patch wondered why his mother was so easily offended. Couldn't she see how doubt and uncertainty were preconditions for the existence of faith? "I'm not doing anything wrong," he said.

"Not doing your duty, that's wrong. Believe me, if you don't fulfill your obligations, I won't be able to live with it—or you."

Though the warning was consistent with all her past words and deeds, it still astonished Patch. "You'd kick me out?"

"Don't tempt me."

That afternoon Patch took the initiative. He hitchhiked to Canada, bidding good riddance to his past. The day after he watched the land flatten and the Tetons fade, he took a job with an Alberta wheat farmer until he raised enough cash to buy a second-hand pickup. Then wanting to put distance between him and Idaho, he churned up a cloud of dust leaving that one-horse town.

He went the quickest way he knew. That was north.

His first morning on the mountain Patch opened his copy of Kit's journal to a page where he'd inserted one of her photos. The picture, taken at a place he reckoned was nearby, revealed a cloudless sky. He traced with his finger the wandering path of the river, a glittering ribbon that marked the trail over which he'd passed. Eager to witness firsthand what Kit had seen, he slipped out of his tent, but the river and its valley—even the trail he'd ascended—were obscured by clouds that clung to the earth.

His camp was on a ledge between a near vertical drop and a rock wall that had offered protection against the wind that met him the evening before. The area was treeless and covered with lichen-painted rocks and an occasional clump of grass. Standing in a thin fog, Patch sensed a presence, like a breeze on his neck. He peeked behind the tent to dispel from his mind the image of something lurking there.

Patch hoisted himself over the ledge and walked along a ridge deeper and higher into clouds. After a while, he lost sight of his camp and decided to retrace his steps. In that moment a form emerged out of the fog and broke the linear geometry of the summit's peaks and crags.

It was a dog—no, a wolf—and it sat, watching him. Patch remembered that a pelt could fetch a couple hundred dollars and he cursed himself for not packing a rifle. The only firearm he'd brought was a handgun, a .357 Magnum, that he kept in a waterproof bag in his pack. It was the one compromise he'd made in duplicating Kit's preparations.

The wolf crouched. In the mist it took a lower profile and seemed to meld with the ground. Patch stopped and waited for sounds of movement, but every noise was obscured by moisture in the air and he wondered: Is it still there? Or is it circling?

He'd never known one to attack, but he figured a wolf's reputation had to be based on some amount of truth. While searching for a clear view through the gloom, he took a cautious step toward camp. Suddenly the animal sat up again, then it stood and the movement etched an outline in the filtered light. Mostly gray, the wolf had a dark ruff around its shoulders and a black muzzle. Its ears stood tall in a manner that suggested interest rather than hunger.

Patch lost track of how many minutes they stared, oblique angles to each other. In the end the wolf turned. After a quick backward glance, it trotted unhurriedly down the hill, its tail a horizontal line behind it.

Patch moved slowly to where the animal had stood and almost stumbled on the object of his search. It was recognizable even in the dense fog: a hill of slate, no more than four feet high, but of almost perfect symmetry. The task of building it would've taken most of a day. Finding the correct sized rocks and balancing them in a manner to survive the occasional gale-force wind had been a feat not easily accomplished.

He touched it and felt a new kinship to the woman who had made it. The mound was sprinkled with wetness—markings from the wolf—that seemed to stand as a warning to those who might come to desecrate. Upon observation, he considered: I stand on sacred ground. Here's an altar, doused as it were, by holy water. Where is the gift?

Patch walked around the pile, looking for a hint of what Kit found worthy to offer God. He figured it would be gone by now, devoured by the winds and blizzards of the previous winter, but no. At the base of the altar, rolled and fitted into a crevice between two rocks, he saw a familiar sight. He pulled out the baggie, withdrew the note and read.

Only Human

By my electric
Involuntary word,
Unseen legions rally
To battle the clandestine intruders
And renegade factions

121

That would destroy this vessel.

Making possible a storybook universe,
Embedded in dreams
And impenetrable longing,
Peopled by the captured and constructed,
Who cry for attention,
Then whisper in equal measure:
Truth and lies.

They have sentience
And also free will,
Capable of posing
That most disconcerting of questions:
Why should you be any different?
Maybe God, too, is an impulse
In the synapse of a greater consciousness.

Patch wondered what the poem meant. Was it a simple statement of fact, or an apology for the doubts Kit knew to be part of the human condition? Feeling pressed to perform some ritual in Kit's honor, he knelt before the altar in an act of reverence that surprised him. A cold breeze caused him to shiver. He bowed his head and considered phrases of consolation: *In my Father's house are many mansions.* Instead, he uttered words that had long waited for escape.

"I'm not a believer," he said. "I lost my faith a long time ago. But my disbelief turned to hate when You let my little girl die."

He raised his head and scanned the summit. The wolf had returned and was sitting a short distance away. It was panting, tongue lolling to a side. Patch whispered, "You wouldn't disturb a man in prayer, would you?" The animal cocked its head, a curious witness to the liturgy.

Patch bowed his head once more and continued to speak. "From where I sit—on this place they say You pieced out of chaos—it seems You let too much go on. And the way I figure it, if You're really what folks say, You're not just a part of the problem.

"You are the problem."

That night, still on the ledge and heating a meal of freeze-dried pasta, Patch heard the wolf howl. A fitting benediction, he thought, as lonely as any funeral dirge and more beautiful than most. He ate his fill, then on a whim and free of expectations, he set out an extra helping of dinner at the confluence of lantern light and a starless evening. With his back to the rock wall behind him, Patch opened Kit's journal and read from a curious entry.

> *Is it exhaustion and hunger that play tricks on my mind? Or is it possible that in solitude the façade of this world momentarily disappears and a startling reality presents itself?*

Patch puzzled over the words, wondering what moments of confusion Kit had suffered. Suddenly to his surprise the wolf emerged, crouching through the shadows and training a suspicious eye on the tent's flapping rainfly. After sniffing without compunction at the leftover food, it licked the plate clean of linguini and cream sauce, dropped to its chest and stared into the harsh lamplight.

Patch leaned back and relaxed, careful not to move too abruptly or gaze directly at his guest. Time passed and drizzle fell. Still the animal remained. Cold and butt-weary, Patch began to wonder: Does this creature have a home? Does it expect something from me? Perhaps it had been fed by other travelers, he thought, and it enjoyed human companionship. The idea seemed unlikely, but Patch wanted to investigate it further. "Might that be true?" he asked softly. "Do you get callers coming out this way?"

The wolf's ears stood erect and turned, like fur-covered radar antennas.

"I ask, because there was a young lady named Kit Lerner, who came here last year. You might've seen her."

No reaction.

"She built that mound of rocks where I saw you today and went down the river a piece." Patch gestured behind him. "I don't know if it was for lack of food, or on account of the cold, but she didn't make it home. I was the one who found her dead."

The wolf shifted on its belly, looked to the river and whined softly. Patch replayed the response in his head and convinced himself it was accurate, but he couldn't get over his own skepticism.

"She didn't mention you in her journal. That would be an odd thing if you'd met, because she wrote about everything she saw."

The wolf turned its head and lantern light gathered in its eyes. Patch noticed something there that he'd seen elsewhere. It was a vulnerability, the same pensive and melancholy look that spilled from photographs of Kit Lerner.

"Maybe you're not a wolf at all," Patch whispered, "but one of Kit's startling realities. Maybe you're Kit herself, come back to this place she loved. Is that why you were at the altar?"

He stood and the wolf tensed.

"Is it you?" Patch said.

He was sure the animal would bolt, or at least slink away, but it only inched up off the ground with its head lowered and ears flat. Its upper lip drew back and exposed a set of gleaming teeth.

"If you're Kit, show me."

The hair on the wolf's back rose. Still, Patch approached, thinking if it had meant to attack, it would have already. The distance between them closed and he crouched forward, intent to caress the animal's head. With two feet left to go, the wolf snarled in a way that sounded like a cough and it struck so swiftly as to be incomprehensible. Patch fell back, breathless. He searched his hand for injury, but found none. And like an apparition, the wolf returned to the shadows without making a sound.

###

For the next hour Patch questioned his actions. Had he believed the wolf was anything but a wild animal? The idea seemed ridiculous to him now, but maybe he'd seen the wolf as a means of self flagellation—canine teeth rather than stripes across the back. On the other hand, if penance had been his aim, how was a return to innocence possible, when his one memory of a noble and unselfish act was the thing that haunted him most?

He tried to put it out of his mind—that selfless deed—but Kit's startling reality was playing tricks on him. Her melancholy eyes were in the sky, wanting an explanation: Penance for what? Haunted by what? The rainfly fluttered again and seemed to repeat the words: "Tell me."

"You sound just like Emily," he said, "but it's something I aim to forget. Besides, you won't want to hear it. It's a story of God's injustice."

"Tell me. Tell me, now."

"Fine, how can I refuse the dead?" And Patch raised his voice, recounting the only time he'd spoken of Amanda's last mortal act. "Emily begged me to attend grief counseling," he said, "and I was frantic to help her."

It was a group session, Patch recalled, held at the borough building in a room with a view to the parking lot. He'd sat tight-lipped, listening to other people's stories of loss and wondering how the discussion would ever amount to therapy when it revealed a hopeless whimsy to life. Near the end of the session the grief counselor looked in their direction. Linda was a plump, dark-haired woman, who was dressed in a corduroy jumpsuit.

"What about you two?" she asked.

"Our daughter drowned a few weeks ago," Emily said. "Amanda was twelve."

Mumbled condolences followed and Linda bent toward them with her fingers laced and elbows resting on her lap. "Do you want to talk about it?"

"I'm not sure what happened."

"She was alone?"

"No, Patch was with her."

"And you two haven't talked about it?"

"He doesn't want to."

Patch turned to Emily and his eyes begged for understanding. "I gave you the coast guard report. Wasn't that enough?"

A hush filled the room and Linda looked at her watch with lips pursed. Time had come for the session to end, but she asked Patch and Emily to remain. As if on cue, the other couples stood and filed out, rubbernecking on their way to the door. Their voices faded down the hall.

For a moment it was quiet, then Linda spoke to Patch as if scolding a child. "If your wife wants to know what happened, you need to tell her. She won't get the sorrow out, otherwise."

Patch didn't respond. He thought of himself as walking a tightrope, a thin line between forgetting and remembering too much. He hoped to honor Amanda by keeping her safe in his memory, just as he'd once sheltered her in his arms. Being alive in someone's thoughts, he reckoned, was better than no life at all. Yet he was careful to pick and choose his memories, to gather tokens of what had been, rather than torture himself over what was no longer.

"All right then," Emily said. "Let me tell you what I know and maybe you can fill in the blanks."

She dropped her gaze and her voice softened. "Amanda thought the sun revolved around you," she said. "You shared a bond that made me envious. And she loved the ocean, too. It was something magical to her. So the way I see it, she spent as much time in the pilothouse as she could. You probably gave her the wheel now and then, telling her not to speak of it to Mom. She told me a few things, though, mostly about the animals—the otters and whales, especially. She talked about the cannery towns, too, and the homes built on piers along the coast.

"Sometimes she'd go down to the galley to fix a sandwich or make coffee. It was probably one of those times when the explosion sounded and she came out with her hair singed. I guess she'd left a burner on, because propane had been leaking from below. Do you see it that way, Patch?"

He nodded, but in his heart he thought: Let's not do this. Can't you see I'm bucking up? That I'm doing the best I can? This is my duty: I'll be strong for you and not shed another tear, but don't make me relive that day.

"Afterward," Emily said, "you set up the pump and sprayed into the flames. You tried your damnedest, I know, but the fire—"

Patch cut her off. "Why are we doing this? Isn't it enough to know our girl died?"

The disappointment in Emily's eyes was answer enough. For whatever need it met, Patch saw no alternative but to recount Amanda's passing. He shivered as if cold and spoke barely above a whisper. "The sea was rolling," he said and paused, feeling a cry creep into his voice.

"Go on."

"We were powerless and listing. Things got so bad I tied Amanda to the deck rail and left her to get the survival gear. And there's the point I go over, again and again, in my head. Should I have done things differently? Maybe. Because, when I tied her down, I used a knot that wouldn't cinch—one she could loosen. But can you see why I did it?"

Emily looked at him. "You were trying to keep her on board, weren't you?"

"That's right, but I gave her the chance to free herself, too— just in case the boat went down. That was my intent, nothing more."

Emily nodded. "I see."

Patch described his tumble into the water. His voice cracked as he spoke of the heavy rope that fell off the deck—a miracle, he'd thought at the time—and the wave that lifted him to the railing. "At first I laid there puking. Then I turned to where Amanda had been, but all that was left of her was the short length of cord I'd used to fix her to the rail. I scrambled all over the deck, looking for her and screaming."

Patch gasped for air, afraid to acknowledge his daughter's final deed, the only explanation for the dangling cord and the appearance of the mooring rope. "It's the only thing I could do—just scream—because our little girl had untied herself to throw me the rigging. And she got swallowed by the sea doing it."

Emily turned and wrapped her arms around him. "You did everything you could," she said. "Things like that happen. God only knows why."

They sat together, Emily trying to hold on and Patch trying to let her. They hid their faces on a shoulder of the other. "I know it's difficult," Emily whispered. "But can you tell me? Did she say anything? Anything before...?"

Patch shook himself free. As he walked away, he heard his daughter's final declaration. It was something he'd tried to shush away, just before climbing the deck to get the life raft. The words echoed in his head as he recalled the horror in her eyes and the smoke-soiled tears he'd failed to wipe away.

"Daddy, I'm so sorry I ruined your boat."

Chapter 8

All nature hearkens,
When salmon fill the river:
A flesh offering.

- From Kit Lerner's Journal

Jesse woke with a start. The amount of sunlight streaming through his east-facing window told him it was close to noon and the day was too fine to fritter away. He got up from his cot, stretching and scratching, and walked to the window where two unmatched chairs and a worktable stood. Constructed of plywood and spruce pole legs, the table was piled high with sour-smelling furs and hides. Beneath it were a number of firearms, a roll of gill net, several spring-loaded traps, and a pair of snowshoes. The wall was covered by a variety of hanging implements, including a coiled rope and a pack. From an old Blazo crate he took a clean pair of jeans and slipped them on.

Then he strode across the slat floor and, with a hand on the stove, stepped into his mukluks and out the door.

His cabin crowned a forty-foot hill that offered a view across miles of undulating tundra and a river pass. The river itself was clear and dark, flowing at the pace of a man in a hurry. It was a bit wider than the distance Jesse could throw. From the muskeg at the water's edge the slope was overlaid with willows and new greenery. Lichen-covered rocks rested at the foot of faraway mountains.

For several minutes Jesse stood on his fish wheel, observing its rotation. The structure was made of two-by-fours, planks, mesh, and wire. It floated on empty oil drums and looked like a carnival ride on pontoons. At the water's surface, two baskets the size of French doors revolved like spokes around a hub.

While checking the anchor tether, Jesse heard a boat upstream and he supposed it was a band of hunters returning to the village. Satisfaction filled him as he listened to the wheel creak and splash. As one basket fell, the other emerged from the river. The hunters will see this, he told himself, and know my life is full, that I can live without them.

When the sound of the outboard grew louder, Jesse looked across the water. He took off his glasses to clean them and squinted though his lenses. It wasn't a band of hunters after all, but what was it? A dream? A hallucination? In a moment of reflection he decided it was no invention of his mind, but a vision. What else could explain a walrus driving a boat?

The animal wasn't as large as most he'd seen, but still it was a fine looking creature. With its glossy unmarked skin and expressive eyes, Jesse figured it was a young walrus. Yet there were odd aspects to its demeanor, because it sat erect and had the use of human-like arms.

The walrus turned upstream, just a stone throw off the bank, and held steady in the current. It drove a Zodiac, the kind of inflatable boat that could be loaded into a small plane. The animal smiled and hollered, "Glorious day."

Jesse tried to blink away the image, but it remained before him. "Damn," he mumbled. "I never heard an animal talk."

"What?" The walrus cupped its hand to an ear.

As it grew closer, Jesse reconsidered. It wasn't a walrus after all—he could see that now. What had first appeared to be small tusks were only graying whiskers that ran down both sides of its chin. Its hairless head looked to have been shaven. But what of the creature's covering, the color of otter fur?

Jesse remembered one of the folktales of his people. Could this be the land-otter man, the creature called *Shdonalyashna*? Jesse thought about running, for the land-otter man—a beast that took the form of a human but was covered with dark fur— was known to steal children from the village. This one, however, smiled and appeared to be friendly. Jesse decided to stay, but he would watch it closely for any abrupt movements.

He pointed to a sandbar and the land-otter man came aground. It tossed a line that Jesse caught and wrapped around willows. The creature was dressed in men's clothes and it lumbered out of the Zodiac, extending a brown hand.

"Brother," it said. "I'm Ezra Willis. Do you have Jesus in your life?"

Jesse, who acknowledged a soul in every blade of grass, every bird on the wing, and even in the river he lived on, was shocked. He thought of himself as a spiritual man, as one who could discern things not seen by others, but his encounters with the otherworld were rare. Not since his visit with the god of the island had he seen so tangible a vision. He took the creature's hand and, with a tremor in his voice, asked, "Did you say, 'Jesus?'"

"Yes, sir. Have you found Him?"

"No, but I didn't know he was lost."

There was an uneasy silence as Jesse held his visitor's hand and gawked unrepentantly. Ezra was short—no taller than Jesse—but he was heavy, with rolls of flesh beneath his chin. When Jesse finally decided to speak, all he could say was, "Feels like skin."

"Pardon?"

"Your hand, it feels like skin."

Ezra chuckled nervously. "What were you expecting?"

"Fur." Jesse lifted Ezra's hand and scrutinized it closely.

"Brother, are you okay?" Ezra pulled his hand away and rubbed it.

"Sure, I'm just wondering."

"Wondering? Now, that's a good thing. Conjecture leads to discovery. Ask and it shall be given you—that's what our good Lord said. What were you pondering?"

"Whether you got a tail."

"A tail? What do you take me for, old Scratch, himself?" Ezra turned and patted his backside. "I'm just a man—a simple man in the flesh. Even you said I had skin."

"Yeah, but it's different from mine."

"That's right. Because I'm a black man."

It all made sense to Jesse then. He knew of white and brown men, so there might as well be people of other colors, too. Jesse listened, spellbound, as the first black man he'd ever met spoke. Ezra Willis said he was a missionary and that he'd come from a place called Motown, U.S.A. on a self-funded effort to spread the gospel of Jesus. Though his purpose was to share good news, he also seemed to have a healthy curiosity, because he turned his attention to the fish wheel.

"What's that contraption?" Ezra asked.

Jesse was amazed. He thought everyone knew about fish wheels. "It's something to catch salmon with," he said and he explained how the wheel spun in the current and captured fish in its mesh. He pointed to the angled bottom of each basket, which spilled the catch into a storage bin for later butchering.

"Glory be," Ezra said, shaking his head. "Who built it?"

Jesse answered modestly. "Some Indian."

"How many fish will you catch in a year? A few? Or would you count them in the tens? Or the hundreds, maybe?"

"Hundreds, I guess."

"Wonderful." Ezra looked around and let out a low whistle. "You're truly blessed here. It's God's country, isn't it?"

"God's country?"

"That's right, brother. I'm sure of it. He made it, blessed it and dressed it. It's God's country."

Jesse considered that last bit of information. "God dressed this place?" he asked.

"Yes sir."

"He gave it mosquitoes, did he?"

"Yes, He did."

"Now, why the hell he do that?"

Ezra chuckled. "It's obvious, isn't it? To feed the birds and the fish. And, in turn, to feed you by nourishing things you eat. It's a glory and a fact. It's a marvelous thing to behold."

"Is that right?"

"Yes, brother. Hallelujah." Ezra raised his hands and shuffled his feet. The rolls of fat around his belly shook like warm bread dough.

"Too bad he didn't figure things out a bit," Jesse said.

"What do you mean?"

The look on the missionary's face suggested they were entering serious philosophical territory, so Jesse spoke with care. "If God wanted to feed fish and birds, he should have made more sticklebacks. Or he could've made dirt good to eat, or mosquitoes that drink water instead of blood. He had plenty of ways to feed creatures, but he messed up by making mosquitoes. I know that much."

"Oh, I see what you mean, brother. But in this you err."

"I'm air?"

"Sure, God's understanding is without limit. He is, after all, omniscient. The fact is there are other reasons for mosquitoes. Or didn't you know that?"

Jesse was still wondering how he was air. "I guess I forgot."

Ezra let loose a belly laugh that boomed over the water. "We all do at times, but there's one thing we should never forget. God gives us challenges to help us grow. If we weren't prodded in one direction or another, we'd be doing nothing of significance. Do you see what I'm getting at?"

"I think so." Jesse tried to summarize the concept in his own simpler words. "You mean God wants us to give blood to mosquitoes so that fish and birds can eat."

"No, no! That's not what I mean at all. He doesn't want us to give blood to mosquitoes. In fact, He counts on us to avoid them at some cost. He wants us to work to keep them away—to build houses that hold them out, invent poisons that kill them, make medicines to stop their itch. That kind of thing."

"Oh, I get it. You're talking about a white god, I guess."

Ezra sucked in his breath. His voice took on a high pitch. "No, sir. God is no respecter of persons, not at all. He loves all His children. Why would you think He's white?"

"Well, if he was an Indian god, he'd just give his people patience. It serves the same purpose. I know that much."

Ezra stayed an hour or so, but when several white men floated by in a raft, he joined them, jabbering about the gift of salvation. Jesse wondered if he'd said something to offend the man. Couldn't he have stayed for coffee? Evening came and Jesse's cabin grew so quiet that a whisper would have sounded like a shout. I could use some company, he thought. Why don't people visit?

Then it all came back to him, the circumstances he'd somehow fenced off in his memory. He thought of the night after the last Tuehkna meeting, when he sat in front of an open cupboard at Belle's house and went through her liquor. Jesse hadn't known what to look for—he wasn't a drinker, himself—

but he read each label by flashlight and settled on something called vodka. With a half-full bottle and a can of beer, he returned to the bedroom he once shared with Martin. The boy was asleep in the bottom bunk, motionless except for his deep and regular breathing. Jesse watched him and thought: There's the slumber of the innocent. Why can't I sleep like that?

In the top bunk he drank from the bottle, hoping it would solve his problems. The liquor stung his throat and made him wonder if he'd grabbed the window cleaner by mistake, but he liked the way it warmed him. Soon his muscles went slack and his sight became blurry. While chasing the vodka with beer, he checked his glasses to make sure they were still on his face and pointed the flashlight toward the ceiling.

Within the circle of light an image appeared, like an old black-and-white movie. He saw his hillside fish camp. A native man was there, walking the game trails through snow-covered willows and deadfall. The man squatted and reached beneath a fallen log where a rabbit was held in a wire-noose. He grasped the animal by the ears and spun it with a quick twist of his wrist. There was a crack and the rabbit went limp.

Jesse blinked hard, cursing the effects of alcohol and hoping for a better view of the man's face. A moment later he whispered, "That's me."

The image disappeared and Jesse shook his head. He thought it odd to watch himself, as if he were an actor in one of Clarence's school plays. With much to think about, he left the house and stumbled through the village. The moon was bright and it scattered light off the snow. Dogs on short chains barked as he passed, but they quieted quickly and returned to their kennels, too cold to put up a fuss.

Still under alcohol's influence, Jesse wondered what the vision meant. He remembered how the man—how he—had smiled, as if taking strength from being alone and living on the results of his own effort. It was life as it was meant to be lived, the way the god of the island passed his days. He wondered if it was a view of the future, or just plain nonsense.

From atop a steep hill he saw Rodney's house and a honey bucket standing out in the open. Suddenly the world seemed funny to him, like one of the Disney cartoons in Martin's comic books. The thought of plastic buckets and people perched over them made him laugh. He put his hand over his mouth to squelch the noise and stumbled with the motion. People weren't meant for honey buckets (just like mice weren't meant to speak or walk upright). Holy smokes, Jesse thought, the world was a silly place.

He tottered to the stoop and kicked the bucket onto its side. The contents were cold and didn't spill. He turned the bucket over and slapped the top with an open palm. There was a soft splat and wetness soaked from beneath the container. That was fun, he thought, and before the cold chased him home, he'd visited most of the houses in the village.

The next day the place was abuzz. Belle asked Jesse if he knew anything about the spilled honey buckets and he answered, "The what?" Aside from the previous night's vision, which seemed dream-like to him now, Jesse couldn't remember what had happened.

"Come on," Belle said. "You made the mess, didn't you? Becky Chugiak says she heard you stumbling around, muttering like a drunk. Is that true?"

Jesse thought hard. "I don't think so."

"Well, it looks like someone was going through my liquor last night. It doesn't take a Ph.D. to figure out what happened. And believe me, if our neighbors learn you're responsible, you'll be in deep trouble. Everyone's upset. The village expects better from you."

"It does?"

"Of course it does. And the problem goes beyond shit on doorsteps. People say alcohol is at fault and there's more talk about turning the village dry. Some folks want to string you up for dumping the honey buckets. Everyone else would rather stone you for giving the teetotalers ammunition."

Alcohol had always been a source of trouble and controversy in the village. Not only did it have play in most of their shootings and boating accidents, it was a common factor in the episodes of domestic violence and suicide, too. Despite these problems, more than a few people thought of alcohol as necessary to life in the bush.

If Belle was right, the community was at war again, one faction trying to eliminate liquor, the other working to keep it a matter of choice. Jesse considered the situation. In little more than a week since the muktuk incident, people were upset with him again and he'd become the cause of bickering. Surrounded by neighbors and the village of his birth, he felt alone and

140

lonely. More than at any other time, he longed for the wisdom and guidance of the old ones. In such a complicated world what would the god of the island do?

Then an answer came to him.

Jesse stayed up through the night, knowing there wasn't much time before morning arrived. As the rest of the household slept, he tied the last few braids in a kelp rope and fashioned an antler-tipped spear. The next morning, after Belle and Clarence left for the day, he gave the objects to Martin, who accepted them with large shining eyes.

"You have a nice collection now," Jesse said, reminding the boy of the other items they'd made together: the gillnet formed out of pounded nettle, the bone fishhooks, and the willow salmon traps.

"Why are you giving me these?" Martin asked.

"Because you have to keep the memories alive."

The boy looked confused. "I'm only in the second grade. I don't have many memories."

"But you have an old spirit."

Martin asked if he could take the rope to school. "We're having show-and-tell today," he said.

Jesse nodded, swelling with pride. He watched the boy finish breakfast, then he cleared the dishes from the table and prepared himself for the silence that would follow. In the wake of the boy's departure, Jesse heard sounds he usually ignored: the hum of the electric generator, the banter of children going off to school, the barking of dogs. He realized that not since autumn had he heard the quiet that came from true solitude.

Jesse began to write a note and finished it after several revisions. He read the message three times, making sure it was free of errors. Finally satisfied with its content, he placed it on the dinner table and walked out the door. It read:

Dear Belle,

>*I've been trouble for you. Sorry about that. The village isn't a good place for me. We'll all be better off if I'm gone. That's why I'm going to my fish camp. Don't worry, I'll be fine.*
>*Tell Martin he's the smartest kid in the world. I know that much.*

>*Your Uncle, Jesse*

P.S. I'll bring some salmon in the fall.

Jesse went to the family smokehouse and filled two duffel bags with a portion of the fish strips and dried caribou meat he'd brought last year. A sob welled out of him as he took the food to the skiff and boarded it. The trees along the hillside swayed in the breeze as though waving him along. He turned away from the familiar houses and distant voices and chipped a path through the ice near shore.

After reaching clear water, Jesse started the skiff and a thin cloud of blue smoke poured out of the motor. He put the outboard into gear and felt a jolt as the boat sprang forward.

Halfway to the river he turned for a final look at the village and wondered if anyone would notice his absence.

"They don't matter," he whispered, "as long as the boy can tell the difference."

Chapter 9

Many of life's dilemmas occur at the intersection of faith and calling.

- From Kit Lerner's Journal

Two days after he scaled the mountain, Patch descended its still-wet slope, hoping he wouldn't stumble on a crag and be sent headlong. Though he knew he'd dallied too long on the summit—waiting in vain for the wolf to show up again—he assured himself that he could make up for the delay.

His progress was halting and gave him too much time to think, his own past and the idea of fate on his mind. He reached the base of the mountain with hours of daylight left to travel, but he pitched his tent anyway. Hungry for the kind of nourishment that didn't come freeze-dried in a bag, he walked to the river and searched its surface.

"I could eat a horse," he whispered. "But a dolly would do."

He pointed out in his mind, areas where trout might reside: along the shore in deep water, in a riffle behind a rock, downstream beneath a cutbank. That's where they would be, waiting for easy meals of rotting salmon flesh. He rigged up a fishing rod, using a single hook and a ball of split shot. After baiting the hook with a salmon egg and drawing line off the reel, he backhanded the rig into the current and let the bait drift.

The first trout took with conviction but, fat after a season of continuous feeding, it hugged the river bottom. When coaxed away, it leaped from the water like a silver projectile, stripping line off the reel and leaving the water in a froth. Patch caught several fish, two as large as the salmon among which they swam. He kept a dolly varden, but released the others, mostly rainbows, without lifting them from the water.

He was ready to put the pole away when, almost as an afterthought, he cast again and caught another trout that he kept. He cooked both fish over an open fire, adding only salt and pepper, then he boiled a generous helping of brown rice. It was a combination, he reminded himself, that Kit had eaten often on her trip.

His hunger satiated, Patch relaxed next to the dancing flames of his fire. Darkness settled and his breath turned to cloud. He retrieved Kit's journal from a waterproof bag and looked for the entry she wrote after coming off the mountain.

I came in search of something I'd called God all my life and found Him. His voice came to me—as clear as falling rain, as distinct as wind through the trees—but I learned that His speech

145

is easily missed. The words mingle with the white noise of daily life. Perhaps His voice had always been there and I noticed it for the first time in solitude.

Despite the joy of my discovery, I've learned that attending to God's purposes can be a lonely endeavor. To accept Him is to deny so many other things. In the end we feel God's own loneliness—a detachment born of trial. For, despite His matchless power and authority, He MUST withhold His hand.

Patch looked up, wishing the wolf would find his camp, stare into the dying embers of the fire and answer his question. In a world where children die and marriages collapse, why must God withhold His hand? Though Patch waited late into the night, the wolf didn't come and the second trout—placed at a point where campfire and starlight merged—was left untouched, until discovered by ravens the following day.

Patch woke before dawn to continue his travels. Overnight the clouds had cleared, leaving hoarfrost and a chill that seemed a willful restraint to his passing. Along the way only the chirping water and the stroke of his paddle interrupted the stillness.

The day warmed and the ridge along one bank gave way to muskeg. Measuring its open expanse, the river forked, split again and crossed itself like the weave in an untidy braid. The water was full of lilies already brown from the cold nights. In most places, the muddy bottom was visible.

Against the river's imperceptible current, a slight breeze carried something pale and downy over the water's surface. Too late in the year, Patch thought, for cottonwoods to be seeding. He slapped it with his paddle and studied the object as it floated in the water. Goose down, he decided.

He noticed more feathers—some stained red—and a place where mud filtered slowly through the water from an earlier disturbance. Violent images entered his head. It's the nature of things, he told himself, to eat and be eaten. Something happened here and life, of necessity, had come to an end.

For God had withheld His hand.

Suddenly there was a voice upon the breeze, its message indistinct. He thought, is it Him? Is it God? But no, he heard other voices engaged in a conversation that was irreverent and familiar. It caused the prior images in his head to adjust and conform to the sound of human predators.

His expression soured. Solitude, he knew, was best left to those who sought it. He considered walking around the noise, but the ground was like a wet sponge, too difficult to portage. Instead, Patch coughed to announce his presence.

Around a bend he saw two boats with outboards raised. They were tethered to shore on a small rise of land. Beer cans were scattered about the bank. Feathers littered the water. He was about to pass when he saw movement. A man with black hair stood within a thicket of trees and stepped clear. He held a shotgun loosely at his hip and pointed it toward the water.

Patch stopped and nodded. "I'm just passing through. No need for alarm."

The man was dressed in blue jeans and a plaid shirt. He nodded back. "There's no alarm," he said.

Uncertain of what he'd run into, Patch remained, waiting to be dismissed. "Is that thing trained on me?"

"What?"

"Your weapon. Is it pointing my way for a reason?"

The man raised the gun and rested it on his shoulder, its barrel aimed at the sky behind him. He was of medium height, wiry and muscular. His scowling face was the color of bronze.

"Call me crazy," Patch said. "But I get queasy looking down the mouth of them things." He attempted a smile. "I'm headed to Kaknu. How long do you suppose it'll take me?"

The man studied the kayak and answered. "In that? A week, maybe longer. And don't lollygag. It'll get cold."

"I hear you."

Still slinging the gun, the man walked to the riverbank and stepped into one of the boats. He said, "You'll want to get going then," and turned his back to the water to busy himself with his gear.

Patch recognized the hunter as someone from the village and the man's behavior was clearly an invitation to leave. Clenching his teeth, Patch thought: You can fill my body with buckshot—even feed my carcass to animals—but, by hell, don't ignore me or say I'm not welcome.

"Seeing all the feathers," he said, "makes me think you've done some hunting."

The man didn't move. "Is that any of your business?"

"No, just making conversation." Patch took a deep breath to calm himself. He listened to the banging and sliding of camping equipment over the boat's aluminum bottom.

The native man stood. He stretched and looked over his shoulder. "Are you still here? You're not going to tell Fish and Game, are you?"

"Fish and Game? Hell no. I'm just passing through on my way to Kaknu. I told you."

"Got a radio?"

"Who carries a radio out here?"

"A pilot might. Should I check your gear?"

"I wouldn't argue with a man and his gun. But if I *did* have a radio, would you use it to call home? Or take it so I couldn't?"

The man looked up the rise and motioned toward the trees. At the signal a party of hunters stood together. Patch ignored the possibility of danger. He watched the men step into the clear and descend the slope, game bags in hand.

"I didn't know it was open season on geese," Patch said.

The man exhaled slowly. "Seasons don't mean shit out here."

"I can see that. Looks like you took more than a few, too."

"Limits don't mean much either."

Patch picked out a member of the party—an adolescent boy—and addressed him. "Did the birds have wings yet?"

The boy reached the riverbank and snickered. "Naw, we just clobbered 'em with our paddles." The other men looked at the boy, irritation on their faces.

"I figured as much—didn't hear any shots from up river." Patch bit his lower lip. "That's not a sporting way to get grub," he added.

"This isn't sport," one of the men said.

"That's right. So let's call it by its name: poaching."

Even as he spoke Patch questioned his course of action. He couldn't bring the geese back. Neither could he change the men's behavior. People in the bush had hunted "box lunches"— the term they used to describe flightless waterfowl—since the beginning of time. So what did he hope to accomplish?

"Someday you'll get caught," Patch said. "Until then, I'll leave you to your business."

As he paddled away, an angry voice trailed after him. "Don't judge us. It's your people who screwed up the world."

The shouts continued, but diminished in clarity. Beyond the next bend Patch saw another flock of geese huddled in tall grass. They squabbled nervously as he approached. In another week, he reckoned, their molted feathers would be replaced and they'd be ready for flight and a warmer location.

"They're about to come back," Patch said and he slapped the water, causing the birds to scurry. "Best you get further into the grass."

Patch sprung forward, trying to shorten the distance to Kaknu. Half an hour later, he came onto deeper water and heard the sounds of outboards. The noise grew louder and he hugged a bank. The hair at the base of his neck stood on end.

When the boats came abreast of him, the leader stood and shouted. "Hey, pilot."

Patch looked across the water, relieved to see there were no guns aimed at him. "What do you want?"

"I thought you'd like to know. We voted about shooting you, but figured you weren't worth the bullet. Anyway, Mother Nature will get you just the same."

As they pulled away, the man uttered the name, "Custer," and the others laughed.

Evening arrived, bitter and still. A half moon hung low in the sky. Patch paddled to a rise, pitched his tent on dry ground and built a small fire. He skewered a few small trout he'd caught along the way and cooked them over the yellow flames. The fish steamed as he picked the flesh off their bones. He ate and leaned into a half-bowl of ground behind him, intending to remain there until the fire died.

A light fog descended and the night warmed. His arms and shoulders grew limp, his eyelids heavy. Every muscle in his back went slack. Suddenly a woman appeared on the riverbank, but he was too tired to be surprised. She'd been dead nearly a year, but there she was.

"What are you doing here?" she said.

Patch forced himself to speak. "I could ask the same of you."

Kit ascended the bank and knelt beside the fire. She stared into the flames and took a deep breath. "Camp smoke," she said, "now that's something I miss."

The fire began to die and she stirred it with the last stick of wood Patch had gathered. New flames licked upward, but they lacked vigor. Kit tossed the stick down and exhaled. "I swear," she said. "You're taking some big risks. Why are you doing this?"

Patch chuckled. "You—of all people—ought to know."

"Because I tried it first? Listen, I heard your prayers. Our reasons are not the same."

Patch was suddenly exhausted beyond reckoning. He tried to sit up and argue with Kit, but felt as if bound to the earth. Even speaking seemed a chore, yet he pressed on. "I'll answer your question," he said, "if you answer one of mine."

"You go first. Why are you here?"

As Patch considered his explanation, the river ticked off the passing seconds in an impatient way. "I came to find what you buried," he said.

"Of all the ridiculous reasons…"

"No, let me finish. Sure, I'd like to see what you left behind, but I'm not here to satisfy my curiosity. I need to know how you achieved peace of mind—how you could write just before the end came: 'I recognize this home as the perfect place to understand God's wisdom and appreciate His ideals.' Remember that?"

"Of course."

"Well, maybe we don't have the same beliefs, but I'd like to call this a perfect place, too, and trust that our lives make sense. Don't you see? People have always done this. The Indians would go on quests for visions and hope to be changed somehow—to become wiser and stronger. And that's what I want to do: finish this and be a different person, finally able to rest easy in my own skin."

A lump formed in Patch's throat and tears came. He tried to reach for a handkerchief, but his arms refused to move. Angry and embarrassed, he turned his face away from Kit and said, "I'm tired—so tired of what I've become. This is all I could think to do."

In the next instant, Kit was standing before him, smiling and wiping his face. "Good," she said. "Now I'll answer the question you've already asked."

"What was that?"

"I'll tell you why *I'm* here: The fact is you willed it. That trick with the wolf wasn't the smartest thing you've done. You have to stop that. I can't come back every time you decide to be clever. But I owe you my thanks, too. You've been awfully kind to my mother."

Patch shrugged. "She had a rough year. I guess you both did."

"Mine wasn't so bad. I got what I was looking for."

Patch wanted to probe further—to know how he, too, might find what he was seeking—but he gave priority to a question he'd pondered since Amanda's death. "What's it like where you're at?"

Kit sighed. "I can't even explain it, not in a way you might understand. You probably think of eternity as a never-ending number of days, but it's more than that. It's wonderful and overwhelming, a little strange and exactly what it must be. That's my story. Now, tell me more of yours. What happened to you after Amanda died?"

"Amanda? You know my little girl?"

"Of course."

Kit raised an arm and Patch realized she was holding hands with someone beyond his field of vision. His chest rose into his throat and choked off his breath. He strained to turn his head, when suddenly he saw her there, the twelve-year old girl in blue jeans and slickers he'd lost eight years ago.

Patch tried to rise. "Amanda," he whispered.

"Don't get up," she said. "You're tired and I can't stay long."

"No, don't leave."

"I have to, Daddy, but I want to tell you something first."

Patch was inconsolable. After so many years without Amanda, how could he bid farewell a second time? He tried to raise an arm and grasp her. "Say you won't go. Just hold my hand."

"I can't, Daddy, but you need to know this: I love you bigger than the world—bigger than life. Nothing so powerful dies. Don't forget that, okay? Now, go home, please."

Amanda waved goodbye.

"Sweetheart, stay with me."

"I'm never far away."

"What do you mean?"

"It's complicated. Just remember what I said." With that she began to dissipate, leaving a hole through the fog where stars sparkled.

Kit appeared in the void and filled it. "Now, tell me what happened after the accident," she said.

Patch couldn't deny her. I'll tell you everything, he thought, just as long as I can see my Amanda again. Then he let events he'd tried to forget spill from his memory, even as Kit vanished with the fog.

A month after the accident he met with the Deacon at the Church of Jesus Calms the Sea. Those who worked within the warehouse-like edifice called it a church—and their labor of building boats a consecration—but it was all a ruse. Even the morning prayers they uttered (Lord, keep us safe from Caesar's grasp!) were meant to earn them tax-exempt status. Patch figured the IRS would someday uncover the deceit and exact its form of justice. Until then the Deacon and his fellow anarchists would build the finest fishing vessels in Southcentral Alaska.

He presented the Deacon with a blueprint and pointed to changes he'd made to it. He asked for an estimate of the "donation" required to assemble the boat, then he watched as the man studied the plans.

The Deacon was wild-eyed and had a nervous tic, a twitching upper lip that rose halfway to a snarl. His shaved head was beaded with sweat. He spread the drawings on a table and traced the lines with a finger. "I'll need time to work out the estimate," he said, and then he added after a pause, "Hmm, this looks familiar."

"It should. You built her once."

"She's a dandy. You still fish her?"

Patch swallowed. "I'd rather not talk about it."

155

"Sure, Hoss. Confession isn't always good for the soul." The Deacon called everyone "Hoss," which was one of his more noticeable eccentricities. He continued to study the blueprint and whistled low. "You had a fire on her, didn't you?"

"What makes you say that?"

"Well, it's like this, Hoss. A boat is just a floating shell of compromises. If you want stability, you trade fuel efficiency and speed for it. Too shallow a draft and you better think twice before hauling crab pots. You know what I mean?"

Patch nodded.

"Well, these changes—the non-oil based insulation, the extra batteries, and wiring—it all points to someone who's fire shy. You'll lose space and incur costs for these precautions."

"It's a trade I want to make."

The Deacon shrugged. "Most folks wouldn't. I hope you know what you're doing. 'Cause if you're spooked somehow, the water's not a place to exorcise demons."

"I know that."

Patch tried to sound confident, but the Deacon's words were at play in his head. He wondered if sorrow was a variety of haunting and ghosts only memories. As he left the church— among the flying sparks where a winch was being welded to the deck of a bow picker—he could smell marijuana. No doubt an element of the faith, he thought.

At first Patch and Emily grieved together. They leafed through the family album and recalled events—some Patch knew were imagined or exaggerated. It became a ritual, beginning with words spoken like an act of religious devotion.

Remember when...?

Days passed and Emily asked for details of their daughter's passing, a request Patch accommodated by giving her the coast guard report. Beyond that he couldn't speak of their loss, but his wife was persistent. They sat at dinner one evening—an empty place at the table and Amanda's room looking down at them from the loft—when Emily jarred him with a question.

"What's it like to drown?"

She asked him, Patch knew, because as a young deckhand he'd nearly been there once. He thought back and returned to a rough sea and the toil of clipping gangions to a longline. He saw a hook enter his palm and emerge from the back of his hand. He remembered the panic, knowing that in a moment the anchor-weighted line and the shift of the tide would drag him into water so cold it would knock the wind out of him.

Yet all he could recall of subsequent events was waking up in an Anchorage hospital with lungs burning and muscles aching. He hadn't learned until later of the desperate measures employed in his behalf: the CPR on deck and an airlift in bad weather. It seemed a fair trade, though, when he saw Emily, his nurse, for the first time. She was then, as always, a petite woman with a gentle touch.

"I don't remember much about it," Patch said.

Emily speculated aloud, as if hoping to learn by his reaction. "That first breath of water must come as a relief."

By the look in her eyes, Patch finally understood. On behalf of the child to whom she'd ceded a mountain of dreams and loved as urgently as she needed to breathe, her remaining hope was reduced to this: that Amanda's final moments had been painless.

Patch shuddered. Their daughter's struggle must have ended quickly—the frigid water first like an electric shock, but later like a narcotic, dulling the senses. She probably lost consciousness soon after drawing water into her lungs, but had it come as a relief?

The phone rang—mercifully, Patch thought—and Emily stood to answer it. He heard her say, "Hang on," and her voice was laced with surprise and irritation.

"It's the Deacon," she said.

Patch took the phone and turned his back to Emily. He kept his responses short while she remained nearby, listening. After he took note of the pertinent facts—a dollar amount and likely delivery date for a new fishing boat—he returned the phone to its cradle.

"What business do you have with him?" Emily asked.

Since she held to principles of fair play and social responsibility, Patch assumed her reaction had to do with the Deacon's tax evasion.

"He makes good boats," Patch said. "And as far as I'm concerned his gospel isn't any more profane than what I've seen from TV preachers."

"That's not the point."

"Then tell me what the point is."

"Damn it," she said. "We lost our daughter. I can't live with the prospect of losing you, too. Don't go out there again. Please."

Patch didn't argue. He knew Emily was teetering on an emotional precipice. His own heart, too, was no longer in the business of stretching nets across the tide, but what else could he do? He'd been a fisherman—not the kind of occupation to put down on a resume. For the next two weeks he moped about town, dealing not only with his daughter's drowning, but the need to find a new vocation as well. At 35 years of age he was starting over, childless, jobless, and without a skill to employ.

Lucky thing, he came to decide, that eighty percent of success is showing up and looking interested. He got a tip from the brother-in-law of a friend and found a summer job as a mechanic's helper at an aviation service. In a hangar beside the municipal airport he discovered that planes weren't much more than tractors with wings. Drawing from his experience as an Idaho farm boy, he showed unusual aptitude. Before a month was out, he was performing standard maintenance with little supervision.

Late August came and, though air traffic diminished, Patch was offered a permanent position. He took three seconds to consider it before deciding that a nine-to-five routine wasn't for him. He'd been watching the planes rise up off the airstrip, wondering if the sky could offer the same degree of freedom he once knew on the water.

He'd never flown before, so he asked a pilot to take him up during a test flight. They rode an old two-seater, a biplane with an open cockpit that put him in touch with the wind and an extended horizon into the sky. As they passed over the inlet he recalled that as a fisherman, he'd believed in no power greater or more certain than the flow of tides. But from the air he saw parts of the world to rival the ocean's ebb and flow, not least of which were the glaciers that plowed massive fissures through the mountains.

Patch knew how bush pilots flew themselves ragged during the summer, having more work than they could handle. With no additional forethought than the mannish sense that had brought him to Alaska in the first place, he decided to take the *Citadel's* insurance money, sell his commercial fishing permit and purchase a Cessna 185 and flying lessons.

"I don't get it," Emily said, when she heard of his plans. "Why give up a livelihood that can drown you, just to get splattered across a mountain?"

Patch laughed, appreciating Emily's knack for reducing an argument to one caustic observation. She'd always been easy on the eyes, but it was her wit and intellect he loved most. "That won't happen to me," he said. "Are you okay with it?"

Emily's eyes smoldered. "Don't you dare make me a widow," she said. "Don't you dare."

Afterward Patch flew every day of clear weather, memorizing landmarks and extending the vistas familiar to him. In five weeks he soloed and by the following summer he was taking clients into the sky. Work was slow at first, but he threw himself into it and drummed up business from local lodges.

He thought Emily might accept his vocation if she only saw the world the way he did, from a height among the clouds. So he supplied her with a double dose of Dramamine and invited her on a short flight to Lake Skilak. Just minutes after takeoff, Patch spotted a brown bear bounding along a creek that flowed snake-like through muskeg. He watched the animal leap into the rivulet and fracture the water's surface. Upstream, a school of king salmon scattered, like wriggling maggots on a disturbed carcass. The fish regrouped and darted away, leaving the bear standing on its hind legs and searching the water.

Patch circled, thinking Emily would enjoy the spectacle. He saw the salmon come around a tight bend in the creek and put distance between themselves and their pursuer. Undaunted, the bear vaulted out of the water. It ran up the far bank and down the opposite slope through scrub willows, taking a shortcut across the stream's oxbow course. The bear was standing tall and waiting in the water when the fish came upon it. It plunged its head, raising a plume of froth and spray, and came up with a struggling salmon in its mouth.

Patch considered the scene and thought of the fish as living in a twisted universe, one that seemed to them as flowing in a single unwavering direction. The bear, on the other hand, by virtue of its different perspective, could understand the hooks and bends of the creek. The notion left Patch speculating: Might he understand life if suspended from a distance over it? Would he recognize the crooked paths of his own existence and make sense of them?

He looked to where Emily sat and hoped she would understand these thoughts in his heart, but her eyes were closed and her forehead was furrowed. She was taking deep steady breaths.

"What's wrong?" he asked.

"Pull out of the circle. I'm going to be sick."

Patch eased out of the arc and headed back toward the airport, lamenting the chance he'd lost to rebuild something crumbling between them. "Sorry," he said. "I was hoping you'd have fun."

"I tried, Patch. I really did."

He could see that Emily spoke the truth. Her eyes remained shut against the nausea and her body tensed at each dip through dead air. Still, she was in the sky with him, trying to appreciate (or at least tolerate) this new aspect of his life. Maybe, he thought, they lived in separate diminishing worlds and would never obtain the perception necessary to understand each other. Maybe they never really had.

Chapter 10

*Why is life so complicated? Would it kill us to
live more like the Indians?*

- From Kit Lerner's Journal

Jesse motored across Killborn Lake, the hum of his boat
unimpeded by any noise but the barking of dogs. After months
in the bush he'd come the fifty miles from his cabin, intending
to purchase supplies. His aluminum skiff bounced over the
choppy water and sliced through a thin fog.

He pulled back the hood of his pullover and watched for the
Marina House to come into view. Smoke blew east from the far
ridge, where the village lay half-hidden by spruce and birch
trees. The lake's black water was a contrast to the blue-green
hills. A yearning rose up into Jesse's throat. Was it
homesickness or dread? He couldn't say.

A young woman with blond hair emerged from inside the Marina House. She helped Jesse unload several plastic drums and carry them to the dockside gasoline pumps. After checking the first container for leaks, she began filling it with gas. Jesse looked across the water. The sun remained high, but the sky was dark where the river entered the lake. A cold wind was picking up.

"Is your dad around?" he asked.

"In the store."

"Tell him I'll be by. I've got a dividend coming to me."

At the post office he waited while a squat woman with pigtails came to the front counter. He used the tail of his wool shirt to wipe his glasses free of fog. "There should be a check for me," he said.

The woman left through a pair of swinging doors and returned with an envelope in her hands. She started to hand it to Jesse, but appeared to change her mind. "Before you left," she said, "you caused us some trouble. You won't buy booze—not if you know what's good for you."

Jesse put his glasses back on and his eyes seemed to jump off his face. Only fifteen minutes in the village and he was being told what to do. "Don't worry," he said. "All you have to do is give me that." Jesse pointed to the envelope.

"It might cause problems."

"You got to hand it over. That's the law. I know that much."

The woman frowned and held out the letter reluctantly. "I'm warning you—no booze."

Jesse opened the envelope and skimmed its contents. "Damn, it's getting cold," he said. "You know where a man can get a drink around here?"

The woman stood defiantly with hands on hips and Jesse left for the Marina House. Along the way he wondered why the village made him so crazy. Life in Kaknu, he decided, was bound by too many rules. It drained him, just being there. In his fish camp the earth was his companion, as were the sky and water. Their demands were reasonable and unchanging. Their gifts sustained him. He wished the village could be as good a partner. On the other hand, he missed being with people, which raised a conflict in his head: Where do I belong?

The roar of a motor disrupted Jesse's thoughts and he glanced over his shoulder. A woman approached on a familiar red three-wheeler. She slowed, then turned broadside in the road and killed the engine. Behind her sat a young boy in jeans and a sweatshirt.

"Uncle Jesse!" Martin said, as he jumped off.

Jesse knelt in the road and took the boy into his arms. He closed his eyes and rocked, lamenting such moments he'd missed by being away. "Who's this boy?" he asked.

"I'm Martin. You know me."

"Martin? You got so big. You'll be a man before your mother."

The boy's mouth opened wide in surprise. "You think so?"

Jesse squeezed Martin again and heard Belle ask, "Are you here to stay?"

"Afraid not. As soon as I get a few supplies, I'll be leaving."

Jesse turned his attention to the boy again and crouched playfully, as if stalking an animal. Martin copied Jesse's motion, but stopped abruptly.

"Why did you go away?" the boy asked. "Don't you like us anymore?"

"Sure I do. You're my favorite eight-year old boy named Martin in the village."

"I'm the only boy named Martin here. Why did you go?"

Jesse raised his shoulders. "I had things to do. I talked with the earth."

"And did it talk back?"

Jesse smiled. "Yes, and it said Martin chatters like a squirrel."

Belle cleared her throat and crooked a leg to sit sidesaddle. "Don't let Uncle Jesse kid you," she said. "He has no friends where he is. He misses us."

"I get my share of company." Jesse tried to look convincing. "A black man dropped by a few days ago. He left with some hunters, though. And Sasha shows up sometimes."

"Sasha? Who's that, a girl? I know better than that. You're all by yourself. And lonesome, too, I imagine."

Her statement caught Jesse off guard and left him without a reply. He wanted to live the way of the old ones—just like the god of the island had—but Jesse *was* lonely at times. Sounds of the village came to him. Somewhere, a door opened and closed. There was a conversation between children, the whine of a distant chain saw. He continued to stand in the center of the road, tongue tied and distracted by human activity.

Belle sighed and sat forward again. "Wish I had time to chat," she said, "but I've got a meeting in an hour. We'll be talking about some pretty important stuff."

"Sure, busy life in the city."

Belle chuckled. "You're a pain in the ass, Uncle Jesse, but you do make me laugh." She told Martin to get back on the vehicle and he complied.

"You won't come home now?" the boy asked.

Jesse shook his head.

The three-wheeler growled back to life and Belle spoke over the noise. "I wish you wouldn't go. Martin misses you—so do Clarence and I."

Martin's eyes were pinched as he waved goodbye. Jesse watched him pass through a cloud of blue smoke and disappear behind a tree-lined bend. *I wish you wouldn't go. Martin misses you.* The expressions left him wondering. Was there a complaint hiding in the invitation?

He was within sight of the Marina House, when a dog lunged from behind a spruce tree and was stopped by its four-foot chain. The animal remained there, worrying its tether and exposing its teeth. Unruffled, Jesse drew closer and studied the dog. It had yellow eyes and a ragged charcoal coat.

Jesse knew animals. He lived among them and appreciated their direct and honest ways. Under most circumstances he would have walked away and respected the dog's right to defend its space, but he was back among people now and less certain how to act. He chose to growl in response, not in the manner of an insecure pack animal, but like an angry alpha wolf. The dog lowered its ears, crouched and snarled.

"You're a mean one," Jesse said and by speaking those words he experienced a flash of clarity that filled him with remorse. Was the dog unfriendly, or just trapped? After all, wasn't it subject to the same frustrations he felt when living among people? From that perspective they had a lot in common.

The dog barked a warning, to which Jesse replied with an apology. "Poor doggy. I shouldn't have growled at you. It's not your fault you're a dumb-ass pet."

The barking continued and grew louder, as did Jesse's expressions of regret, when a door slammed and he looked up the hill. Through the trees he saw a house made of tarpaper and plywood. A man was standing outside it, straining to get a clear view to the road. His voice penetrated the clamor.

"What's going on?"

"I'm just talking to your dog," Jesse said. "The town makes him crazy. He belongs in the wild with his wolf brothers."

"The town's not doing him any harm. It's you who's driving him crazy. Hey, is that you, Toyonek?"

Jesse raised his hands as if in surrender and turned to walk away.

When he entered the dim-lit store, Jesse saw four tiny rows of grocery shelves that were stocked in no particular order. Displays of canned food, box cereals, and candy bars stood at the front. A commercial-sized cooler was visible through the aisles.

He saw several items he'd come for, but the words of the Post Mistress came back to distract him. *I'm warning you—no booze.* He recalled that somewhere beyond the wall—inside the machine shop that smelled of grease and the guts of outboard motors—there was a separate pantry.

Jesse waved to the man sitting behind the register.

"Heard you were in," Ollie said in reply.

The man was middle-aged and balding, with a pudgy belly and big callused hands. Ollie had grown up in the coastal town of Dillingham, where he'd worked beside his fisherman father into early adulthood. After reaching an age when his friends were buying their own boats, he did the unexpected. Smart enough to recognize Kaknu's need for a general store, he used the nest egg his father gave him to build the first phase of the Marina House.

A year later Ollie coaxed a girl from Dillingham to be his bride and he added a residence to the original building. As each of his four children came along, he continued to expand the facility until it was a combination second-story home, grocery store, and marine garage.

Jesse picked up a can of soup and put it back on its display. "I came for supplies. You got any 30.06 shells?"

Ollie turned from his register. The small shelves behind him were filled with cigarette cartons. He stooped to open a sliding door, pulled out a yellow box and placed it on the counter in front of him. "One enough?"

"Make it five." Jesse stamped his feet and blew on his hands. "It's cold for this time of year," he said.

169

The man counted out four more boxes of shells and placed them on the counter. "Anything else?"

Jesse grinned in a way that was all teeth. "Are bullets the only thing you got here with a bang? You have any whiskey?"

"None for you," Ollie said and his eyebrows furrowed. "This village is a hair's breadth away from regulating me dry. We don't need another one of your stunts."

"But you got some, right?"

"Look," the man said. "You could get me into a mess of trouble. You can spoil things for everyone."

Jesse pulled his envelope from a back pocket. "Let's forget about that. I got my Tuekhna dividend here and I could sign it over."

Ollie looked at the envelope, but he didn't ask to see it. "Let's get one thing straight. I've got no hard stuff, but I might have something else."

"Beer?"

"Let's say I've got three cases. Would they be worth what you have in your hand?"

Jesse considered the transaction. A few cases of beer weren't worth the dollar value of his dividend, but he knew Ollie liked to dicker. He handed over a grocery list. "Throw these in and I'll trade."

Ollie took the paper. He seemed to do a few mental calculations and looked up without emotion. "If a fellow came back in an hour and agreed to leave right away, he might get what he wants."

###

That evening Jesse wrapped himself in a sleeping bag and sat in his skiff to contemplate the craziness of town life. By the time twilight settled he'd downed a six-pack and a half of premium malt liquor and his bladder was ready to burst. He tried to stand and pee into the lake, but the boat seemed oddly unstable. So he crawled onto the dock and pushed himself to his feet, intending to find a less wobbly place to be relieved.

With his vision blurred, each step he took brought him to ground as unsteady and unremarkable as the last. Eventually, he was standing before the same dog he'd met earlier in the day. It lunged and growled at him again, as if Jesse had never offered it an apology or words of sympathy. Why was it so mean? he thought. Why couldn't it be nice?

"I need to piss," Jesse said, "and you need to cool down. Seems like I can help us both, right here."

Without further consideration, he extracted his penis and showered the dog with a stream of urine. The animal shifted from side to side and cowered from the water, but after taking a direct hit, it lunged again. With teeth bared, it howled defiantly. The din echoed off the ridge and over the lake.

The noise grew louder, until the dog's owner—dressed in moon boots and flannel underwear—stepped out of his house. He held a shotgun in one hand, a flashlight in the other, and both were pointed toward the commotion.

"What's going on?"

Jesse gave his organ a jiggle and zipped up his pants. "Just teaching this dog some village rules," he said.

"Is that you again, Toyonek?"

171

Jesse covered his eyes from the light's glare. "It's me, Henry."

The man slung his shotgun over a shoulder. "I thought you were a bear or something. I could've shot you."

"No, it's me."

The dog relaxed, hearing its master's voice, but it kept up a low growl. "It's dangerous to be out like this," Henry said. "That dog might take a leg off—or something worse—if you're not careful."

Along the ridge, scattered pinpricks of light appeared and descended down the hill. Jesse heard muted voices and the crunch of steps on dried spruce needles. "How's the town doing?" he asked.

"We're all fine."

"That may be, but there's nothing here for me." Jesse raised his voice as though speaking to the entire village. "You've all become white men."

"Is that so?"

"Sure. You go to a white school and learn from white books. You eat white canned food, obey white laws. There's nothing here for an Indian."

"Uh huh."

Something in the reply made Jesse feel uneasy. His eyes narrowed, but refused to focus. "What do you mean by that?"

The man walked along a narrow footpath to where his dog stood stiff-legged. He patted its head and recoiled as if feeling wetness there. The other voices were clearer now. "I was just wondering: What kind of boat you got?"

Jesse looked up at the man, confused. "Hell, I don't know. A Lowe Line, I think."

"Oh? What Indian built that?"

Jesse tried to steady himself, but the world came at him in waves. A crowd had gathered and he saw a mix of glistening faces, blankets over nightclothes, and unlashed mukluks. The faces were stern.

"Oh, look," Jesse said. "More white folks."

Lantern light bathed him and made him dizzy. The world seemed to swirl. He tried to concentrate, to slow the motion and make sense of his surroundings, but everything picked up speed and rotated around him. The next thing he remembered was rocking back and falling.

Jesse Toyonek woke up in the bow of his skiff and tried to recall how he'd gotten there. The prior day's cold weather had turned warm and misty. When he opened his eyes, even the fog-filtered light caused him a stabbing pain. It was an ache that spread to his head, neck, and shoulders.

Jesse reached behind him and tried to find the source of his discomfort. He felt a case of beer beneath his back and the boat's forward seat propping up his left buttock. His torso was angled toward the floorboard and his right leg was crooked over the boat's side. He tried to rise, but only managed to wince. He pulled his leg in, rolled off the beer and tumbled to his face and stomach.

The boat rocked and the water's soft lapping echoed between his temples. He considered getting more sleep, but where he'd come to rest the scent of fish slime and caribou blood made him queasy. He pushed himself up, scrambled to one side of the skiff and lost the remains of his binge.

While clinging to the bow and wiping a string of vomit off his chin he saw a raven out the corner of his eye. It landed on the pier, cocked its coal-black head and cackled. Jesse rotated his face toward the noise and recalled the creation story of his people.

"You made the world," he said between gulps of air. "Is it so funny to you now?"

Not until the bird flew away, croaking out of view, did Jesse work up the gumption to crawl over the boxes of food and start his outboard. His stomach began to settle, but his head still throbbed. After untying his boat, he pushed it off the dock and motored into a sea of fog.

Halfway across the lake a series of images leaped into his mind. He tried to piece them together, like torn fragments from a photograph, hoping to recognize a pattern and to comprehend the meaning. One mental picture in particular took on significance. It was of a man and a dog. There were spoken words, too, that echoed again and again.

What Indian built your boat?

It was a strange question, one that intrigued him and caused him to contemplate similar queries. Who made my gun? Who sewed my jeans? Who weaves the cloth of my life?

He entered the river and traveled upstream for several uneventful hours before running aground at the base of a hill.

His camp served as a lookout for prey, but just as importantly, the elevation provided him distance from mosquitoes. It's the best camp on the river, he thought, but it's still just a camp. He unloaded his supplies, stopped to catch his breath and glanced back from where he'd come. The river's amber water hissed and rambled around a willow-covered bend toward Killborn Lake.

Standing on the bank, the question came to him again. *What Indian built your boat?* Suddenly he understood the message. There was an act required of him, a rite to perform. He untied the skiff and pushed it off the sandbar. He angled its bow upstream and stepped knee-high into the water. After shoving the boat forward, he released it and watched it catch the current where it slowed and began to rock and twirl. As it drifted away, Jesse laughed and his voice was swallowed up by the murmur of the rushing river.

"What boat?" he yelled and it disappeared into the patchy fog.

As the sun slipped below a bruised and brooding sky, Jesse put away his supplies. He stowed a portion of the flour, sugar, coffee, and other dry goods in his cabin, and he packed the remaining food in the cache behind his residence. The log storehouse was built on stilts to keep the stash away from bears and it shared a clearing with a walk-in smoker and plywood butcher table. Another outbuilding in front of the cabin held his store of gas and kerosene.

When his work was done, Jesse sat on a stump outside his cabin door and ate a strip of smoked salmon. His supply of meat was running low, but that didn't worry him. The woods were full of game. Jesse decided he would go hunting the next morning, which caused him to wonder about Sasha. He was accustomed to her comings and goings, but after spending a day in the village, he longed for company. He shouted her name into the night, but she didn't appear.

They'd first met the previous fall while Jesse was checking snares in an area littered with deadfall and crosshatched with game trails. A fallen tree, with bare limbs like pins on a cushion, crossed his path. He circled it, searching for a snare he'd set earlier, when he heard a scuffle beneath the trunk. Through the thin cover Jesse saw a young coyote. She was straining against a wire noose cinched around her paw. The icy ground around her looked to have been hit by a cyclone.

He'd only expected to snare a rabbit or two, so a coyote pelt was an unexpected bonus. Jesse lifted his rifle, a lever-action .22 meant for small game, and his first view down the barrel was of frantic eyes. He lowered the firearm and the animal cowered between two sun-bleached tree boughs. She shivered and avoided his stare.

"So," Jesse said, releasing the rifle hammer. "You're not ready to leave this world."

He ran quickly to the cabin and retrieved a pair of wire cutters, a quilt, and a few pieces of caribou jerky. Back at the tree, he tossed a strip of meat to the coyote and she shied beneath the trunk. A moment later she emerged, one foreleg stretched rearward, and sniffed at the food. Jesse quickly flung the blanket upon her and leaped to pin the coyote to the ground. Only the quilt separated him from the animal's snapping jaws, but he held on tightly, one arm around her throat, the other around her chest. The exhausted coyote struggled and yelped, but Jesse whispered to her and kept her muzzle wrapped. When she finally quieted, he took a deep breath, clipped the snare and scrambled away.

The animal shook off the quilt and blinked in the sun, but she didn't bolt. She only stood stiff-legged, ears at attention. Jesse offered another piece of meat and noticed the rise of the coyote's nape. Without taking the food, she limped away, but turned before leaving, as if to offer thanks.

"You're welcome," Jesse said. "But it was my snare that caught you."

Though he figured the animal was gone for good, Jesse noticed her prints the following day. She'd returned and taken the meat left at the site of her captivity. Her tracks were distinctive now, with one twisted forepaw. Later that week the animal appeared at the cabin and he gave her more food—and a name, too.

Jesse waited on the stump outside his cabin and the night grew colder. He folded his arms against the chill and shivered. The words Belle had spoken came back to him. Was he, as she claimed, alone among the stars, mountains, and trees? Were the spirits of the land not company enough? He hollered out Sasha's name again and it faded in the empty air.

###

Along a ridge not far from his cabin Jesse held a .22 in the crook of his arm and peered into the underbrush in search of ptarmigan. He looked among the deadfall for a hint of feather, or a glossy eye. The birds, he knew, were brown in summer plumage and difficult to spot. He was staring so intently that the sound of human voices jolted him, like a rough poke to the ribs.

"Hey, you."

He turned and looked downhill where Rodney Baktuit and three other men from the village were motoring upriver. His surprise turned to delight. Jesse yearned to be with them, to ride into unnamed places and share stories in the way of men on a lark. He hurried downhill.

"Where you going?" he asked.

Rodney was sitting behind the steering column at the center of the boat, his black hair like a stallion's flowing mane. He let the engine go idle and called back across an acre of rushing water. "Why do you want to know?"

"If you're doing chores, I'll help."

Rodney shrugged and angled toward shore. "Why are you out here, Toyonek?"

"To catch salmon."

"Salmon? They're everywhere in the river. We get our share right from the village. You must have a honey hidden in that cabin of yours. It would be lonely out here, otherwise."

One of the men snickered and said, "He don't have dick enough for a honey."

The others laughed and the boat grounded to a stop on the bank. Jesse hopped on, smiling and pushing up his glasses. He took an empty seat near the center and asked, "Are we setting up a fish camp?"

"Something like that."

They reversed off the shoal and nosed back into the river. Once more Jesse felt the weight of a calling: to teach the truths he'd learned from the god of the island, just as Ezra taught about the white god. Jesse watched the passing scenery—the undulating valley beyond one bank and the ridgeline on the other—when he remembered the drawings on the cave wall where he'd slept so long ago. He felt contentment and tried to put his thoughts into words.

"It's good to be here, to do what our people have always done."

Rodney put a cupped palm to his ear. His other hand was pressed against the steering wheel. "What?"

"Never mind."

Less than a mile upriver, Rodney swerved to the near shore and motioned the others to silence. From behind a fallen spruce Jesse saw a young cow moose walking through shallows toward the opposite embankment. She ambled into deep water and began to swim.

"You think anyone's around?" Rodney asked, scanning the section of river from where they'd come.

A man sitting in the prow turned in his seat. "People float this water," he said. "Someone might hear."

"Hear what?" Jesse asked.

Rodney fingered the sheath on his belt. "We won't need to make noise—not while the moose is swimming."

The animal was midway to crossing when Rodney sped the boat forward. Jesse felt confused. Why did they worry about being heard? And why were they chasing the moose? Teasing a wild animal, he knew, was wrong. Pursuing the cow—even for fun—might leave her tired and unable to protect herself. Jesse begged the men to stop, but they ignored him. He sat back and hoped they would take a quick pass and leave the moose alone, but something he saw distressed him. The man up front was gripping a hunting knife.

"Closer," he said in Rodney's direction.

Jesse finally understood. The men had come to hunt, but they were reluctant to shoot for reasons that were clear to Jesse. "You can't kill a cow," he said. "It's not even hunting season."

"Don't be stupid," Rodney answered.

They advanced and the cow swam a zigzag path through the water. With knives drawn, the men stationed themselves along both sides of the boat. When they were just a few feet away, Rodney goosed the kicker. The skiff climbed the moose's back, then it slid off. The men struggled to remain in their seats.

The animal spun and lashed out with her hooves, but she soon broke off the attack. One of the men leaned off the bow and reached with his knife. He aimed for the animal's throat and landed true. She reared back to kick again and a gash opened. Jesse saw the knife tear into the moose's neck and come out with the windpipe on its point.

He could hear the animal snort from her throat. She tried to swim away, but her severed windpipe filled with water. The cow lunged for air, coughed blood and made sounds like a balloon deflating, but the noise came from the jagged wound.

A look of terror showed in the animal's eyes. Rodney circled to keep her from reaching ground and the men continued to strike. The cow eventually grew still and one of the men severed her jugular. The water turned red and the carcass floated with the current. Someone grabbed it by an ear and Rodney motored to shore.

Jesse hated what they'd done, especially when he recalled the cow's struggle, but a counter thought occurred to him: Isn't this how the god of the island once lived? Silently, he helped skin, gut and quarter the carcass. Together they loaded the bulky portions into the boat. Jesse covered the meat with a tarp and stared at it, trying to convince himself that killing was always brutal.

He looked up and saw Rodney and another man struggling to carry a canvass bag. "What have you got there?" he asked.

Rodney knelt beside the water and scrubbed blood off his hands. "The innards."

Jesse nodded, pleased at least with this portion of the day's events. The entire animal would be used. Nothing would go to waste. "The heart is one of my favorite parts," he said.

"I was planning to give it to Mr. Bear, but it's yours if you want."

"Oh, no thanks."

Jesse knew what the reference to Mr. Bear meant. Rodney would use the moose entrails as bait to attract something more valuable. The Athabaskans had hunted bear for as long as they'd hungered for meat, but only recently had they learned of the worth of gall bladder. Rodney and his family certainly ate bear (and maybe even liked its strong greasy taste) but meat

181

wasn't scarce to them. Gall, on the other hand, could be traded for gasoline or ammunition.

White men came to the village and bought the organs stripped from the bellies of bears. They made rounds throughout the bush, visiting natives and hunting guides. In turn they sold what they gathered to foreign medicine men. Jesse heard that, in a place called China, bear gall was consumed by old men to turn their peckers hard.

Was this a proper way to honor the dead moose and thank her for the meat she'd provided? Once again Jesse wondered about the rituals of the ancient ones. What acts had they performed to show gratitude and a desire to partner with nature? The god of the island certainly knew, but he'd neglected to share his knowledge.

Or maybe, Jesse thought, I just wasn't listening.

Chapter 11

Why have I come here along? Don't we find God
best by helping others?

- From Kit Lerner's Journal

The aspen trees he came upon the next day stood like
bleached poles, naked of leaves. The air froze his nostrils. Patch
looked over the rim of a draw, where a section of white water
churned below him. He slid downhill on his butt, his boots
digging into the bank to keep him from spilling. At the base of
the slope he cast his eyes down river and compared the terrain
to a passage he remembered from Kit's diary. It spoke of a
cataract, the likes of which he'd seen from atop the ridge, and a
pool where riddled salmon skin and fleshless bones lay
scattered.

He noticed bear scat and fresh tracks leading up and down the canyon wall and upon both narrow banks at the base of the cataract. Farther downstream there was a scattering of rocks leading to a wider channel and finally the place he'd been searching for since early morning.

"That's it," Patch whispered and he blew into his cupped hands to warm them. "That's where she took the tumble."

Two boulders stood defying a swift section of water. It didn't look dangerous—no more than the chute Kit had managed to negotiate—but turbulence was a devious thing. He walked down river, stepped off the bank and waded, first to his knees and then to his waist. The water's chill made his muscles tense and cramp. Patch struggled to stay on his feet. He reached the near boulder and leaned against it, now chest high in the flow and shaking from the cold. The river sought to crush him in its progress.

There were metallic and other colored scrapings on the boulders—some chiseled into the rock—but one streak in particular caught his eye. It caused him to recall Kit's photo, the one taken moments before her plane had left. Hadn't her kayak, the one on the ground at her feet, been red?

From where he stood, supported by a rock that he dared not leave, he reached with his foot midway between the two boulders and felt the river gain speed and strength there. At a place where the water surged white, his foot touched something solid only to be whipped away. He probed again, his leg like a length of cord in a stiff wind, and felt a pointed rock, shaped as if shattered long ago. He pulled his foot away and thought it was appropriate that a thing hidden would lead to Kit's death.

According to her journal, the kayak had run aground and been crushed by the current. Patch saw the physical evidence and coaxed a story from it. She came through the canyon too fast, bounced off one rock only to catch the other, and went broadside between the two. The kayak tipped and yielded to the water. The concealed rock punctured the kayak and held it fast.

She'd fought to dislodge the vessel, but to no avail. Where had it gone? Patch figured its disappearance was due to low water and the prodding of winter ice, but a playful bear or a conscientious local could have taken it away just as easily. It took Kit three trips to transport her belongings to the opposite bank. Each passage tumbled her downstream and threatened to drown her, except that her gear—stowed in waterproof bags— stayed afloat and kept her head above water. Exhausted and disconsolate, she spent the evening beside a fire and tried to get warm. In her journal she wrote:

> *Afterward I sat on a sandbar and had myself a cry. It didn't get me any dryer so I sobered up, started a fire and hoped the smoke was enough to keep the bears away.*
>
> *By late evening I was still cold and low on food. I asked God, "What's next?" And I took comfort that He had a purpose for me. (I hope He lets me in on it soon. The anticipation is killing me).*

Here Kit faced death and took comfort in a promise she believed to have come from her Maker. Patch looked into the sky and yelled. "It was You who made this rock, wasn't it?"

In this way he'd begun to address God or whatever else was responsible for life's injustices. Though he received no reply, the expression itself had taken on a meaning all its own. On his less angry days, he accepted the possibility that his imperfections stood in the way of true communion. More often he could only rebuke so careless a being. Wouldn't a court of the land judge against the creator of a realm so bruised with hazards? And God asks us to sing Him praises?

Patch raged at the notion. "Do You hear me?" he shouted. "Do You understand what You put Kit through?"

He listened for an answer, but even his voice was smothered by the rushing water and didn't sound an echo. If his words couldn't rise above the chasm, how would he ever be heard? He screamed this time with tears in his eyes. "I don't need Your forgiveness, hear me? Because I'll never forgive You. And put this in Your almighty head: Can You imagine what it was like to tell Emily that our girl was gone?"

The vision of it was before Patch now: He was in a hospital bed, trying to believe he'd imagined the accident and would come to his senses and find Amanda unhurt. Sleeping pills did him no good. He shivered, unable to get warm. Suddenly Emily appeared in the doorway, wearing a print dress and one of his cold-weather jackets that fell to her knees. Her eyes were wet and black with mascara that streaked down her face.

"Tell me it's not true," she said. "Say they got it wrong."

Patch heard the hysteria in her voice and knew he hadn't dreamed of the fire, or the rise and fall of the cold water. The realization pierced him like a gaff. His chest heaved and he covered his face.

"I'm sorry," is all he could say.

Emily went to his bedside and held him. "How could this happen to our baby?" she asked.

Her question multiplied into a cacophony of unspoken accusations: You should have known better. You ought to have been more careful. How could you let this happen? During the jumble of days thereafter his grief refused to be contained and threatened to split him wide open. In response, Patch could do little else but promote an emotional alchemy and let his anguish turn to anger.

Now that, too, was in the process of transformation—on its way to becoming a kind of weariness. At the very least he didn't want to care anymore and from that odd mix of ire and resignation he sought to symbolize Kit's suffering. An idea came to mind that caused him to doubt his resolve. But just as she'd never challenged her convictions, he would try not to question his own.

"From here she went on foot," he said. "Maybe I will, too."

He began to ford the river, probing the bottom to keep from stumbling. The water roared as he moved forward. It rose to his chest with each stride. Exhausted by the effort, he set one foot on a rock and rested.

Patch stepped again only to feel the rock turn and give way. He went under and came up gasping. Battered by the current, he scrambled to find the riverbed. Fifty feet later he finally touched down and dragged himself to safety. He coughed up water, then the remains of his most recent meal. Still lying in the shallows, he condemned again whatever dictated the vagaries of life.

"Hear me?" he whispered. "You might as well put me out of my misery, because I don't give a damn anymore. And I'll prove it."

Patch raised himself to his feet and began to climb the slope. He kicked a hole into the soft bank, hoisted himself up and caught his breath before continuing. His legs shook and he felt dizzy with vain promises and plans in his head. At the top of the draw he traced his earlier steps along the ridge and down the hill to where his kayak waited on the bank. He stared at it and thought: I've got something else to do.

The rumble and hiss of water filled the air like a mournful dirge. Patch unloaded the kayak of its gear and pulled the pistol from his pack. Before he could convince himself otherwise, he switched the gun off safety and fired three rounds into the vessel. As the last shot rang in his ears, he felt as if roused from a dream.

"Damn," he whispered. "I guess I'm committed now."

Is this what I'd come to do? he thought. Am I here to kill myself? Though his first inclination was to condemn his impetuousness, his next thoughts emerged from a defiance that would not be extinguished. It rose up and overwhelmed his other feelings. Suck it up, he told himself, finish this and do it on your own. You don't need anyone's help, least of all God's.

###

After changing into dry clothes, he left the kayak a wounded hulk near the water and followed along the ridge. Gradually the river widened and he kept close to the bank. He walked in frost-filled, but dry, weather. To conserve his remaining freeze-dried meals, he ate what fish he could catch along the way.

On the morning of his third day walking, the draw opened onto rolling hills and occasional stretches of wetland. Later in the afternoon he approached a familiar bend in the river. He saw a sandbar beyond the bend and a hill sloping up to the bank. Recognition of Kit's final camp hit him like a sad song. He knew from her writings that she'd survived several days there, while the snow piled so high she could scarcely walk to the river.

Upon Patch's arrival, however, the valley was clear of snow the way Kit had seen it once, before he'd circled her sky the first time. He slipped off his pack and sat to rest. A chill and the sweat on his back caused him to search his belongings for an extra layer of clothing. The surrounding area was covered with tundra, dusty with frost in the shadows and dark pastel where it was exposed to the sun. A few stunted willows stood like shattered bones struggling to rise.

Patch exhaled slowly and saw his breath rise. He was finding sustenance a hard thing to obtain. Trout were scarce, likely holed up in the lakes in anticipation of winter. He continued to cast for grayling—the gunmetal-colored fish with sail-like dorsal fins—which were his only fare most nights. Though he'd seen ptarmigan, he was reluctant to draw his pistol. Bullets were a luxury he hoped to conserve.

He pulled out Kit's journal and read the words she'd written as she sat on the same plot of ground. Even to his unlettered eye, her writing had lost its feverish pitch. She'd stopped referring to the past, lost her maniacal urge to detail what she'd seen. Despite that, her entries—less introspective and more preoccupied with survival—told of her predicament.

> *The hunger is awful—worse than the cold. At first I told myself I would never eat from the carcasses of dead salmon, their bodies gray with fungus and decay. But that was a long time ago. Now I know what hunger can drive a person to do.*
>
> *I'm constantly nauseated. I don't have the strength to push on. I've decided to stay and, God willing, wait for rescue. I remind myself that this is a test. Nothing can be fully appreciated or counted as worthy, without a compensating sacrifice. So I'm willing to accept my lot.*
>
> *A plane spotted me and circled! I'm sure that once the snow stops falling, a rescue party will be on its way. So this is what I've done to prepare: In a place where the river cuts into the bank I hid the reminder of my sin. I won't return to it ever again. I finally feel as if I've been redeemed.*

Patch closed the journal, careful to mark the place where he'd stopped reading. He shut his eyes in the way of a man with a headache. That was my plane, he thought. That was me adding to her false hopes and strengthening the faith that led to her undoing. He was about to scatter the journal's pages and leave them as a final memorial to Kit's struggle, but he couldn't.

> *I raise my voice to heaven, expecting the sky to clear and stars to appear, but it continues to snow. Last night was the coldest yet. The wind blew my tent flat. My poor feet. No planes.*
>
> *Snow again. When will it stop? All I've eaten today are berries. I dug through the snow to get them. They're bitter and frozen—crow berries, I think—and not filling. As much as I hate the thought of killing some wild and beautiful animal, my body yearns for meat.*
>
> *Stooped to a new low. Scared a fox from its kill—couldn't wait for the rabbit to cook. Only its bones didn't end up in my stomach. I'll save them just in case things get bad.*
>
> *Gathered stones from the river, hoping to kill a ptarmigan. Hit one on the head. Feathers flew, but so did the bird. Maybe I need bigger stones? Resort to chewing rabbit bones. Noticed tracks*

in snow. (More rabbits?). I set snares using dental floss. Hope they hold.

Snares don't hold.

He put the journal away and looked down the hill toward the river, where a spent sockeye floated on its side and circled slowly in the current. Patch thought it was dead, but as it drifted closer he saw one of its fins twitch and its gills filter water. It hit a gravel bank and remained there, flapping its tail.

The fish's mouth was beaked grotesquely with its teeth exposed. Its body—streaked yellow with disease—was milt-spent and oddly tapered. Patch shuddered. This was one of the victorious and what was its reward? In the water's near-arctic chill, where there was little to nourish new life, it would offer its own body to feed a new generation.

Patch thought of Kit and recalled how she'd judged salmon as heroic, as creatures that understood the obligation to die and return to the earth. He walked to the bank, stooped and lowered a hand to the fish. It struggled again, but remained stranded. Patch grasped it by the tail and turned it toward deeper water. It remained on its side, but whirled and drifted once more with the current. Patch watched it float away, touched by its sacrifice and thankful that he'd witnessed a scene of such exquisite beauty. It reminded him of something he'd heard once—was it Amanda who'd said it?

Nothing that powerful ever dies.

"You won't be long for this world," he said, "but maybe I offered you some comfort."

A flock of geese flew overhead in a perfect V. Patch raised his face and listened. The birds announced their passage in a way that sounded like both an affirmation and promise to endure.

###

Patch based his search for Kit's buried object on two pieces of information: the journal's reference to a place where the river cut into the bank and his assumption that Kit wouldn't venture far from camp. For the remaining hours of daylight he explored the strip of gravel between low water and the hump of ground standing over it, but without success. The next day he used a spruce pole to probe beneath the bank's overhanging lip, wondering if Kit's words were, as Cooper had claimed, just a figure of speech. On his third pass through a promising section, he frightened a muskrat from its lair and it leaped into the river with a violent splash. Patch watched it swim away, thinking he ought to continue his journey, but he couldn't—not yet.

He turned again to the bank and worked the pole forward, when suddenly it met with resistance and a metallic clank sounded. Patch dropped to his knees and reached into the opening, clawing at a tangle of tree roots until he touched the smooth edge of something wrapped in plastic. He moved more dirt away, grasped the object and withdrew it from the hole.

Taking a step back from the bank, Patch peered into the garbage bag he'd retrieved. He kneeled again on the gravel and fished out a metal box. Some of its paint had been scratched away and rust showed in places, but he recognized pictures of

Winnie the Pooh on the front. He turned it over in his hands—realizing it was a child's lunch pail—then he lifted the latch and opened the lid.

The first item he saw inside was a note, written in Kit's hand that read:

> *I will no longer dwell on the past. I'll put every incrimination and moment of self-loathing in a box. I will close the box and bury it forever.*

Patch moved the note aside and saw symbols of childhood: a pacifier, a small picture book, a baby spoon, a pair of tiny socks, a faded report card. There were also photos of kids with written inscriptions: *Davey, 2, likes apple juice. Maura, 4, favorite food is fish sticks. Kevin, 5, says he'll marry his kindergarten teacher.* He wished Kit would come and explain each item's purpose, but after a moment of speculation, Patch believed he understood. Kit, he decided, had been chronicling the lost potential of the life she'd given up.

Was that a prescription for guilt, Patch thought, and could a person stop living in the past just by throwing away reminders of it? The possibility intrigued him and he considered tokens of his own sins: the watch on his wrist (an anniversary gift from Emily) and the keychain that Amanda had given him her final Christmas. Could he add them to the box and walk away with a clear conscience?

"No," he said with a sigh. "I couldn't—not those." And he wondered if his journey had been a waste of time. Patch wasn't sure how to answer the question, but this much occurred to him:

Kit's symbols of grief were different than his own. While his reminders had come from people he loved, the contents of Kit's lunchbox were products of an obsession. Still, he couldn't get over the idea that he must sacrifice something of value, just as Kit had. Only he didn't know what.

"I've got to go," he whispered.

He thought of the difficult journey ahead, leading him beside dangerous waters, through a valley of shadows where death could come a dozen different ways. Conceding the possibility that his own life might become the object of a sacrifice, he wrapped Kit's lunchbox in its bag and returned it to the earth.

Chapter 12

*I bought my last piece of equipment: a fiberglass
kayak for $946. Once the season is over and the
last frozen sockeye has been bagged and boxed,
I'll be paddling down the Killborn River. Some
people ask, "Why don't you use your money for
school?" And I say, "Two weeks in the bush is
worth a year at Cal."*

- From Kit Lerner's Journal

Jesse was relieving himself against a boulder, when he
heard a metallic clang and a voice coming from the river. He
peered down the trail and saw Belle emerge through tall grass.
Martin was on the shore, throwing rocks into the water. They
had brought Jesse's skiff, which Belle was tying to willows on
the bank.

"Belle," Jesse said, heading downhill. "What are you doing here?"

She looked up, but didn't offer a greeting. "You got to tie your boat up better. It floated clear to the lake."

"It got all that way? I wonder how that happened."

Belle scowled. "Didn't you know it was gone? It must have taken a week to get there. Where's your head?"

Jesse stopped at the base of the hill and said, "It hasn't been boating weather lately."

Belle looked skyward and ran a hand over her face. "Your prank with the dog was upsetting enough, but when Clarence found your boat, we were frantic thinking you'd drowned. Luckily, some hunters had been by and said they'd visited with you. Believe me, you caused us some worry."

Jesse smiled uneasily. "Sorry."

"Then we had to dry the plugs to get your skiff going. It was half full of water, so we ran it with the drain open."

Jesse didn't like Belle's ranting, but he was more concerned with Martin's behavior. The boy stood aloof, not even saying hello. "You're being quiet," Jesse said. "Are you okay?"

The boy stopped pitching rocks, but he didn't turn. "Why are you here, Uncle Jesse?"

"This is where I live."

"But your home is with us."

Jesse felt as though a bullet had pierced his lungs and taken the air out of them. He loved his family, but there were limits to the sacrifice he must make. "The village and me don't mix, you know that. But I've got something for you. Come and see."

"We can't," Belle said. "We have to go."

"I'll get it then. Just wait."

Jesse ran up the hill and returned with a drawstring bag. It was made of soft leather and trimmed with muskrat fur. He held it out to Martin.

"More charms?" the boy asked.

Martin gave slack to the drawstrings and reached into the bag. He pulled out a necklace made of polished bone and the two claws they'd poached off the black bear. "It's pretty," he said.

Jesse wished he could read the boy's mind. Did Martin understand the need for solitude? Could he appreciate the value in listening to the earth's many voices? Suddenly a frightening question occurred to Jesse. How will the boy learn without someone to show him the way?

"We've got to go," Belle said. She told Martin to get ready and the boy clambered aboard the boat. He sat down and returned his new amulet to its pouch. Belle got the kicker to sputter and it growled as she pulled back from the bank.

"Sure you can't stay?" Jesse hollered. "I'll make coffee."

Belle shook her head and pointed toward shore. "I left you something."

As the skiff motored away, Martin waved and yelled, "See you."

Jesse fingered the whiskers over his upper lip and watched the boat disappear around the bend. He walked to where Belle had pointed and discovered a folded quilt. On one of its exposed corners was a hand-stitched moose. Jesse knelt to unwrap it. In a game bag he found several strings of dried eulachon, the silver smelt that was his favorite food. Every spring the fish entered the estuary and lower river to spawn. Whales and humans alike sought the greasy smelt, but he'd missed the few days he could catch them with a dip net.

He hefted the fish and exposed a crude basket woven out of willow strips. There was a short note as well, handwritten on yellow legal-sized paper. It was spotted with fish oil.

Uncle Jesse,

> *Martin insisted we bring you the basket. (It took him a week to make it). He said it would have turned out better if you'd been around to help. We all wish you were home with us. I thought you might like the fish.*

> *Love, Belle*

P.S. Take care of your boat.

When Ezra Willis returned and asked to stay and help tend the fish wheel, Jesse was hesitant at first. But over the next several days and nights he came to enjoy having an extra pair of hands. Under their joint care the garden of potatoes was quickly harvested and the other chores were accomplished quickly. Jesse also liked Ezra's manner of speech, the musical lilt in his voice, and his observations so unique they seemed to come from a man seeing the world for the first time.

As sockeyes continued filling the river Ezra said something Jesse had always believed—that salmon were perhaps the most noble of creatures, sacrificing themselves to nourish others and accomplishing the purpose to which God had called them with exactness and fortitude. It was consistent with Jesse's view, since it illustrated what was worthy of humans and what he aspired to in himself.

On the other hand, he wasn't taken in by every glib word. He suspected that Ezra's presence and kindly deeds were motivated by something less than complete charity. During the evenings the man from Motown seemed to further a subtle agenda. While Jesse fried potatoes and caribou steaks over the wood burning stove, Ezra asked about the village and its inhabitants down river. After dinner, he would weave out of a seemingly innocent conversation, a broad discourse about Jesus and the good Lord's hopes for humankind. One night the topic turned to repentance.

"Ah," Jesse said in response to Ezra's explanation. "You're talking about that white god again."

Ezra ignored the attempt to derail the discussion. He reclined on the floor, appearing comfortable in his sleeping bag and capable of great patience. "Consider Christ's grace and mercy. Jesus suffered so we might live. Praise Him, for He took our sins away."

Jesse rested on his cot and stared bug eyed at the slats in the ceiling. "Sins? What's that?"

"I'm glad you asked." Ezra rolled to his side and propped himself with an arm. He offered a smile that glowed in the faint light. "In short, our sins are the wrongs we commit. And God knows, we all do our share."

"Of wrongs?"

"Yes, brother."

Jesse pursed his lips and pushed up his glasses. "Is that like when I put the fish wheel in a bad place and it doesn't pick up many salmon? Or if I forget to feed the smokehouse and the fire goes out?"

"No, brother, those aren't sins. Those particular acts don't harm anyone. They don't offend God."

Jesse laughed. "Believe me, if we don't catch enough fish, I'll be hurting pretty bad this winter."

Ezra rubbed his jaw and let silence pass. "Hmm, I see you've spoken the truth. Perhaps I can explain the nature of sin another way. You see, God gives us commandments—eternal laws that, when followed, will prevent us from hurting ourselves and others. If we disobey those laws, we sin."

Jesse picked his teeth and made a sucking sound.

"For example," Ezra continued. "God told us, 'Thou shalt not kill.' And, brother, His yoke is easy. His burden is light. When He says, 'Come follow me,' we should go straightaway."

"So we shouldn't kill?"

"That's right."

Jesse considered the concept. "Seems to me we did that to a bunch of fish today—noble fish, like you say. We slit their bellies, ripped out their guts and hung them to smoke. It hurt them some, I know that much."

Ezra sat up and hugged his knees. "Oh, but that was okay. That was for sustenance. Even Peter, the head apostle, and the sons of Zebedee, fished for food."

Jesse shook his head.

"Brother, you look confused."

"No, I finally figured it out. I see where white folks got it now—how they learned their way of doing things. It must have come from their god."

"What do you mean?"

"You know how it is," Jesse said. "They make up a law and say it can never be broken. Then they think up a couple reasons why it can. Boy, it's a confusion."

Ezra closed his eyes and fell to his back again.

"Now, the Indian god," Jesse added. "He does things different. He says, 'Better get some food or you'll die.' That's it—real simple—nothing to argue about one way or another."

Several days later Ezra emptied the fish wheel of its catch and carried the salmon up the hill to be butchered. Jesse split each fish along the backbone, forming two filets that he sliced into strips and left attached to the tail. They hung the pieces in the smokehouse, where the deep-red meat sweat and glistened with oil.

Before closing the smokehouse door Jesse gazed at his handiwork. Here is my religion, he thought. Survival directed his days and dictated what was good or evil (which he figured was another way to measure degrees of necessity). It was a practical faith, he knew, with little need for speculation about the hereafter. Why be concerned with death, when there was so much to prepare for winter?

Despite their differences of opinion, Jesse had come to like his visitor. Ezra was a hard worker and when it came to subjects other than the white god, he accepted good advice, unlike white men who always seemed to know better. Yet Jesse had grown tired of gospel talk and wanted to change the topic.

As they left to chop and stack firewood, Jesse said, "Tell me about your home."

"My home? Where should I even start? Detroit's a wonderful place, of course, but a world apart from here."

"How so?"

Ezra rubbed the stubble on his face. "Well, there are tall buildings, wide roads, and people—lots of people."

Jesse had seen parts of Anchorage and he could remember its many buildings, some bigger even than the school in Kaknu. From Patch Taggart's floatplane he'd searched the downtown area for the honey pot, but couldn't find it.

"Your village must be like Anchorage," he said.

As they reached the outbuilding in front of the cabin, Ezra laughed. He opened the door and grabbed an ax. "Brother, your idea of a city is limited by what you've seen. Detroit is many times bigger than Anchorage."

"I'm sorry to hear that."

"Sorry? Why? I love the hustle and bustle. There's never a dull moment."

Jesse grabbed a chainsaw-cut log and stood it upright on the stump in front of his cabin. "But it's not god's country—not like here."

"That's true, but Detroit has a splendor all its own. Once the world discovers this place I see no reason why it won't become another shining city on a hill. All roads will lead here."

Ezra swung the ax and buried the bit deep into the wood. He raised and dropped the ax again and the log split. As Jesse stacked the pieces against the front of his cabin, he shivered. To his way of thinking the river had already received too many visitors. On more than one occasion he'd cleaned up a messy campground or dowsed a still smoldering campfire. What would happen if the traffic increased?

"Can you see it, brother?" Ezra said. "Can you see the glory of a church on every bend of the river and the valley filled with the angelic sounds of their choirs singing? Wouldn't it thrill you to have the world flocking to your door?"

"Are you talking about white people?"

"People of all colors—white and black, yellow and brown. People speaking all manner of tongues."

Jesse scanned the opposite hill and imagined it all—the churches and houses, the office buildings and roads. With so many people, he thought, what would happen to the salmon? What would happen to the other animals?

"Do me a favor," Jesse said. "Let's keep this place a secret, okay?"

###

Ezra seemed fascinated with every aspect of Jesse's life, but in nothing did he show as much interest as the salmon they caught. He peppered Jesse with questions regarding the fish. Why did they return to the place of their birth only to die in the end, having eaten nothing along the way? Jesse answered each question with the same response: "It's in their nature." But he knew the reply didn't address the oddity of the salmon—how they offered so much and took nothing in return.

Each time they visited the fish wheel Ezra tolerated the swarms of mosquitoes in order to count the splash rings that dotted the river. "Glory be," he once said, watching the salmon slap the surface and dart away. "I could almost perform the Lord's miracle by walking on the water across their backs."

The assertion reminded Jesse of the first time Ezra saw a fish being butchered. The missionary voiced surprise that nothing went to waste. "A salmon," he said, "was little more than muscle and iron will. I can imagine they offer a challenge to the average angler."

Jesse held that notion in memory and before the sockeye run waned fully he brought out an old rod and reel from beneath his worktable. He joined the separate pieces together, threaded the eyelets with monofilament line and added split shot and a bucktail fly to the affair.

"What are you doing?" Ezra asked.

"I'm going to watch you fish."

Ezra smiled. "The Lord loved the fishers of Galilee. I wouldn't mind testing myself against the creatures that ply the river."

Only moments later they stood on the fish wheel, where Jesse demonstrated how to backhand the fly upstream and let it bump along the bottom in the current.

"But why do the fish strike?" Ezra asked, swiping at a mosquito. "After all, they eschew food."

"They may chew, but they don't swallow. I guess they're only knocking things out of the way."

Ezra claimed he hadn't held a rod since he was belly-high to a cricket and proved to be more than a little rusty. On his third cast something tugged sharply on the line and caused him to shout with surprise.

"What was that?"

"A hit. You got to set the hook. Yank back on the rod when they do that."

During the next dozen drifts, the fly was struck five more times. Jesse laughed as he saw every variety of reaction from his friend. Most of the time, Ezra was too slow and ripped the fly out of the water, causing it to jettison in his direction. He came close to swearing, but after each setback he showed greater resolve.

With his arms tense and eyes fixed upon the water, Ezra finally timed his response and set the hook just as a large sockeye grabbed the fly. As the salmon ran, the rod bent double and the old reel whined. Downstream the fish broke water and raised a fountain of spray. Ezra yelled spiritedly at the sight, but in the next instant the line snapped and went slack.

"My word," Ezra said. "That was a thrill."

"Let's tie on another fly."

"No, let them go." Ezra stared at the place where the salmon had leaped and exposed its green back and glistening silver sides. "Let them make babies," he said. "And may their children be as true to God's purpose."

"If you're sure."

Without the distraction of a fish on the line, the mosquitoes seemed suddenly intolerable. Jesse hurried up the hill toward the cabin and turned as he reached the summit. He expected to see Ezra in pursuit, but the man remained at the river's edge, watching salmon break the water's surface and disappear.

Over the next two weeks the sockeye run reached its peak and diminished. Over a breakfast of salmon strips and berries Ezra said grace, then he looked up from where he sat on the floor and sighed. "Jesse," he said, biting off a piece of fish. "Don't you ever get lonely?"

Despite the sound of concern in Ezra's voice, Jesse sensed the question as containing some hidden motive. Sitting at the table, he sharpened his knife and said, "No, I get company."

"Like who?"

Jesse spat on his whetstone and continued to grind the blade against it. "Like hunters. They show up sometimes. Folks from Fish and Game, too."

"Is that all?"

"Well, sometimes a preacher drops by."

Ezra smiled. "But in winter, who pays you a visit then?"

207

Jesse wondered if there was value in answering. He stared out the window and the room fell still. "Sasha comes around," he said.

"Sasha? Who's that? A paramour?"

"Nah." Jesse stopped sharpening the knife. "Those birds we don't get around here. Sasha's a coyote."

"A coyote?" Ezra sighed again. "Well, that certainly makes my case. Life is a lonely affair without companionship. And regardless of what you might think, Christ Jesus stands ready to be your best friend—to take your loneliness away."

"I'm not lonely. Jesus is welcome to visit, but I've got other company, too."

"But don't you see? You need more than a couple of hunters dropping by—you need spiritual guidance. You need God in your life."

"God?" Jesse sensed the beginning of another long-winded discussion. He set his knife down, went to his cot and reclined. "There's plenty of them around. They're in the wind, the sun, the river—even in the game we shoot. They're everywhere."

Ezra frowned. "I'll speak with candor, for your soul is in jeopardy. There's only one God and He's father to us all."

Jesse plucked a whisker off his chin and studied it in the morning light. "That's not true. I met another one. An Indian god."

Ezra stopped chewing. "What're you talking about?" he asked.

"It happened a year or so back—before coming here."

"You're mistaken, surely. Whatever you saw was not God." Ezra reclined once more and rested with his elbows behind him.

"Describe what you saw," he said. "Confess it and I'll show you the error in your claim."

"It's not an easy story to tell and I have work to do. The smokehouse needs checking."

Ezra raised a hand. "Don't worry about the smokehouse. I've already added wood to the fire. It's the Sabbath, brother. Rest this day and tell me your story. Don't leave anything out. We've got plenty of time."

Jesse knew that in the months to come caribou would gather along the river and provide a final harvest before winter's arrival, but his friend was right. For the moment they could rest. After weeks of frenzied activity, his smokehouse was filling rapidly, as was his cache.

Yet there was too much single-mindedness in Ezra's manner to assume the man might listen. It was a peculiar thing, Jesse thought, how the missionary understood so little of what surrounded them. Didn't the water move mountains? Didn't the mountains gather snow? Didn't the snow make more water? A spirit flowed through the earth in a perfect circle. It was a spirit that had fed and sheltered Jesse all his days and saved him in a startling way as a guest of the god of the island. Maybe if that was explained to Ezra simply, he might finally understand.

"Okay, I'll tell you."

"Good, brother. Start from the beginning."

Jesse looked at his fingernails. "I was in Dutch Harbor—out on the Aleutians. I worked in a cannery there and one day the boss man asked for my help. He wanted me to take a roll of gillnet up the coast. So I left in a skiff and a fog came up. It came up fast and I lost track of land. I turned back and looked for shore, but it was gone in the mist."

"Ah," Ezra said, as though he knew where the story might lead. "I've seen wisps of fog over Lake Michigan that looked like spirits of the damned. Perhaps that's what you saw and only thought it was a vision."

"No, I can tell what's fog."

"Are you sure?"

Jesse ignored the question and told his friend how he ran out of gas and rowed through the night until he came upon an island. In response, Ezra looked to the ceiling as if his words were meant for heaven. "The Lord took you in his hands and performed a mighty miracle."

"That may be, but it seemed more like magic."

Jesse sat up and rested his back against the wall. He spoke of finding hot water that tasted like tea and the warm cave where he slept. Wasn't it proof, Jesse thought, of the great spirit that pulsed through the earth?

"Is that when you saw the apparition?" Ezra asked. "While you slept in the cave?"

"No, it was dark and I slept without dreams."

"Well," Ezra said before taking a deep breath. "The island wasn't your Savior. Only Christ Jesus can save us from our lowly state and that's a fact. But I can explain some aspects of your experience. For example, the warm water had nothing to do with magic. The Aleutian chain is volcanic in nature and you simply ran across a hot spring. Of course, the cave also was warmed by geological activity."

"I suppose."

"And another thing. I wonder if you've fully considered this assertion of yours. After everything you'd been through—the stress of the situation and all—you could have been suffering from a delusion."

"But could we have touched it?"

"We? Touch it?"

"That's right."

"Perhaps you should finish the story."

Jesse smiled. The memory of that night filled his senses. He felt the dry warmth and smelled the mix of sulfur and salt in the air. As he recalled the sustenance provided to him, he described the god of the island and the drawings and treasures scattered about the cave.

"Then something happened," Jesse said. "The god spoke. At first he talked in a whisper, but finally I understood. He said, 'You can get away with a few things, but you can't change nature.'"

Ezra rolled his eyes. "You mentioned touching it," he said. "When did that happen?"

"I was holding him when they found me."

"When who found you?"

"The Coast Guard."

"And they—the rescuers—they saw it too?"

"Sure, I was holding him. He was stiff from all the sitting, so I helped him lie down. It was morning and we were outside. He was resting his head in my lap. He was my god, but they took him away."

"To where?"

"To the university. They said he was a mommy, but that was a damn lie. He was a man, plain as day. I went to see him once in Anchorage. He was sitting in a glass room and people had taken pictures of his insides."

Ezra closed his eyes and sat motionless. When he finally spoke, his voice came in a whisper. "Jesse," he said. "Please, try to understand. That wasn't God."

"Yeah? Who was he then?"

"He was the devil. And he has deceived you."

Jesse wondered who the devil was and almost asked the question, but he knew it would only open a door to another discussion. So he nodded as if he understood and left to check the smokehouse.

The next morning, Jesse walked sprightly up the hill, using his shoulder to crush a mosquito on his cheek. There were two salmon dangling from his left hand and another from his right. At the summit he saw Ezra and grinned.

"Decided to get up?" he asked.

Ezra returned the smile. "Brother, you'll be a topic I'll recount with fondness at The Church of the First Evangelical."

Jesse noticed a backpack and duffel bag at his friend's feet. "What are you saying?"

"I'm afraid it's time to go. As much as I'd like to remain, the Lord requires my attention."

Jesse went to the plywood butchering table and dropped the fish on top. He wiped his hands on his pants and asked, "Why?"

"I've been called elsewhere. I'm to go to Kaknu and preach Christ crucified."

"Who called you? I don't have a phone."

Ezra put a hand nervously to his cheek. "The Lord called me in prayer. The answer was clear. He said, 'Go to Kaknu.' And brother, that's what I intend to do."

A memory came to Jesse. It was of a potlatch following a village basketball game. A small crowd had gathered and he was telling the story of raven and the creation of the world. The people only snickered in response. How could a bird be their creator?

Jesse chased the recollection away. "It's a pretty wild place," he said. "You won't have much luck there."

"No worse than I've had here."

"Things won't be the same. Do you really have to go?"

Ezra nodded.

Jesse took the pack and led the way to the river. Halfway to the bank—with his head down and feet barely coming off the ground—he asked how Ezra would get along.

"God will provide," his friend answered. "The early disciples traveled without purse or scrip. I shouldn't expect anything more."

They loaded Ezra's Zodiac with his few belongings, then they stood a moment, watching the fish wheel turn and swiping at a cloud of mosquitoes. "Damnable things," Ezra said, scratching his arm. "They are a nuisance."

"I told you, the white god shouldn't have made them."

Ezra wiped his bald head and left a streak of blood and crushed mosquito where his hand had been. "I left you a gift—a

213

Bible," he said. "It's on your cot. You should read it when winter comes and you have time."

Jesse looked up the hill. "I'm pretty busy, but I'll think about it."

"I better go then." Ezra stepped away to untie his boat. He hoisted himself into the Zodiac, saluted comically and turned to start the outboard.

Jesse went to his own boat and untied it. "Wait," he said and handed his friend the tether. "God provided this for you."

"I've got a boat," Ezra said.

"Sure, but you can sell this in the village. Ollie Hansen will buy it. Ask for $2000 and settle for $1500. That'll be a good deal."

"I can't do that. It's too much." For once Ezra seemed unable to speak.

Jesse adjusted his glasses. "What do you figure the Bible's worth?" he asked.

"Well, its value is immeasurable, of course."

"Then in a trade I would've made out okay."

"But how will you live?"

"Oh, us Indians have been doing that for a long time. I have most of what I need right here. When things freeze up, I can walk to the village. Don't worry about me."

The men stared at each other. "Are you sure, brother?" Ezra asked.

Jesse nodded.

"God bless you," the missionary said as he took the rope.

Waving off the recognition, Jesse pushed both boats into deep water. "Once you get going," he said, "the mosquitoes won't be a problem."

As Ezra chugged away with the other boat in tow, Jesse reminded himself that he wasn't alone. The wind would still whistle him to sleep. The sun would greet him each morning. The river would keep him company. Jesse watched until his friend disappeared, then he whispered as if speaking in confidence.

"Gods bless you, too."

Chapter 13

When Dirk got transferred to Elmendorf Airforce Base, we tagged along. Mom got a job at a bookstore, while I finished high school and did odd jobs for pocket money. Anchorage turned out to be a nice place. So, when Dirk shipped out, we didn't follow. Mom said she wasn't seeing eye-to-eye with him, anyway.

- From Kit Lerner's Journal

For three days not even a grayling touched his lure and Patch went to sleep hungry. Several hours after he crawled into his sleeping bag and zipped it tight against the cold, he was roused by the sound of steps. It didn't come from a predator. A bear's shuffle was distinctive and accompanied by grunts and heavy breathing. More likely it was a hoofed animal, he thought, but its approach seemed confused.

He retrieved his gun and the idea of meat came to him like guilt over a broken promise, but he reminded himself of what Kit had said about her hunger. Holding the weapon in front of him, he slipped out of the tent and searched out the sound. The outline of a caribou calf appeared in the moonlight. It took an uncertain step and fell.

It must be sick, Patch thought, and he wondered how it had eluded the vigil of wolves, the opportunism of bears. He stood, hoping to get a better view of it, and in that instant the caribou struggled to its feet and presented a shoulder. Patch raised his pistol and pulled the trigger. His arm jerked from recoil and the animal collapsed to its chest.

Patch retrieved his lamp from the tent, lit it and held it high. While bathing the carcass with sputtering light, he noticed something odd. He kneeled and rotated the calf's head from side to side and saw no open stare or glazed look, only festering masses where eyes ought to have been. Damn, he thought, what could have caused that? Then he knew: It had been pecked blind by ravens and left to starve.

There wasn't much meat on the carcass and even less fat. Patch worked through the night, beyond the moment when the lantern sucked the last of its gas. Morning came and found him sitting next to a fire, where the animal's fist-sized heart roasted on a stick. Until noon he worked, stripping the meat and smoking it hot off the fire. He ate small portions, but sealed most of the food in bags and packed it away. When his tasks were done, he wiped his forehead and retired to the tent, trying not to dwell on an irony taking root in his mind.

If a sightless caribou had wandered into Kit's camp, would she have called it a gift from God and dispatched the animal? Maybe, Patch thought, since the calf wouldn't have offered much resistance to a woman wielding a hatchet or knife. With the meat she might have survived the consecutive days of snowfall until a search party arrived. That line of logic caused him to wonder: If the meat was a gift, why hadn't Kit received it, too?

With his stomach full of red meat, Patch slept fitfully. In a dream, he saw a fish. It was yellow and scarred, walking upright, but stumbling. Patch felt no fear or alarm. He stole a closer look and noticed that the creature was without eyes. Where the sockets should have been there were only gray masses.

The fish lurched on, one fin twitching. Its gills flapped as if it were trying to speak. From its lips, a noise organized itself and eventually—ever so gradually—took the form of words. The words, repeated like a chant, were these:

Upon this flesh I feed my children.

I have fed you.

He slept through the afternoon and into the following night until a sense of foreboding woke him. Still wrapped in his sleeping bag, Patch looked outside, but he could only feel the difference. There was moisture in the air, a lack of starlight in the sky. The land, he knew, was preparing for a change.

A cold gale whipped the tent as Patch dismantled and folded it. Suddenly he noticed the meat and remembered the events of the previous night. The dream returned to him like an indictment.

Upon this flesh I feed my children. I have fed you.

"No, damn it," he yelled to the sky. "I won't accept your charity." He opened each plastic bag and spilled the meat onto the ground. "You can feed the wolves. You can feed the foxes and the birds. But, by hell, you won't feed me."

Knowing there was one more thing to do, he stuck a finger down his throat and the sound of his retching echoed off the surrounding hills.

Wet with sweat and shivering from the cold, he trudged over rocky hillsides and through dense brush. His feet and shoulders throbbed. He longed for rest, but each time he was tempted to stop, Kit appeared in a clearing or on a faraway ridge and beckoned to him. Patch wavered between doubt and belief—at once, certain he willed her to life, but wondering if she lived only in his head—then during one arduous moment she was beside him, sloshing through a bog that swallowed them both to their knees.

"You can't stop now," she said. "You have three more hours of daylight."

"I can't go another minute, much less three hours."

"Yes, you can. It's what Amanda would want. Be strong."

"Be strong? Why don't I put my life into God's hands?"

Kit frowned, but she kept moving. Her legs were soaked and her face was splotched with mud. The sky remained overcast and threatening. "That's not fair," she said. "God didn't make you shoot your kayak."

Patch laughed at the mention of fairness, but tried to match Kit step for step. "You say that like God exists."

"If you pay enough attention, you might notice something noble and god-like inside *you*. What was your life like before you gave up on it?"

The question reminded Patch of a time when he made plans and fed aspirations, a time before Emily first begged him not to sneak away into his own head. "What does it matter?" he said. "I'm here to forget such things—which is what you apparently came for, too. I saw what you buried."

"I buried an obsession, but I never lost sight of what was good in my life. Should I repeat the question? Did you always have this dim view of the world?

"No," Patch said. "I was a different man once. Then everything I loved was taken away."

He spoke of the spring days after his first near drowning and how his memories of Emily had stirred him constantly. A week after his release from an Anchorage hospital, he bought a basket of fruit and returned to see her. His sweat ran cold as he waited near the elevators, pretending to have business there.

When Emily appeared at the nurse's station, Patch went to the counter. "You probably don't remember me," he said, trying to quiet his shifting feet and ignore the stares from the other nurses. "I almost drowned and you were a big part of my recovery. I came to say thanks."

To prove that he wasn't always unconscious and cold to the touch, Patch had come clean-shaven and in clothes that didn't smell of fish and a long stint on the water. Emily looked up from notes she was writing on a clipboard and stared without a hint of recognition. Patch felt the heat of embarrassment on his face and thought: Damn, she must think of me as just another guy with a fish-belly complexion.

He was about to drop his gift and scurry out, but Emily smiled and said, "I see that you thawed out. I was wondering how you were doing."

Patch wanted to say she'd been on his mind, too, and that he slept and woke to thoughts of her, but honesty seemed a dangerous thing to him. "It's good to know you've been thinking of me," he said, hoping the words wouldn't sound like a come on. He handed her the basket of fruit—oranges and grapefruits hard to come by in a place snowbound for much of the year—and tried to appear at ease.

"Another gift, Emily?" an older nurse said. "How many does that make for you today?"

"Oh, be quiet."

There were giggles from behind the counter and Emily thanked Patch on behalf of the hospital staff. She came out from behind the nurse's station, grabbed him by an arm and led him toward the elevator. Here it comes, Patch thought, the big send off—the old heave ho—but in the next instant she surprised him.

"They're trying to embarrass me," she said, her voice barely above a whisper. "I may have joked around a bit—said I was going to call you, or something. My intent, of course, was to check on your condition." Emily smiled.

"Oh, sure. I understand. You're concerned about your patients." Suddenly the world seemed like a nurturing place, one that encouraged risk-taking. "I'm staying in Anchorage tonight. I can bring you up-to-date over dinner."

Despite his amazement that an intelligent woman would agree to see him, Patch visited her every two-day break when he wasn't fishing. He would arrange to bunk with a friend and drive the gravel road to Anchorage, nervously rehearsing conversations based upon the news of the day. In the privacy of his pickup he sounded glib, but the sight of Emily would render his preparations all for naught. He was too much in love to be anything but cautious, so their relationship might not have progressed beyond dinners and movies, except that Emily asked to go moose hunting with him.

They paddled a canoe for most of that first day, engaged in a light-hearted chatter that disqualified them as serious hunters. With their tent pitched on the bank of a narrow river, they sat by a fire in the cold of an autumn evening and talked about what they wanted from life: a family, a comfortable home, and simple pleasures. They cuddled under the stars as shadows stood upright around them. Patch wondered who would make the first move to the sleeping bags, but in the end it happened more spontaneously than he could have imagined.

"I'll make an honest woman out of you," he said the next morning. "If you're interested anyway."

"What do you mean by that?"

Patch realized the time for pretense had come to an end. He tried to describe the feelings bursting out of his heart. "Nothing could make me happier than to wake up every day of my life just like I did here—to the sight of you."

Emily tightened her slim arms around him and said, "I like how you put that."

Two decades later the memory still made him weak. If possible, he would exchange his remaining years to relive that one perfect night. But the memory had passed and he was back in the present. He was out of the bog now, but still in the middle of nowhere, tracking a wild river. Kit was no longer at his side. He turned to look behind him, but she wasn't there.

"Do you hear that?" he said. "I would give up the rest of my years to relive that night."

The wind picked up and carried Kit's reply: "And the chance it might happen again makes the rest of your years worth living."

Chapter 14

We write volumes on how to negotiate, but not a word about taking a moral stand.

- From Kit Lerner's Journal

Some evenings, when sleep seemed an unlikely event, Jesse pulled his cot next to the wood-burning stove and, by the glow of its fire, read from the Bible his friend had left. It was then, during the first of those twilight periods, that he made a startling discovery. The white god didn't speak English! (At least, it wasn't a variation of language Jesse had ever heard before).

Over time he began to appreciate the rhythm of the words— a reminder of how Ezra had talked, singsong in nature. It was almost enough to get him beyond the book's more ticklish aspects, like the questions it raised and the hurt it put in his head. Yet he became so distracted by each succeeding puzzle, he forgot the ones he'd encountered the night before.

So Jesse put the questions to paper and each night the list grew longer. It began: Why did those guys have funny names? How did they get so old? What's a begat? Where is Eden and how much does it cost to get in? Is a foreskin really what I think it is? (Why does it need to be off?) What's a chosen people and why does the white god only care about them?

There was also another group of questions, more ticklish in nature, regarding a story he could not comprehend. It was the account of Abraham, the first chosen man who was to be father of a nation. The inquiries began: Why did the white god tell Abraham to kill his boy? (And in dark capital letters: **WHY DID ABRAHAM TRY?**) Must the white god test his people that way? Doesn't he know what's in their hearts?

Jesse woke up mid-morning with nothing to do. The salmon were near the end of their season and the few fish remaining in the river were dark and scarred, unfit to eat but for times of shortage. His cache was full and until the caribou came, churning up the tundra with their many hooves, he could enjoy both warm weather and rest. It was a rare luxury.

Despite his leisure (or perhaps because of it) he felt sad. The feeling would come to him suddenly, especially during evenings and other breaks away from work. When he walked outside, for example, he would notice the firewood that Ezra Willis had left split and stacked. He remembered the day his friend placed the last stick. They made a ceremony out of it and Ezra spoke. Now, what was it he said? Oh, yes.

An idle mind is the devil's workshop.

Jesse tossed the memory aside like it was a slip of paper and turned his face to the sky, grateful for the sun. The previous two days had been drizzle-filled and the smell of yesterday's rain reminded him of something he'd learned from the village elders. It was a notion he reflected on—an ancient remembrance handed down from age to age and kept alive at potlatches. It was referred to as the gateway to the home of the spirits and in olden times the shamans had derived power from it.

Knowing of places along the fringe of his hill where ferns and other cover grew, he decided to test the recollection. He'd spotted them in the past, half-hidden beneath tree boughs and blanketed by shadows, rising from the ground after autumn rains.

He walked away from the river, downhill to a stand of spruce and alder. A tangle of devils club and baneberry grew among the trees and left him damp as he hiked along a game trail through it. He eventually came to a clearing. Deep moss sprung back from where his feet stepped. There, he spotted his prey beneath the cover of a birch tree.

The mushrooms were large and red with white scales on their caps. He picked one and wondered if there was a rite to its taking. Should he chant? Should he pound a drum? Should he dance or sing? Jesse wished the god of the island could be there to teach him and confirm such aspects of his chosen ways.

He sniffed one of the mushrooms, hoping it wasn't poisonous, as rumored. He'd seen caribou eat them—even watched the otherwise predictable animals go berserk afterwards—but they didn't die. If caribou could do it, he reckoned, so might a man. He broke off a piece and placed it under his tongue. It had a mild taste, not bitter as he'd assumed. He took more and chewed the flesh completely, sucking its juice before swallowing.

Thirty minutes passed and the first wave of nausea hit him. His vision blurred and he fell to the mossy floor of the forest and retched. Yet as suddenly as it had come upon him the nausea settled and he rolled onto his back. The trees before him multiplied and changed shape. They were red, then purple, red again, then blue. It was more brilliant than any northern lights he'd ever seen. Even the shadows took on substance and form. He pushed himself onto his backside and watched.

Jesse groaned as another wave of nausea came upon him and he vomited again. It was followed by another dizzying vision. The process repeated itself several times until late afternoon, when he finally walked home, wet with sweat.

Lying on his cot and unable to sleep, he thought about the vision and how it reminded him of things he'd seen through Martin's kaleidoscope. From its shadows demons had emerged. The demons turned to light and the light rejoined the shadows. Through it all he'd received no message, no wisdom, no instruction. Is this what I'm looking for? he thought. Is this how I'm supposed to live?

A few mornings later Jesse scanned the valley down river, focusing on a distant hill where a blueberry thicket undulated like a purple and gray sea. Through his binoculars he saw it again, the young brown bear that had appeared several mornings that week. Its muzzle was unmarked. Its broad sides shook with fat.

"Bear would be good," Jesse whispered. "Especially one that has fed on berries."

It was one half of an argument that had made trails through his heart since the animal first appeared months before. Jesse and Ezra had watched it stand immobile in the river, searching for food as water crashed around it. On several occasions they saw it spring forward—a motion accompanied by a fountain of spray—to pin salmon onto the river bottom. It showed a preference for the fat bellies of the fish it caught, especially those of roe-filled females.

The bear had been a polite neighbor, taking its due but leaving Jesse and his portion alone. It performed its duty, dug roots and ground squirrels, increased its girth ahead of cold weather. Through much of summer Jesse had watched it gain skill and confidence, wondering what he might do when fall approached and the animal had sweetened its flesh on salmon fat and berries.

"Do you hunt bear?" Ezra had asked one day.

All Jesse could do was make a joke of it. "When they're not hunting me."

Jesse trudged to his cabin and took the rifle off his worktable. Dour faced, he weighed the argument again. Isn't this what my people have always done? Isn't this a part of our lives? He slung the weapon over a shoulder and started out the door. The game trail he followed was as old as the river itself and led him to a clearing. He stopped to see if his movement had alerted the bear. The animal was upwind and still far into the distance. Jesse also recalled that a bear was shortsighted at best.

He picked his way through a bog to where the ground rose gradually. Settling near a cover of willows, he dropped to his stomach, raised the rifle to his shoulder and peered through the scope. The bear was belly up to the sun, oblivious to any danger. It gyrated its shoulders and hips, as if scratching a hard-to-reach itch. It made a sound that was both high grunt and sigh.

When his 30.06 exploded, the sound was a surprise to Jesse. The firearm jumped from recoil and he whispered, "What the hell?" He rubbed his shoulder, wondering if the shot was the result of an accident or instinct. He lowered the rifle and trained its scope on the place he'd last viewed the bear. The animal was gone.

He looked over the barrel and caught a glimpse of something cinnamon, a hint of movement. The bear had taken flight down the hill and come to rest behind a boulder.

"What the hell?" Jesse said again and he pushed himself up. Like a man with a stomachache, he scrambled toward the rock in a crouch. He tripped twice to his knees while rising out of pockmarks in the hill. His breath came like a shudder as he fumbled with his rifle bolt. The spent shell flew, spinning like a pinwheel and fell without a sound. The smell of gunpowder pricked his nostrils and caught in his throat.

A wounded bear, he reminded himself, was a menace. He knew of their strength and stamina. When angered, they refused to fall. Bullets couldn't stop them. They were dangerous animals.

But not as dangerous as a man.

From a distance Jesse circled the boulder and heard a groan so human-like, he wondered if he'd shot a hunter by mistake. When the far side of the rock came into view, he saw the bear. It sat with its back against the rock, a bloody gash across its gut. Still unaware of Jesse's presence, it bit and pawed at the wound, enlarging the gap and exposing a roll of pink intestine. Its light brown fur was covered with blood that was already turning black. Jesse raised his rifle and another shot echoed down the river valley again.

He put the weapon down and sat. The second round had entered the bear's head and strewn brain matter and shattered bone against the rock. Jesse stared at the carcass and tried to catch his breath. For a long time he sat motionless. The sun rose higher in the sky.

"Does it matter?" Jesse finally said. "Does it mean anything to you, that I will not waste your gift?"

After he skinned the bear Jesse couldn't look at the carcass, because the arms fell to the side in the way of a large man. He scraped off the yellow fat and wrapped it in the hide. He tried not to think of the young bear that had lumbered across the hillside, caught salmon in the river, dug roots and relished a good scratch on its back. Taking several trips, Jesse dragged the quartered sections of meat to his cabin and rubbed them with salt in preparation to be smoked. Early the next day he went back for the hide.

###

Some mornings were cold enough to leave frost where dew had appeared the week before. Every day the sharp edge of autumn became dulled by sun-filled skies that turned crisp as night descended. By bedtime Jesse's cheeks were flushed and wind-burnt.

For a week he waited for the caribou's migration and tended to his bear hide. He scraped it clean of flesh and rubbed sourdough onto the thick skin to cure it. After the third straight morning of frost, he finished his chores early and spread the hide over a boulder. It took on the form of the young bear and Jesse looked away. He went to his cot and closed his eyes, thinking to take a nap.

All at once he heard his name and an exclamation of surprise. Jesse sat up quickly and looked toward the door. It swung open and he saw Belle standing in the entryway, a hand over her heart and her hair disheveled.

"Please," she said. "Tell me that bear outside is dead."

For the first time in weeks Jesse had company. He patted one side of his cot as an invitation to sit and got up to make coffee. When Belle asked if she could stay a couple of days, Jesse found a bounce in his step. He asked if Martin had come, too, and sighed to hear that the boy was in school and that Clarence was watching him.

Nevertheless, Jesse's tongue tripped over a jumble of words trying to say he was happy to see his niece. There was so much he wanted to tell her—things he'd learned while living alone with a few random thoughts and a persistent dream that were his companions. But all he could manage to say was, "Summer has been good."

"That's nice." Belle took a mug of coffee and glanced beneath the worktable. She pointed to three cases stacked atop each other. "You haven't touched your beer yet," she said.

Jesse tried to recall a phrase Ezra had used in support of sobriety. "That's because my body's a temple. And the spirit swells in it."

"What?" Belle suppressed a laugh. "That was a short experiment. Maybe I ought to drink it. I had my share of beer in college. Hate to see it go to waste."

"Help yourself."

Belle sipped her coffee instead and said, "Looks like you shot yourself a bear. Did you catch some fish, too?"

"Oh, yeah. I got my share."

"What about a garden?"

"I grew a bunch of potatoes and cabbages—picked berries, too."

"You're right, Uncle. Summer has been kind to you."

Jesse felt warmed by the conversation, but a little chagrined, as well. "I had help," he confessed.

"Oh, I know. He came to the village, your walrus man."

Jesse looked up from his mug. The thought of Ezra Willis cheered him. He hoped the missionary was safe and had made many friends.

"He mentioned how you pulled on his mustache—said you thought it was walrus teeth."

"I don't remember that. It could've happened, though. He stayed a couple weeks."

"So I hear." Belle patted her uncle's knee. "He talked about you. He said plenty of good folks are going to hell and mentioned you all but by name. Isn't that a hoot?"

"There's good folks in hell? So it's a nice place, huh?"

Belle looked astonished. "No, not at all. Hell is where it's always burning. And there's this guy, the devil, who pokes you with a stick and makes you work your butt off."

"Oh? So why are good folks going there?"

"I don't know, Uncle, I suppose it's a mystery."

"Uh huh. There's lots of that."

Belle picked at her fingernails. "Your friend said something else, too—something about a story you told him."

"About the Indian god? I told him."

"Why'd you do that? He'll go off telling other folks now and, before you know it, someone will come take you away—even put you in a funny farm."

"Is that where they grow asparagus?"

Belle almost choked on her coffee. "No. Don't you know anything? It's not that kind of farm. It's where they put crazy people and once you're in, you can't get out. You spend all day eating lousy food and talking to the walls."

"Sounds like hell."

"Exactly."

"That's too bad," Jesse said, grinning. "I only had asparagus once. Funny food—reminds me of a dog's...you know."

Belle took a long breath. "You got to be careful. It's bad enough that people in the village think you're off your nut. Don't get the whole world thinking that, too."

"The village thinks I'm crazy?"

"No, I didn't mean that. The fact is we all wish you'd come back. We miss you."

Jesse was too distracted to hear Belle's last words. "They think I'm crazy," he repeated. "In the old days, I might have been their healer. I've seen visions."

"No, you only think you've seen visions. You mistook a black man for a walrus."

Jesse looked out the window.

"Let go of the old days," Belle said. "It's gone. You can't go back to it."

"But we should learn."

"How? It was lost a long time ago."

So much gone, Jesse thought, the purpose in hunger, the distance between kills, the short summers of gathering, and winters of restoration. An entire culture had disappeared. Is it progress, he wondered, to replace a life of foraging with basketball in village gymnasiums and hooch bought on the sly?

Chapter 15

Who's the devil, some fallen angel who turned against God? That's mumbo jumbo. If Satan is really the source of evil, couldn't he defeat God by withholding temptation?

- From Kit Lerner's Journal

Patch walked until he came to a treeless valley. The sky was vast and gray, so imposing that he felt as inconspicuous as a pebble. A cold wind blew and he covered his eyes against its frequent gusting. He'd been walking for hours and his legs were beginning to spasm. For the first time in days his exhaustion overwhelmed his hunger.

He heard the drone of an engine and looked up to see one of his Super Cubs, the one his employee, Jimbo, usually flew. Patch recalled that waving a single arm signaled all is well, two arms was a request for help. Which do I do? he wondered. The plane flew past him before it tilted and circled. It acknowledged his presence by dipping one wing and then the other. Patch finally settled on a course of action, seeing no other alternative. How could he explain the loss of his kayak when the embarrassment alone might kill him? He raised an open palm, waved it with as much confidence as he could muster and watched the plane arc away. Then a thought popped into his head that was tinged with remorse: Amanda will be disappointed. She wanted me to go home.

Patch turned and scanned the basin ahead, seeing an object that didn't fit with the easy contour of the hillside. He headed in its direction—a good sign, he thought, since it meant he was alive enough to be curious. Still half a mile away, he realized what it was: the remains of a wrecked plane that littered the ground like the skin shed by a giant insect. Patch veered up an incline toward the wreckage, seeing it as a place to sleep without needing to pitch a tent. As he approached, a light snow dusted the ground and muted all color.

What remained of the wreckage was weathered. Patch could see that it was an old Fairchild with military insignia, likely built in the 30's and fitted with floats. It had come down hard, in a way that crumpled the landing gear and broke the fuselage. Its nose was dug into the ground.

"What do we have here?" Patch muttered, but that was the extent of his curiosity. He was too tired to speculate further.

Beneath one crumpled wing he found the door ajar and rusted into place. Its glass was shattered. He squeezed through the opening and stumbled past several seats to the back. Sheltered from the wind, he ate a handful of blueberries that he'd picked along the way. He looked outside, where the northern lights hovered over a darkening horizon. The throbbing green lights meandered across the sky and left neon-like trails where they passed.

It was the time of year when he longed for the mischief-seeking days of summer. It was a time for rest, but a rest entered into reluctantly. Time to hole up. Time to hibernate and dream. For the remainder of the night Patch lay in his sleeping bag, battling muscle contractions and wandering in and out of sleep. Though he tried to make plans for the following day, each moment subjected him to a gale of memories that worked his heart to excess.

"You're doing fine."

Kit's voice brought Patch to sudden wakefulness. She was sitting with her back to the pilot's seat, dressed in a clean pullover. Her face was washed. Darkness had settled, but she seemed to shed light. "Look how far you've come," she said. "Amanda would be so proud."

Patch rose onto a bent elbow and rubbed his crusted eyes. "It all ends here," he said, unsure if he was speaking from the heart or only making a point. "I think I'll stay here and die—just like you did."

"No, you won't." Kit moved closer and knelt beside him. "Let me tell you a secret. Are you listening?"

"Yes."

"Do you know what sin is? The fact is it's just another word for selfishness. Sin is always seeking pleasurable—or, at least, painless—ways out of entanglements and getting cheated out of life's lessons in the process. But you're not selfish. You'll keep pushing yourself. That's your way."

"I gave up once. I can do it again."

"Is that what you think?" Kit smiled as if she saw through the pretense. "You're preoccupied with culpability—and not just you, all of the living are. You waste so much energy trying to assign blame, but sometimes the only fault is in the inevitability of our circumstances. And what you did wasn't giving up."

"What was it then?"

"You fought for what you thought was right. Ponder that as you go."

Patch reclined again, too tired to carry the weight of the conversation. As he meandered in and out of sleep, he slipped into another place and a time when he was still battling to save his marriage. It was the second autumn after losing Amanda and he'd invited Emily to Kaknu, hoping it would mark a fresh start in their lives. He watched as she stepped through the door of his single-room cabin and cast her eyes from one wall to another.

"It's cozy," she said. "But I don't see a bathroom."

"Bathroom? There's nothing of the kind here." A queen-sized mattress was on one side of the floor, a wooden rocking chair beside it. A blue tarp covered a mound of supplies, but there was no bathroom. "I thought you knew that," he said.

"Well, I didn't."

Patch tugged his ear and considered various words that might erase Emily's look of disappointment. "It's not like you're without options. For one, you can go outside. There aren't any mosquitoes this early in the year."

"You say that as though bears aren't a problem."

"Nah, bears usually stay clear of the village—they don't take to the dogs, you see."

"That's a load off." Emily pasted a brave smile on her face and nodded through the rear window. "I have to bare my butt and turn the snow yellow out there?"

"Like I said, you got options." Patch set her bag down and pointed to the tarp. "There's a bucket underneath that. Most of the people in the village use something similar."

"A bucket? Are you kidding me?" Emily laughed.

Patch realized he should have prepared his wife for their stay in the bush. Despite the oversight, she was trying to be civil and he resolved not to let the lack of facilities spoil their time together.

"There's one other thing you can do."

"Does it require I climb a tree? Or run naked through the woods?"

"No, but we'll need to walk a bit. The school has toilets and showers. I can take you there if you like."

They strolled over a snow-packed trail, passing yellow-eyed dogs and smokehouses. The sun was two hours from setting and quickly losing its command of the sky. From the west, a storm was brewing and raising the humidity. When they reached the school, Patch opened one of the metal outer doors and heard the sounds of bouncing balls and sneakers on a hardwood floor.

"I'll be in there," he said, pointing to another set of double doors. "The restrooms are down the hall."

Patch entered the gymnasium and saw several teenage boys playing a game of basketball. Kaknu offered few amusements, so the villagers played the sport throughout the year. By the way they set screens and blocked out on rebounds, Patch could tell the youngsters were well coached.

From a section of extended bleacher seats, a few adults shouted words of advice and encouragement. Patch saw Belle and her family among those who were gathered. He waved in their direction and took a seat nearby. Minutes later, amid the rumble of a fast break, Emily found her way inside and sat beside Patch.

"They're good," she said, as one of the boys drove the lane and hooked the ball into the basket.

For an hour they watched, until Clarence blew a whistle and said he was turning off the lights. The boys complained, but they halted play and the adults stood to leave. Patch took advantage of the game's end to introduce Emily to Belle. The two women shared pleasantries, when Clarence interrupted with talk about basketball and the school team's record.

"Twenty-three and one," he said. "And we avenged our only loss—twice."

"Didn't I say they were good?" Patch turned to his wife, looking for confirmation, but she was kneeling beside Martin.

"Sorry," Emily said. "What did you say?"

Patch wondered about the cause of her distraction. Martin was humming a song and kicking the bleacher seat in front of him. Emily slid closer to the boy and watched him. He was pulling objects out of his pocket and studying them.

"What do you have there?" she asked. "Marbles?"

"No, they're charms."

Martin handed a stone to Emily and she held it up to the light. It was an agate the color of amber, clear and without blemish. "It's pretty," she said. "How does it work?"

"You hold it. That's all. You want one?" Before she could reply, the boy curled Emily's fingers around the stone. "There," he said. "Keep it. It'll give you luck."

Emily opened her hand and stared at the offering. She raised her line of sight, focused on the little boy and reached for Patch. "He's as cute as a bug's ear," she said. "Don't you think?"

Belle invited the Taggarts to dinner and served a heaping platter of spaghetti. The tangy aroma of tomatoes mingled with the scent of caribou sausage. Patch's stomach growled, but Emily's reaction was even more noticeable. Her display of surprise and relief caused Patch to laugh.

"You didn't think we'd be eating fermented salmon heads, did you?" he asked.

"Oh, Patch, no one does that." Emily gave Clarence a questioning look. "Right?"

"It's not my favorite dish, but folks do eat it around here."

Emily cupped a hand over her mouth. "And here I was worried we'd have whale blubber."

"That's for dessert," Belle said with a grin.

241

Contrary to her claim, Belle served ice cream at the end of the meal. Later as the adults sipped coffee Martin asked if he could show everyone his treasures. When Emily's eyes lit up, the boy left for his room and returned with stone fishing weights, willow hooks, bone knives, shale scraping tools, and other objects he'd fashioned with Jesse's help. Ignoring his mother's critical looks, he showed how each item was used.

"You made all these?" Emily asked.

"Me and Jesse did."

"Jesse and I," Belle said.

Martin paid her no attention. "Uncle Jesse knows all about how we lived before."

"That's not true."

"Yes, it is." The boy's jaw tightened. "Uncle Jesse met a god in a cave. It was an Indian god. And it showed him all kinds of stuff."

Patch wanted to ask what the boy meant, but the look in Belle's face didn't welcome questions. She told Martin it was time for bed and Emily helped gather his objects and put them away. Patch watched his wife walk out of the room and heard her say goodnight.

He waited for her return and tried to appear mindful of what Clarence was saying about the problems of teaching in rural Alaska. Ten minutes later Emily was back and glowing in a way Patch hadn't seen in years. He decided they'd done the right thing by coming. After just a day in the village, the gulf between them was closing.

###

That night Patch and Emily zipped their sleeping bags together and rested on the mattress with extra blankets piled atop of them. The evening grew cold and seemed to freeze all sound and motion. There was no television to drown out the silence and the only thin light came from a gas lantern. In the near-darkness Emily pressed herself against Patch and rubbed his chest.

He was surprised by her touch and it made him dizzy with arousal. For years their lovemaking had been uninspired and routine, not unlike most other aspects of their marriage. As if embarrassed by a moment of intimacy, they would roll to opposite sides of the bed and pretend nothing had happened.

"Are you cold?" Patch asked, holding her to him.

"A little."

"Glad to be here?"

"No complaints." Emily giggled and then she spoke as if expressing a random thought. "That Martin is quite a kid, isn't he?"

The sound of her laughter caused Patch to close his eyes and recall how passion had once ruled them. As newlyweds, they'd celebrated unabashed desire for each other and he wanted that again. Talk about Martin didn't interest him, but he replied to avoid spoiling the moment.

"The boy's a character," he said, giving Emily the crook of his arm to rest her head. "No doubt about that."

"Oh, he's more than a character. I could steal and raise him as my own."

A warning bell—like the stall alarm in his plane—went off in Patch's head. He recalled scenes from earlier in the day:

Emily's furtive glances in Martin's direction, the glow of her eyes each time the boy spoke. Patch felt out of control, limbo taking him into its grasp. He was caught between arousal and common sense, wondering how he could have been so stupid. The evidence was clear. Emily was in love with a past to which she could never return.

"Belle and Clarence wouldn't take kindly to someone nabbing their kid," Patch said.

"I suppose so. That's why we need one of our own."

For a moment the nuzzling and tittering stopped. "You're joking, right?" Patch said, trying to keep the conversation calm and casual. "We're a little too old for that, or haven't you noticed?"

"I'm thirty-six."

"That makes my case."

"It makes mine, too. I'm still in shape, but if we don't get to work soon, our chance for another baby will have gone."

Patch tried to sort out his feelings. He wanted Emily to be happy, but giving her something to fret over—to love and maybe lose again—wouldn't help. Besides, he thought, what business did a middle-aged couple have bringing a baby into an uncertain world?

"I don't relish the thought of playing catch into my sixties," he said.

"You won't think so when the time comes. Babies make you young."

"Or they make you old. Listen, I'm through with procreation. I wouldn't mind going through the exercise, but it would be wrong for us to get pregnant."

Emily went limp. The lamplight flickered and cast an eerie shadow on the cabin wall. "Then let's adopt," she said. "There's plenty of children who need a family—a lot of them Martin's age."

"Let's be honest. We would only be replacing what we've lost and that's no reason to have a child."

Emily put an arm over her eyes and turned onto her back. Patch assured her that everything would be okay, but she was inconsolable. He held her, thinking she would come to her senses and recognize the merit of his position, but the sound of her cries extended long into the night.

Morning on the Killborn River broke calm and cold, when Patch awoke after a restless night. At first he didn't know where he was, the ghosts of his past playing tricks on his memory. He tried to make sense of the frost-covered walls surrounding him and remembered taking refuge in a downed plane. Disappointment smacked him broadside. He was still childless and divorced and far from home.

Patch rose and stowed his gear, every muscle in his body throbbing. He stepped outside and took his bearings. A light cover of snow remained on the ground and the Killborn was a dark line in the distance. The valley stretched across his periphery and filled his vision. He began to walk toward the river, when something stopped him five steps later.

Bear tracks—just minutes old—crisscrossed his intended path and led beyond a faraway ridge. Patch stepped into one of

245

the prints and his size-twelve boot took up less than half the distance from paw heel to claw tip. He checked the direction from where the animal had come and whistled low.

"Did we share the same bed?" he said.

There was only one set of tracks and its path originated from the plane. The bear had slept in the wreckage, too, but in the tail section separated from the cabin by a gaping hole and the bulkhead. Something about the trail bothered him and he recalled the circumstances of the previous day. The snow had fallen for just a short time—the flurry beginning and ending during the same hour he found the wreckage. The bear, Patch reckoned, had been in the plane when he came across it. Otherwise there would be another set of tracks.

"Did I sleep with a bear?" Patch mused. "Or the devil?"

He stuck to the valley's high ground, where the footing was dry and firm. Around noon he came to a ridge that rose across his path. He climbed the hill and stopped at its peak. The sky was clear and settled like something chilled and poured from a bottle. At the bottom of the hill a creek entered the river from a lake a short distance away. The ground appeared wet and overgrown.

"That's going to be tough slogging," he said.

Patch studied the creek, looking for the best place to ford. His view progressed from riffle and whirlpool to rock and eddy before the lake claimed his interest. Trout, he reckoned, would be hiding in the deep water. He was about to assemble his fishing rod and test his hypothesis, when he noticed a floatplane tied to the bank. It was his Super Cub and a man was hiking up the hill from its direction.

Patch slung the pack off his shoulders and let it drop to the ground. He sat beside it and waited. His vision blurred as a dozen competing emotions washed over him. The idea that someone—an employee, no less—could hover over him to ensure his safe return diminished the meaning of his journey. On the other hand, it offered him some amount of relief, too.

The man reached the summit and smiled. He was dressed in a knit cap, tattered letter jacket and corduroy pants. An embroidered name appeared above his left breast that read: Jimbo. He chuckled and said, "I was flying a client out yesterday and spotted you. You didn't look too good."

"I don't recall asking you to come back for me."

"No, but I couldn't sleep for wondering how you were. My paychecks are worthless without your signature." Jimbo reached into his daypack and tossed a brown paper bag into Patch's lap. "I figured you'd like something to eat."

Patch opened the bag and pulled out a sandwich wrapped in plastic. He raised it to his nose and the scent made him salivate. "Egg salad," he said and began to eat.

Jimbo looked in the direction of the river and asked, "Where's your kayak?"

"I decided to walk to Kaknu. I can use the exercise."

"Well, that's quite a hike. Are you up for it?"

Patch swallowed. "I believe so."

"*Believe* so? Winter's on its way. You better think twice about going any further."

"I can't stop now. I've got a hundred dollars riding on the result. Besides, Kaknu is a nice place. I might stay there for the duration."

Jimbo knelt beside Patch and patted him on the knee. "There's nothing for you there," he said.

"Is that right?"

The man laughed. "I'm damn sure of that. Kaknu's not a place for you."

Patch thought of previous summers, when clear skies had let him fly nearly every day from late May to early September. The landmarks appeared in his mind again, familiar points on an uneven tapestry. Only in places of rare plenty did bears act amiably, but they came bounding to the area's rivers like shaggy dogs to chase and eat. From the best fishing and hunting grounds in Alaska, Patch could fly a handful of minutes west and circle his cabin in Kaknu.

"Damn, the life those Indians lead," Jimbo said. "You know what I mean?"

"No." Patch waited for the man's opinion.

"You've seen it: Dogs on three foot chains, rusted out snow machines, empty 50-gallon drums—all kinds of shit scattered around the shacks those people live in. And there's no indoor toilets either. It's dumped out on the permafrost."

Patch couldn't disagree, but he couldn't let the observation go without comment either. "You see some of those things in downtown Anchorage."

"Maybe, but not to the same degree."

"I suppose you prefer the stress of living on top of your neighbors."

"Better than living in shit. And between here and Kaknu there's a whole lot of nowhere. So I'm taking you home."

Patch shrugged. The thought of returning to his Forest Drive apartment was a temptation, but to do so meant turning his back on a commitment. "I don't think so," he said. "I've got a date with a trout in that lake over there and then I'll be hiking out. Thanks for lunch, though."

With that he stood, hoisted his pack onto his shoulders and raised a second sandwich to his mouth. "And Jimbo?" he said, his mouth full.

"Yeah?"

"Don't come looking for me again. Do you hear?"

Chapter 16

Oh! I saw a caribou today, a bull, I think. He seemed sick—just waved his head and stumbled like a drunk. I caught myself wishing (the first time ever) that I had a gun. I would have put the poor thing out of its misery. Better die from a bullet than at the mercy of wolves.

- From Kit Lerner's Journal

"Caribou."

Belle's whisper brought Jesse to full awareness, as if she'd screamed aloud. Rubbing an eye, he pushed himself off the floor, slipped into his jeans and went to the window where his niece was standing in her long johns. Through a corner of the pane, they took turns studying the opposite hill across the river. A dozen cows had entered the valley and were browsing, heads down and their small racks bobbing.

"Shall we go?" Belle asked.

"Where?"

"To get them, of course."

Jesse rotated slowly on his heels and stepped away from the window. "It's best we wait," he said. "There's more in the pass and they'll be heading this way."

"How do you figure?"

Jesse spotted his eyeglasses on the floor where he'd been sleeping. He picked them up and hung them on his face. "The bulls and calves will follow. It's always cows that lead."

"Oh." Belle chewed on a thumbnail and continued to stare out the window. "But if they go over that hill, we'll miss our chance."

"Don't worry. They'll hug the river. I know that much."

They decided not to build a fire. After eating a cold breakfast of salmon strips and sourdough bread, they stepped outside to glass the opposite bank. More caribou emerged from a distant bend in the pass.

"I want two young bulls," Jesse said, "ones that haven't been in rut."

Belle waited for her turn with the binoculars. "You're hunting for yourself," she said, "but people in the village look to me for leadership. They can use the meat. I aim to get as much as I can."

After a score of animals had entered the valley, Jesse pointed to a ridge downstream where they could reach cover and wait for the caribou to gather. He stuffed a small pack with knives, whetstones, and extra ammunition and handed Belle his 30.06. He took for himself an antique .308 and led his niece downhill to the river. Though the herd was still far off, the two moved without speaking. They stepped into Belle's boat and paddled quietly across the current.

"Does that rifle shoot?" Belle asked. "It's got no scope and its barrel is rusted some."

"Don't worry."

On the far shore they walked to the ridge in a crouch and hid behind a lip of rock. They whispered back and forth, tracking the herd's advance until caution called for silence. Jesse watched a bull enter the valley. The massive rack danced across the horizon, like the sails on a distant ship, before the body of the bull rose into view. There were calves, too, lifting their heels, undaunted by a life of constant travel. Jesse turned to Belle and smiled, but she'd fallen asleep with the rifle resting across her chest.

One of the lead cows broke from the group. She trotted down the incline to the river and walked along the bank only a handful of yards away. Belle woke with the sound of hoof steps and raised her rifle slowly.

"Wait," Jesse whispered.

The caribou stopped and stared. Her nostrils flared and a breeze ruffled the thick hair beneath her neck. Belle looked anxiously out the corner of her eye.

"Don't shoot," Jesse said and the animal scrambled away to rejoin the herd.

"I had a shot," Belle complained.

Jesse pointed behind her into the valley. "It's not time yet. Look."

Belle rolled to her stomach and gazed beyond their rock cover. The far valley was covered in caribou, turning the ground into a restless carpet of gray backs, white capes, and swaying racks. As Jesse had promised, they were avoiding the far hill, but most of them had a distance to travel before entering shooting range.

"How long did I sleep?" Belle asked.

"Not long. They've been coming fast."

Minutes passed and several animals began to graze near the base of the ridge. Belle looked through her rifle scope and said, "I'm shooting." Jesse readied himself, too.

Their rifle blasts shattered the air and two animals—one a yearling bull and the other, a cow—fell. In the wake of the explosions, there was a hesitation followed by the crack of rifle bolts and new shells entering their chambers. The animals stopped. Their heads came up with eyes searching. A few nudged their fallen members, as if to encourage the dead to rise. Jesse loosened the grip on his rifle and thought, they haven't been hunted for a time. They don't know enough to run.

Belle shot again and Jesse followed her example. Two more animals collapsed and the rest of the herd picked up the pace. She shot once more and a mature bull crumpled to its knees and dropped its head. Before falling, it grunted softly. Belle ejected the empty casing from its chamber and acrid smoke filled the air. She forced the bolt forward, lifted the rifle and shot again. Another caribou tumbled.

Belle gritted her teeth and looked at Jesse. "Take more," she said before releasing her clip to insert more shells.

"There's no room in your boat to take them back."

"I'll borrow yours."

Jesse thought of the boat he'd given away and the full day of work that awaited them. "You can't."

"Then I'll get others to come—people from the village. Shoot, will you?"

Jesse raised his rifle, but he only looked down the barrel.

Belle snapped a full clip into place and turned her attention to the hill. "Damn it," she said. "They're running."

She stood as the caribou took flight. The bigger part of the herd sped up the slope. The lead animals were already out of sight beyond the next bend down river. Belle shot her clip empty and dropped two more bulls. She whooped and the herd formed a wide arc around the ridge and headed over the hill.

"Let's follow," she yelled.

Jesse stared at the dead animals. "And leave what we've killed?"

Belle glanced across the valley and up the slope again. "We'll butcher them first, then go. We can take the boat down river and cut them off."

Jesse wanted to tell her what was in his heart, to talk of nature's gifts and nature's demands. Instead, he shook his head. "I've got what I need. I won't go."

Ignoring Belle's silent glare, Jesse walked a beeline to the closest of the fallen caribou. He hauled its head up a grade and tried to roll the animal to its back. Belle followed reluctantly and helped prop it up. She watched while Jesse made a series of practiced cuts along its brisket to the lower gut.

Up to his elbows in viscera, Jesse heard a noise and raised his line of sight. A trio of ravens were hopping across rocky ground toward another carcass. The birds paused to scan the valley, then they fractured the quiet with rasping caws. A thought like a vision entered Jesse's head. The ravens took on other shapes, became fur-clothed hunters, gaunt and ghostlike. They plodded across the hillside in his mind, carrying bone-tipped spears.

"I wonder what they did after a hunt," Jesse said.

"Who are you talking about?"

"Nobody. Sorry."

Careful not to tear the dead caribou's entrails and release gastric juice into the meat, Belle helped push the last of the viscera from the body cavity and Jesse cut it loose. A breeze picked up and brought a chill.

"You weren't talking about the birds, were you?" Belle asked.

"No."

They stood and grasped the gutted caribou by the rack. Straining against its weight, they dragged it toward the boat. Jesse glanced over his shoulder—beyond the bloody carcass with its legs askew and its neck contorted—to where the ravens had begun to pick on a kill.

"It was the old ones," he said, "our people who lived here before. That's what I was talking about."

"Oh, that again."

Jesse had said too much not to explain. "I was wondering how they showed thanks. In those days, hunting was hard. There was always danger."

"And you want to go back to that?"

"It wasn't bad. The land was a partner—not a slave like now—and the people were happy for what they got."

"That's because they were starving."

"Starving? They may have been hungry sometimes, but their lives were full. They had the land and respect for life. Today—"

Belle released her portion of the caribou's weight and put a wrist to her hip. "Today," she said, "we live differently. We have responsibilities beyond eating."

Jesse let the head fall, then he straightened his back. "I know, but the way we get food—the killing—it's too easy. In the village, boys get .22s and pellet guns before they ever understand. We're a part of what we kill."

Belle shook her head.

"You know what I'm saying," Jesse continued. "I've seen kids shoot animals for fun—like it's a joke. But after a while the killing takes something away from them. It makes them mean. I don't want Martin to get like that."

Belle rubbed the drying blood off her hands. "I don't understand. You talk about returning to the lives of our ancestors. But that's the way they always lived. They killed. And they taught us to kill."

"But the respect. What about that?"

Belle gestured vaguely from the river to the stretch of muskeg and the rocky slope. "You respect the land—that's true. But you have no feelings for the village. You've made an ass of yourself there. Don't you see? The old ones couldn't have survived without respect for each other, too."

Jesse looked away.

Belle continued softly. "Do you want to be our Jesus and teach us a new way to live? Well, it'll never happen, because we won't give up the luxuries that make this place bearable. You might as well join the twentieth century, because it'll never join you."

Jesse wished he could explain himself and resolve the misunderstanding. He didn't want to be Jesus—not at all. In fact, he needed little more than to be left alone. By accomplishing that, neither he nor the twentieth century would have to worry about the other. Couldn't Belle see that?

The shadow off the facing ridge threatened to swallow them as it crept across the valley floor. Knowing that daylight was a dear thing, they trudged back up the hill to disembowel the next animal and drag it to the river.

"This is hard work," Belle said, wiping sweat from her brow.

Jesse agreed. "But if you take care of your meat, it'll take care of you."

By the time all eight caribou were on the bank, evening was beginning to settle. They loaded the boat with as many carcasses as it could hold and took a second trip hauling their bounty to the opposite shore.

"I'll sleep like a baby," Belle said when they made the final crossing.

Jesse pointed to the contents of the boat. "We'll keep these four here and cover them with a tarp. You can take them to the village tomorrow, but you'll have to come back for the rest."

Belle nodded.

"The ones you come back for," he continued, "we'll hang in the smokehouse tonight."

Belle scowled, an expression visible even in the moonlight. "The smokehouse? Up there?" She pointed her chin up the hill.

"That's where the smokehouse is."

"Why can't we just leave them here?"

Jesse squatted near one of the carcasses and took it by a hind leg. He cut through the skin at its ankle and split the hide along its inseam. "If we do that," he said, "bears will get to them."

"They'll be hell to drag."

"That's why I'm going to skin and quarter them. We'll pack the meat in pieces."

Belle grimaced. "There's got to be someplace down here to hang them."

"No," Jesse said without looking up.

He asked Belle to fetch some gear and she returned from the cabin carrying a pack frame, a hatchet, a couple of meat saws, and a rope. Through much of the night they skinned and quartered the caribou and reenacted the life of their ancestors. To Jesse, nothing could have been more satisfying.

###

While Jesse packed the last of the hindquarters, Belle returned to the cabin to light the lamp and fry a heap of cabbage and dried eulachon. There on the hilltop, where cheerful recollections and shared secrets had passed between them a day earlier, only exhaustion and a vague discomfort remained.

They ate dinner without speaking until the persistent hoot of an owl interrupted the cold silence. Jesse gave ear to the sound and a thought occurred to him. The bird was singing a familiar song, one he'd heard at a village potlatch.

"Listen," Jesse whispered.

Sitting on the cot, Belle chewed the last of her fish and swallowed. "To what?" she asked.

"The owl." Jesse tried to imitate the sound—a triplet pickup, followed by three quarter notes. *"Ooo-Ooo-Ooo. Ooo. Ooo. Oooo.* What's that?"

Belle held her breath and tilted her head to better capture the song. "I don't know."

"It's The Hokey Pokey."

As if to test her uncle's assertion, Belle added her voice to the owl's accompaniment. "You put your right foot in. You put your right foot out." She continued to sing, with each note more confident and bawdy than the last.

Not to be outdone, Jesse stood to dance. When Belle exercised poetic license with the lyrics (suggesting unusual places where one might put various body parts) their laughter shook the cabin. Unable to go on, but apparently encouraged by the distraction, Belle wiped her eyes and turned her mischief elsewhere.

An object on the worktable caught her eye. It was bathed in a mixture of shadow and lamplight. She stood, wiped her greasy hands on her shirt and went to it. "I've been meaning to ask you," she said. "What's this?"

The question came while Jesse, still breathing hard from his effort at the Hokey Pokey, was spreading a sleeping bag on the floor. He traced Belle's gaze and concern crossed his face. "It was a present," he said. "A gift from Ezra."

Belle picked up the book and spoke with feigned delight. "A Bible. It looks like you've kept notes, too."

"They're not for you."

As Jesse crossed the floor Belle turned aside. She extended an arm and put the books out of reach. "Let me see," she said. "It looks like you wrote down questions. What's this about?" Stifling a laugh, Belle read part of the list aloud. "What's a begat? Where's Eden?"

"Give it back."

"Listen, maybe I can help. I went to Sunday school in Anchorage." She held the notebook up and pointed to one of the questions. "This one's marked with a star. Is it important?"

Jesse gawked at his own scrawl and attempted a diversion. "We should get some sleep. It's late and you'll be busy tomorrow."

"No, tell me."

The owl had long since quieted and for a moment the night was still. Even the lamplight lost its flicker. Jesse sat on the floor, rested his back against the wall and took a deep breath. "It's about a prophet. His name was Abraham."

"Sure, Abraham. Remind me who he was, will you?"

Hesitantly, Jesse spoke of the prophet and how God chose him to be the father to a nation blessed above all others. "But Abraham didn't have any kids," he added.

"Makes it hard to be a father." Belle laughed at her own joke.

"Anyway," Jesse said, "Abraham was old when he finally got a son. He named the kid Isaac, but there was a problem. The white god told Abraham to sacrifice the boy."

"Kill him?"

"Uh huh. The white god told Abraham to sacrifice Isaac. That means kill."

"What did he do?"

"He did what he was told. He took Isaac to a mountain and tied him to a rock. He was about to cut the boy's throat when an angel stopped him."

Belle shook her head. "Damn. God gave a commandment that wasn't meant to be obeyed."

"One of them mysteries, I guess."

Belle opened the Bible and stared at a page. "Maybe he wasn't supposed to obey. Maybe that's why God stopped him. Killing is against the law. Abraham should have known that."

"It doesn't matter. The white god doesn't care about laws. It was a test and Abraham passed. The white god was happy. That's what the book says."

"I don't understand." Belle's mouth puckered. "Crazy people do all kinds of things. They kill and do worse. Sometimes they say God told them to do it. People like that deserve the pokey. They're no good."

"But what if they're only doing what the white god wants? Who should they obey?"

Belle crossed her arms, and then a smile spread across her face. "I see what's going on," she said. "It was made up! The whole story! White folks do that, you know. They make up stories to teach a lesson. That's called a parable."

"Oh?" Jesse's face brightened. "What are we supposed to learn from it?"

Leaning toward her uncle, Belle spoke like a conspirator. "It's an important lesson, all right. It teaches a thing or two."

"Tell me."

She expressed the idea as fact, with conviction and purpose. "It was meant," she said, as the sun peeked over the horizon, "to show how easily we sacrifice what's most important to us."

They didn't arise until early the next afternoon. By that time their labor had become a fuzzy memory. Belle recounted the exhilaration of raising a rifle to her shoulder and watching big game fall.

"Imagine what Clarence will say when I come home with a load of meat," she said.

That's when her eyes lit up. Eager as a child on Christmas, she laid out a plan. She would go upriver and scout areas where men might be sent to hunt. If it led to success, her people would be grateful. It would show how she bridged the modern world and the village's enduring reliance upon nature. They might see her as a great leader.

Jesse thought of the possible dangers awaiting her, but he responded carefully. "Good idea, except you're not dressed for bad weather."

"I won't go far and I'll stay in the boat."

"Sure, you can do that, but the river is different up there. It gets shallow in places and fast in others—especially this time of year."

Belle laughed and declined Jesse's offer to guide her through the troublesome water upstream. Ahead of uncertain weather she passed through the narrow draw visible from the cabin.

"Be careful," Jesse said, watching her disappear. "Don't do anything stupid."

Chapter 17

Food is getting short. I caught a few trout two days ago, but I lost my last lure to a big one. I need to get to the village soon. Not feeling well.

- From Kit Lerner's Journal

The river widened and the surrounding hills gave way to vast wetlands. From a lily-covered stretch of water a moose raised its head and flapped its ungainly ears. A flock of geese passed overhead and a beaver smacked the water in warning. Patch let none of it distract him. He picked his way through muskeg and scattered hummocks of dry ground, until the glint of metal caught his eye.

I'll be damned, he thought, is that a boat?

At first he believed it was a figment of his hopeful mind. The skiff sat in shallow water, like a gift from a guardian angel. He cut across a muddy arm of the river in its direction. There was no apparent damage to the hull and the kicker looked clean. Cordwood, it seemed, had been stacked inside. Patch dropped his pack on high ground, waded to the vessel and made a startling discovery. What had looked like firewood from afar were caribou quarters, erected in the form of a teepee.

Patch wasn't sure whether to curse or cry. Not only did he have meat now, but he had a vessel, as well, on which he could float to safety. The good fortune made him wonder: Why can't the Lord of tundra and cold weather leave me alone?

As he scrutinized the butchered flesh, one of the upright forelegs shifted away from center and he heard a soft thump against the hull. Patch moved a ribcage and gazed into the opening he'd created. Half hidden within the shadows and gathered into a fetal position was a native woman. She was wrapped in a raw caribou skin.

"Quit stealing the covers," she mumbled.

Patch figured he'd happened upon a hunter, a hardy local who was taking a nap before continuing home. He was about to walk away, relieved the boat wasn't a gift he must chose to accept or reject, but he caught a better glimpse of the person.

"Belle, is that you?"

He put a hand on her shoulder and turned the woman toward him. Belle's cheeks were puffy and her lips were blue. Patch dismantled a portion of the lean-to, pulled away the skin cover and saw that her clothes were wet.

"Wake up," he said, moving the meat aside. "We need to get you dry."

Belle opened her eyes, but she didn't speak. Her teeth chattered like an old pair of barber clippers. Patch forced her to stand and she rose deliberately, as if infirm. He lifted her from the boat and carried her toward the closest embankment.

"What happened?" he asked.

"Tried to turn. Sun in my eyes…got stuck. That was yesterday."

Patch saw the events in his mind. He pictured Belle circling to come about, the outboard stirring muck and the sun now west before her. He saw her kill the engine—heard the boat whistle to a stop, but how did she get so wet?

"Let's get that coat off. You've got hypothermia."

He lowered Belle onto a clump of grass and she took off her wet parka. Patch pulled her thermal shirt over her head and she reclined, arms across her bare breasts, while he wrestled off her jeans.

"Your underwear is wet, too, Belle."

"Go away. Let me sleep."

Patch took care not to gawk. He slipped off her long johns and panties, then helped her into his sleeping bag. After building a fire, he placed several large rocks near it. When they were hot, he wrapped one of the stones in a dirty sweatshirt and put it in the sleeping bag. Though Belle tried to doze, Patch gave her warm water to drink and quizzed her about the prior day's events.

Her babbling was scarcely coherent, but he caught the gist of it. Belle said she was using a tree limb to lever the boat off the shoals, when she fell in the water. Wet and desperate for shelter, she propped the meat around her and tried to sleep under the cover of hocks and marbled flesh.

"It was a good idea to hide out under the meat," Patch said, then he recalled the blood smell that had settled like a blanket around her. "Still, it must've been a hell of a night you spent here."

Darkness fell and he figured Belle was out of danger. He let her sleep, but continued to heat and rotate the stones. When his eyelids grew heavy, Patch looked into the star-filled sky. No rain tonight, he thought, then he stripped off his clothes and squeezed into the sleeping bag with Belle.

"You need to get warm," he said, "and there's no better way than this."

###

The sun rose and Patch awoke with his arms around a woman. The back of her neck smelled of camp smoke and sweat. She stirred and he rolled onto his back to avoid touching her with his erection.

"Clarence?" she said. "Can you give me some room?"

"I'm not Clarence."

Belle stiffened and threw an elbow that Patch deflected. "Who the hell are you then?" she asked.

"Don't you remember? It's me, Patch, the pilot from the village. I found you here."

"And you figured, finders keepers?" Belle tried to get as far from him as the confines of the bag would allow. She scooted across the slick fabric and gasped. "Where are my clothes?"

"They're drying."

"Did you take them off me?"

"You couldn't do it yourself."

Belle gave Patch a backward kick to the shins that caused him to groan.

"You were sick and your clothes were wet," he said. "I had to get them off you."

Belle demanded the return of her property and Patch clambered out of the bag, shivering and hugging himself for warmth. The woman's clothes were draped on short willows near the previous night's fire. He bent to gather them and Belle screamed.

"What's wrong?" he asked.

"You're naked."

Patch covered himself with Belle's shirt and imagined the view to which she'd been a witness: his two hairy hams and the strip of shadow in between. "You couldn't get warm on your own. I did what was needed."

"Please," Belle said, beginning to sob. "Don't tell me what you did."

"You got it wrong. Nothing like that happened."

"Really?"

"I promise. Scout's honor."

A hand over his private parts, he handed Belle her clothes, which she took without glancing up. While Patch slipped into his pants and began to stoke a new fire, she remained in the sleeping bag and got dressed.

"I'm sorry about how I acted," she said, emerging fully-clothed.

"No call for that. I suppose yesterday is a blur to you now."

"That's true, but I remember enough. It was a miracle you were here."

"Miracle?" Patch chuckled softly as the fire licked the tinder he applied to it. "There's no such thing. It was dumb luck we came together, that's all. And I don't know who's dumber for being here—you or me."

Belle shrugged and let a pause fill the space between them. "Maybe that's so," she said. "But the night I came aground I had a dream. I saw my boy, Martin, sitting on his bed, tossing charms onto a pillow and studying how they fell. I caught myself whispering: 'Wish me home, son. Wish me home.' Maybe you were the answer to those prayers."

Patch wanted to believe what she said, but the idea ran counter to everything he suspected was true. He waded to the boat and returned with a strip of meat that he cooked over the fire. They both ate ravenously.

"We should be going," Belle said, still chewing her last bite of food.

Patch told her to stay close to the fire and he left to unload the skiff. Eventually it became buoyant and he pushed it into deeper water. When he replaced the cargo, the boat held clear of the riverbed, but there was no margin for adding his own weight. On the bank Patch dug out a set of fleece clothing from his pack and insisted Belle wear them.

"Stay in the main channel," he said, "and you'll be okay."

"You aren't coming?"

"It's best you go alone. The boat would get stuck otherwise."

Belle put on the extra clothes and Patch carried her through the shallows to the skiff. He gazed longingly at the vessel, wondering if the purpose of his journey would be violated by asking her to send help.

"Not much clearance, is there?" Belle said, frowning at the water.

"Not nearly enough."

"Tell you what, though. My Uncle Jesse lives a few miles down river. Stay with him and I'll come get you in a few days."

Patch had forgotten about the fish camp. Rugged terrain stood between him and its sanctuary, but the prospect of sleeping next to a warm stove made the distance seem shorter.

Under a graying sky Belle touched his arm and added, "I won't forget what you did."

"I'm not sure you remember much of it."

They both laughed until Belle grew serious again.

"The night before you came," she said, "I kept thinking: Is this how it's going to end? In a place full of bears and glaciers, am I going to die like this?"

Patch nodded. "Cold weather and wet clothes, that's all it takes."

"Where would I be without you?"

Likely dead, Patch thought. Suddenly he felt as if he'd been released from a prison. Was it relief over the prospect of being rescued? Or was it a sense of redemption for having helped someone in need? As Belle motored away, he considered the change wrought inside of him.

"Did you see that, Kit?" he whispered. "Wasn't it good I was here?" Yet by the time snow had begun to fall his only thoughts were of survival.

The snow fell wet and without interruption, claiming instant possession of where it landed. Through the night Patch followed along the river, dazzled by flakes drifting within the influence of his flashlight. By daybreak the contours of slope and valley were obscured by immutable white.

He thought of how Kit's feelings for snow had changed during her sojourn in the wilderness. In the beginning she'd recognized it as a symbol of hope and purity.

> *"Though your sins be as scarlet, they shall be as white as snow." That's what the Lord said. So I'll take this as a sign—a token of His acceptance of my sacrifice. On this day snow fell and God told me with each drifting flake, "Kit, you're forgiven."*

Toward the end of her journey, after being buffeted by a series of storms, the falling flakes only spoke to her of despair.

> *No color in my feet and there's snow again. How can anything so beautiful be the source of this much affliction?*

Coming onto another ridge, Patch took care to remain within the sound of water. Over much of the trail he noticed scat steaming on the ground. He heard the grunt and snuffle of bears seemingly hell-bent to find shelter. As evening approached and the shadows began to rise up off the ground his anxiety increased. Cautiously, he pulled the .357 from his pack and holstered it. He plodded on, hoping to find a place to set camp.

A steep slope gradually fell to his right and from a considerable elevation the river flowed below him. As he passed a toppled birch—its roots hanging ghostly in the evening gloom—he heard another noise and saw a dark form rise from behind the tree. He drew his gun, took a step back and landed on an exposed root. In the instant it took him to grit his teeth, he stumbled and twisted an ankle. The gun went off.

Patch was still in motion, on the verge of spilling where gravity took him, when he recognized the shadow for a moose. He damned himself for shooting, but the thought didn't have a chance to trouble him further. Head over heels he tumbled downhill. He tried to stop—tried to gain control—but the effort was useless. At the water's edge his head collided with something hard. Before he could even curse his luck, all sense left him.

Chapter 18

Life has gotten so complicated we can't see the big picture anymore. We make widgets all day, never asking how they'll be used. We're so bound by our narrowly defined commissions, we'd wither away and die—completely baffled— by life at Walden.

- From Kit Lerner's Journal.

Belle didn't step out of her boat, or even relate the events of the day. Before leaving, she only said, "Expect a visitor."

"Who?" Jesse asked.

She hollered out a name, but the growl of the outboard swallowed up the answer. Jesse watched his niece disappear into a blizzard already two hours old. Though he understood the need to get a jump on bad weather, Belle's urgency seemed peculiar. Jesse hoped she hadn't done anything stupid, but he was relieved to see her heading home.

He retired to his cot before sunset and, in the twilight of half sleep, he heard the crack of gunfire. Jesse rubbed his eyes and propped himself on an elbow, thinking: One bullet in the dark isn't good—not good, at all. He waited for another round, a finishing shot or signal that all was well, but it didn't come. The stove crackled lazily and the wood smoke was a friendly presence, yet the prospect of trouble left him unsettled. He hugged his pillow and tried to sleep, wondering if the guest Belle had mentioned was in trouble.

Jesse got up, changed into warm clothes and filled a pack with camping supplies and a tarp. He slung the kit over his shoulder, then he opened the door and turned his face away from the entering cold. The sky was clearing and a three-quarter moon scattered needles of light across the snow. He left the cabin, circled behind it and walked along the ridge while the storm waned.

Jesse paused occasionally to scan the hillside and peer through shadows toward the riverbank below him. Once, he heard a soft groan that froze him where he stood. The sound repeated itself, but it bounced off the slopes without direction. He called into the crisp night air. There was no reply. Suddenly he noticed a disturbance—exposed earth where snow should have been—and he extrapolated a line beyond it. A few feet from the water, he saw a crumpled body.

He stepped gingerly downhill at an angle upriver. The man was prostrate on his stomach, moaning and delirious. Jesse rolled the stranger onto his back and noticed him wince when his foot slid across the ground. It was the pilot, Patch Taggart.

A few feet away Jesse saw a dead spruce, one that had been uprooted and carried away by past high water. He broke the tree by stomping on the branches, then he gathered twigs and moose hair moss for tinder. He took up the wood and started a fire near the mouth of an exposed cutbank. After spreading his tarp, he dragged the pilot onto it.

There was no hesitation, no wondering what to do. Jesse checked Patch for broken bones, wrapped his ankle against the swelling of a bad sprain and helped him into a sleeping bag. He boiled willow twigs and cajoled the man to drink the broth, saying, "This will take away your fever and pain."

The clouds scattered and stars appeared. On the far summit, spruce trees swayed and shed snow that fell like curtains of lace. Jesse fed the fire against the cold. His glasses fogged and froze—an inconvenience he ignored.

"We'll hold out here tonight," he whispered.

Before Jesse fell asleep, he watched the pilot drift in and out of consciousness and he thought: What is a white man doing here so late in the year?

Daylight came, crisp and cold, peeking into the cutbank where the two men rested. A stiff wind followed and flung bits of frost that pricked everything in its path. From where he'd sat through the night, the smell of tree roots and cold earth filled Jesse's nostrils. He rose off the tarp and stepped away from the hill. Hunkering down, he placed more wood on the dying fire and stoked it with his breath. In time, Patch too, awoke. He tried to sit and howled from the effort.

"Your ankle's bad," Jesse said, looking over his shoulder. "But it's not broken."

He tried to forget his annoyance. The pilot wasn't a bad fellow, but his presence reminded Jesse of how the world had changed. No one knew how to live with nature anymore. At best, human beings related to the earth in the way of two people speaking different languages.

Patch blinked several times, as if trying to focus his eyes. "Jesse Toyonek," he said, his voice more croak than human speech. "Am I in hell?"

"No." Jesse turned to face the fire, palms open and hands extended. "You're on the Killborn River, a mile from my cabin."

"You sure?"

"Plenty of good folks may end up in hell, but you're on the river. I know that much."

Patch gulped at the air. "I suppose you know that Belle and I ran into each other. Our lives must be connected somehow." Suddenly his eyes opened as big as silver dollars. "Did I kill that moose?"

"What moose?"

"The one up the hill."

Jesse stood and stepped around the fire. He turned to scan the slope, thinking of the white man as an intruder who had come to take from his land. "I don't see a moose—dead or alive."

"Good." Patch relaxed, seeming to take comfort in the reply.

"Of course, one could've walked away with your bullet."

Patch frowned and tried to look beyond the lip of the bank, but he fell back, panting.

"Is that what the shooting was about?" Jesse asked. "A moose jumped you?"

"It's a little more complicated than that." Patch changed the subject and added, "I may be on the river, but it sure feels like hell here."

Jesse searched his pack and pulled out several thick strips of caribou jerky. He tossed one to Patch. "There's always tomorrow. You aren't dead, yet."

"I'll keep that in mind."

Jesse glanced downstream and said his cabin wasn't far away. "Can you stand?" he asked.

Tight-lipped, Patch slipped out of his bag, one leg trailing like an obsolete appendage. Despite the cold, sweat trickled off his face. He pushed himself to his buttocks and stopped to rest. "To tell you the truth," he said. "There's no sense in you sticking around. I'm fine here by myself." He bit off a chunk of meat.

"I can see that."

"Where did you say your cabin was?"

"Only a mile away. Up the hill. Down the river." Jesse pointed the two directions with a finger.

"Maybe I'll meet you there. On the other hand, I might keep low to the water. That hill beat me once already."

"You won't follow me out?"

"No, I think I'll just sit here for a while."

Jesse scratched his head. "Then, I've got no choice."

The white man gnawed at the meat. "Yeah, you might as well be on your way. I'm fine."

Jesse grasped one of Patch's arms.

"What're you doing?"

Without answering, Jesse knelt, draped the arm across his neck and stood to get leverage. Patch yelled, but Jesse ignored the protest. He lowered himself again, took more weight and shifted it across his shoulders with a heave. Straightening up, he lifted the white man.

"Put me down," Patch yelled. "I can't go—there's something in my pack."

"Stop jiggling," Jesse said. "I'll come back for your stuff later." As he climbed slowly up the hill, he decided a beer would be good once he got home. In fact, Jesse thought, I might have two or three.

The sun had started on its downward trajectory (heading in a direction more south than west) when Jesse returned to his cabin for the second time that day. After searching unsuccessfully for signs of a wounded moose, he stepped through the door carrying the white man's pack.

Several hours later, amid the litter of beer cans, he sat on the floor, cleaning his rifle and listening to his guest's feverish muttering. It was a curious thing, he thought. He'd seen other white men on the river—three or four parties each summer besides the occasional Fish and Game officer—but never so late in the year. They came, packing pretty rifles and fishing gear. Some would stop and talk, not realizing how they diminished his world. Their babbling was always about getting away. Women, traffic, and complicated jobs seemed to be their common enemies. They envied Jesse for his lifestyle.

On more than one occasion he'd asked, "Then why go back home?"

And they responded with talk of responsibilities. "Oh, I need to get back," (just like they'd needed to get away). In the end they returned to what they'd professed to hate most, which caused Jesse to think of need as a sickness. It grew until it was big enough to take souls hostage. From that perspective, people could learn a lesson or two from the god of the island, who relied on just a few handmade belongings.

When he heard Patch unzip his sleeping bag, Jesse looked toward the bed. "You finally getting up?"

There was a groan in reply.

"You were lucky—a white man in the woods, not ready for winter. It was good that I came."

"Where am I?"

"You asked me that once already. You're in the middle of nowhere and it was me who carried you here."

Patch tried to sit and the exertion left him breathless. "I know better than that," he said. "Other folks got me here. But I still owe you my thanks."

Jesse dragged his chair to the cot and sat down with his rifle pointing carelessly at Patch's head. "Shouldn't you be flying home? Why are you here, anyway?"

Patch ignored the gun. "It's not an easy story to tell," he said, "so I won't burden you with it. I can see the way out and I'll be leaving." He scooted to one side of the cot, his face pale and streaked with dried sweat. He swung his legs onto the floor and his forehead came in brief contact with the rifle barrel.

Jesse laughed, but the sound spoke of sadness. He wondered if the beer had given him clarity, because another vision was forming in his head and he could see a meanness to life. The people who least understood the earth held it in their control. Jesse decided to take a stand for the trees and tundra. He meant Patch no harm—the gun was empty, after all—but he had to make a point.

"You won't get far," he said. "I might as well put you out of your misery."

In one swift motion Patch grabbed the rifle muzzle, directed it toward the near wall and pulled with a grunt and a grimace. As the firearm came out of Jesse's hands, the hammer clicked, but there was no explosion.

"Take off your glasses," Patch said.

Jesse did as he was told, laughing like a madman. "Why?"

"Because I see you got no control when you're drunk. And I never hit a man with glasses."

Patch threw a punch that made up in accuracy for what it lacked in force. It caught Jesse on the nose and he fell hard, toppling the chair with him. For a moment Jesse felt fine, but when he tried to raise his head, dizziness overcame him and darkness followed.

###

When he regained consciousness, Jesse was on the floor with dried blood on his shirt and his vision blurred. He saw Patch on the cot, holding a can of beer in one hand and the rifle in the other. Jesse shook his head, clearing it of cobwebs, then he looked around for his glasses. He tried to scratch his nose, but his arms seemed to have fallen asleep.

"You're not drinking all my stuff, are you?" he asked.

"Hell no, one's my limit."

Patch laughed and threw an empty can that clattered onto the floor. He took another beer from where several rested on the cot next to him and lifted its pull-tab.

"You got crazy on me," he said. "So I figured you'd give me some leeway for raiding your stash."

Jesse tried to get up and finally realized that his hands were tied behind him. "What did I do?"

"You don't remember?" Patch pointed to the rifle next to him. "You pulled an empty gun on me."

"Hmm." Jesse rubbed his cheek with a shoulder and winced from pain. "That was stupid. I got shells."

Patch chuckled. "You're a character. Do you treat all your guests like this?"

"Only the ones who drag me out of bed."

The white man held up his can as though making a toast. "At least you're serving beer. How'd you get it anyway?"

"One of my honeys brought it." Jesse tugged softly at the ropes binding him. "They like my dick."

"Is that right?

"Sure, I got plenty."

"Oh? How much dick is plenty?"

Jesse rolled onto his stomach, exposing his tied hands behind him. He indicated four inches of distance between an index finger and thumb.

Patch smiled. "I don't blame them. That is plenty of dick. I've only got about three inches myself."

"That's still a mighty fine dick."

Jesse added his tenor chuckle to the bass guffaws of his guest. Their laughter spilled through the walls of the tiny cabin and out across the moonlit valley.

"As long as we're getting along so well," Patch said. "You should know I don't intend to live here. In fact, your niece promised to take me back to Kaknu. She ought to be back in a day or two."

Jesse tried to stand again, but failed. "I don't mind a visitor now and then. I'll get us something to eat."

"Don't bother. I can see you're tied up."

###

For an hour, Jesse squirmed on the floor, amazed at how firmly his wrists were bound. He was beginning to wonder if he would ever get loose when Patch asked, "Do you figure I can untie you, now?"

Jesse relaxed. "There's no need. I'm almost free."

"Yeah, I can see that."

Patch seemed to tick off the distance to his host. "I suppose you didn't mean me any harm. Your rifle was unloaded, after all." He took a knife from his pocket, rolled off the cot and cut the rope that bound Jesse's hands. "I'll keep your rifle," he said, "for the time being, anyway."

"Suit yourself," Jesse said, but it sounded more like: Shoot yourself. He rotated his shoulders and rubbed his wrists. The sun had set, but moonlight streamed through the window and lit their rising breath. Jesse stood and went to the stove, where he threw two split logs onto the dying embers of a fire.

"Where's my glasses?" he said.

"I put them on the table so nobody would step on them."

Jesse frowned. "Looks like somebody did." He held the glasses up to expose a tiny scratch on one of the lenses. The contraption hung on his face at a queer angle, so he adjusted the frame and put it on again.

"It fell when you went down," Patch said, checking the rifle out of the corner of an eye.

"Went down?" Jesse touched his upper lip. Dried blood flaked onto his fingers, but he made no attempt to wipe it off. "You hungry?" he asked.

"I'm starving. Why do you think I untied you?"

Jesse left the cabin and gathered a skinned rabbit carcass and potatoes from his store of food. Soon the cabin was filled with the scent of frying meat and the sound of friendly banter. Before the evening was over, Jesse relearned a thing or two about Patch. The fellow wasn't a bad sort—quite likeable, in fact. Only he seemed haunted like other white men by a need Jesse couldn't understand.

Still, Patch seemed to be cut from an unusual skin. He didn't express the normal complaints. Traffic and the stress of work didn't seem to bother him. Something else was at the root of his problem. So throughout the night and for the next handful of late evenings, Jesse listened to the man curse in his sleep and wondered what could cause such angry dreams.

Chapter 19

I've been stuck here for five days hoping for a miracle, but maybe I shouldn't expect one. Maybe God intends to bless the worms by granting them my body for food. And this thought occurs to me: Perhaps God isn't enough. Maybe even with Him we have to set limits.

- From Kit Lerner's Journal

Except for a woodpecker's intermittent knock, the morning began as quietly as a sigh. Patch woke up alone in the cabin, slipped out of his sleeping bag and tested his foot against the cold floor. He limped to the window and rubbed the pane with his palm, clearing an opening through the frost. Across the river snow dusted the spruce and left the hillside a soft indigo. Nothing moved—not even a tree swayed—yet he remained there, watching.

Jesse entered and the air turned frigid until the door closed and the stove's heat retook the room. The two men exchanged greetings and, while Jesse spoke of chores to be done, Patch returned to the window and watched a squirrel scamper up a nearby tree. His head was full of plans. He would accept Belle's ride to Kaknu and bum a snowmobile ride to Dillingham. Since a clear day would be a good travel companion, he hoped to be gone before winter settled fully.

Despite nearly a week of rest, Patch knew he couldn't resume his trek into the village alone. The urgency within him had died and left him unwilling to even try. Replacing his need to complete the journey was a realization that he'd already failed. Were it not for Jesse's help, he might have duplicated Kit's trek in a way not contemplated. All he wanted now was to haul his butt home and put the nightmare of his failure to rest.

But had he really failed? In the course of his travels, he'd saved Belle from disaster, an act that had changed him in ways he was still trying to fathom. Patch understood that he wielded little influence in the world (an earthquake or sudden illness could take him tomorrow) but in one instance he'd exercised dominion. He'd helped someone in need. Maybe that was enough to make living worthwhile.

Patch took a seat at the table, where leftovers from the previous night's meal of roast ptarmigan remained. He cleared his throat to get his host's attention, but Jesse couldn't be distracted. The native man sat with his face in a book, his fingers tracing words. The slow pace of his reading filled Patch with anxiety. He wanted to be home, but he wasn't sure how to express the feeling.

"I don't understand," he said. "How does a fellow survive out here without a skiff?"

Jesse looked up from the page he was reading. "I get along."

Patch could see his question had been less suggestive than he'd hoped. He was more concerned about taking leave of the river than with Jesse's ability to make do without a boat. "When do you think your niece will be coming?" he asked.

"She'll have to get here before the water goes low. I know that much."

"It looks pretty low to me now." Patch remembered how Belle had been trapped in shallow water just a few days earlier. "I hope you won't take this in the wrong way, but I'm not of a mind to be rooming with you."

Before Jesse could respond there was a scratch at the door and both men spun toward it. Jesse's face brightened.

"That sounds like Sasha," he said.

Patch raised a fist in the air, thinking his ticket home had arrived, but in the next instant confusion clouded his expression. He lowered his arm. "But your niece's name is Belle."

"That's right."

"So, who the hell's Sasha? One of them honeys you talked about?"

Jesse closed his book and went to the door. Patch stood, too, and was astonished by the scene outside. A coyote scrambled from the exit and stopped at the edge of the clearing. She turned to face the cabin and pawed at the air.

"I'll be damned," Patch said. "It looks to be begging."

Jesse smiled so big his eyes had to narrow to make room for his teeth. "She isn't exactly a pet, but she hangs around sometimes."

Patch noticed that the animal favored a front paw and Jesse spoke of how he'd found her caught in a rabbit snare. "It doesn't seem to hurt her, but it slows her down some."

Jesse went to the table and reemerged from the door with a ptarmigan not yet picked clean. He tossed the carcass halfway to the edge of the clearing and it broke into two pieces that landed in close proximity to each other. The coyote approached the meat, head down and sniffing. She plucked the closest scrap from the snow and, with ears back, scampered into the trees.

"She keeps me company," Jesse said. "I guess I owe her a meal now and then."

Jesse mumbled something about his fish wheel and started out the door with a crowbar. Patch grabbed a sweater and hollered for his host to wait. Though he followed as best he could—head and arms struggling out of his garment—the distance between them increased. Jesse turned and told Patch to stay put, but he waited nonetheless.

"I like this part of the year," he said. "The air is sweet."

"Sweet? It smells like dead salmon."

Jesse's eyebrows met at an angle. "That's what I mean."

"Oh." Patch searched his head for something worthwhile to add. "For me winter seems too much like a time for rest and I've never gotten used to that."

"Then you're like every other white man, always needing to fix this or that. But you don't complain about work or money. What's wrong in your life?"

Patch shrugged. "We should get to them chores, I guess."

The fish wheel sat in low water with one side resting on the bank. Patch pried the wheel frame apart while Jesse rolled the drums away. Together they stowed the platform on the drums and leaned against the affair to catch their breath. They watched Sasha approach on the trail and sit on an exposed knoll. A sound or movement caused her to look away.

"You mumble in your sleep," Jesse said. "What do you dream about?"

Patch recognized the question as another attempt to pry, but he couldn't help wondering what he muttered at night. In one recurring nightmare he'd come upon Emily's garden, only to watch her get trampled by a moose. The dream not only horrified him, but reminded him of his promise to build a fence around the plot. It implied, too, that one measure of a man was his ability to fulfill commitments.

"You're getting a bit personal, aren't you?" he said.

Jesse continued, undaunted. "You seem angry sometimes."

"It's no big deal."

But Patch knew otherwise. Anger as much as guilt had drawn him to Jesse's cabin on the Killborn. Like the urgency that had died inside him, his dishonesty began to melt, too. Patch sensed a need to speak of things he wouldn't have mentioned to the boys he drank with back home.

289

"I got divorced last year," he said. "And of all the nightmares I could dream up, would you believe they'd be about her, my ex-wife?"

"Scary lady?"

"Hell no. She's as good as they come. I shouldn't have let her go."

"And you came all this way to kill yourself over her?"

Patch considered the question. Had his journey been a failed attempt to take his own life? "No," he said. "To others it might have seemed like suicide, but the irony of it is: I came to put an end to my bad dreams and take control of some part of this existence, even if it was by doing something stupid."

Jesse looked stunned. With a sweeping gesture, he pointed to the river and the hills and sky. "You thought you could control this place? Maybe I'm just an Indian, but I know one thing. There's no control out here. You should go back to town. The world obeys you there."

Patch chuckled and allowed silence to follow. "Let me tell you a story," he finally said.

Then he spoke of a time when Emily and he were just dating. She'd taken him to her aunt's house in Willow and as they passed through the door, he saw a boy, Emily's cousin, playing on the carpet with .22 shells. The ammunition was scattered across the floor and the boy was tossing them into a glass.

Jesse shuddered. "Someone should have taught him about rim-fire cartridges," he said.

"No kidding," Patch replied, "but that's not the point. Because the aunt tells the boy to bring the glass, so she can offer us drinks. A minute later she comes out with some pink sugar water and the tumbler is pretty familiar." He repeated the last two words slowly, emphasizing each syllable.

"The same one the kid had?"

"You got it. So I take a drink and something gets stuck in my mouth. I pick it off my tongue and it's a hair—not one of mine."

Jesse made a face. "White men hate that."

"Oh, yeah. At first I'm thinking she didn't wash the glass. But hey, I wanted to give her the benefit of the doubt, right? She's Emily's kin and all. So I gagged the stuff down, put the glass aside and what's there at the bottom of it?"

"A bullet?"

"That's right." Patch laughed. "And that settled my mind as to the kind of housekeeper the lady was."

"Funny story," Jesse said. "But why are you telling me about it?"

Patch shook a finger to emphasize the point. "When something happens once, you figure it's happenstance—simple luck, or an accident, but twice is already a pattern. And as far as my life goes, it's clearly an affliction. The truth is I don't have much authority anywhere and you don't need to be an Indian in the bush to feel like the world has left you behind."

What do you dream about?

Patch let the question twirl in his head, where it sought a connection with Emily's last straw, the day she called it quits.

For the rest of the evening and into the night he replayed the twenty-four hours leading to her decision, believing Kit would have demanded a review of the events. To him it was a crude kind of repentance, a way to correct his bad choices, if only he could relive the past.

He remembered how the day had started—how rain had pelted the windshield as they left for a get-together with friends. Patch drove the truck and Emily sat impassively, not yielding to the turns or bumps in the road. For the first mile the cab was quiet but for the hum of tires across asphalt, then Emily exhaled.

"It just didn't seem right," she said.

Patch heard trouble in her voice and his stomach bubbled. There was a time when he could've put his share of the conversation on autopilot—just grunt an affirmation and hope it would mollify her—but he was concerned with keeping the peace.

"What's not right?" he asked.

"The fact is it was raining when Rusty called and it's still raining. He had every right to cancel. That's your policy. You can't expect him to pay if the weather won't allow you to fly."

"I know that." Patch pulled the truck onto a main road, surprised that Emily had overheard his conversation. She hadn't showed that much interest in his affairs in quite a while. "I figured the wind would die down. I just wanted him to wait before he backed out."

Emily folded her arms. She slid lower in the seat and gazed out the passenger-side window. "All I know is you can't go around calling your friend a pansy."

"I didn't do that."

"Well, you did. I heard you."

Patch saw a battered El Camino appear in his rearview mirror. Though they were rounding a blind bend, the driver accelerated to pass. The car was abreast of them, when a container truck emerged from the opposite direction. The driver broke sharply and darted back, narrowly missing a collision.

"Damn," Patch said.

In the time it took him to catch his breath he noticed a line of RVs and campers filling the oncoming lane. A thought occurred to him. He turned on the pickup's hazard light and slowed on a straight section of shoulder-less road.

"What are you doing?" Emily asked.

Patch came to a stop and took the truck out of gear. He promised himself that he would fight for control over some aspect of his life. Was safe passage into town too much to expect?

"I'm going to have a talk with our friend back there," he said.

As he opened the door and stepped outside, Emily spoke in a way that got through to him. She didn't raise her voice. The words could as easily have been: How do you do? With barely a quiver she said, "You make a scene and we're done. Do you understand?"

Patch looked at Emily's face and knew he'd stumbled upon some invisible line she'd drawn. At first he was angry. His wife couldn't understand a man's need to piss along borders, to establish and maintain space. In the next instant frustration almost knocked him to his knees. He fought with his emotions, trying not to look stunned or hurt.

"Okay," he said.

Battered by the rain, he went to the front of the pickup, opened the hood and tinkered as though fixing something broken. He remained there until the oncoming traffic cleared and the El Camino could pass. That took long enough, he decided, to teach a lesson regarding patience and the need to obey traffic regulations.

Patch felt he'd avoided a scene (though probably not the way his wife had hoped). He didn't expect censure, but he supposed Emily wasn't pleased, either. With his hair matted and dripping, he returned to the cab, wondering how she would react. To his surprise, his wife displayed no anger, but by the end of the day he questioned her ability to feel any emotion at all.

The Nikolai Homesteader's Association was an informal group of folks who'd endured much to carve their homes out of wilderness. To people on the outside it was a snobbish clan, but from the perspective of its members, it was a fellowship no more worthy of aspiration than a longing to be in someone else's family.

Most meetings were arranged on a whim and convened around a barbecue, but sometimes a gathering was announced as a forum for discussion. The Taggarts entered the refurbished high school cafeteria and Patch could smell fresh paint and grout. There was another, more subtle odor, too, that caused him to search his memory where he found a tunnel into the past. He saw himself as a boy sitting at a dinner table in the Idaho farmhouse of his childhood.

That's when it occurred to him: The odor was of cooked peas, leftover and thrice boiled, a scent that described so much of what he hated and had rebelled against. In the jumble of his thoughts he wondered how his life, which had harbored youthful dreams, could leave him as crushed and undifferentiated as the cooked vegetables that came in industrial-sized cans.

Patch glanced up from where he'd lowered himself onto a bench and noticed people entering the cafeteria. A man with a NRA belt buckle sat beside him. He had the appearance of a bulldog, with short tawny hair and wide shoulders that narrowed to girlish hips.

"Hey, Rusty," Patch said. "I want to apologize for what I said this morning. You're no pansy, or whatever it was I called you."

Rusty patted him on the back while Emily looked stoically ahead. Other men and women arrived, some of them smiling or raising a hand in greeting. After several minutes of hugs and hellos, they all took seats and the meeting came to order. The Deacon stood and walked to the front of the room. His upper lip was wild with nervous twitching.

"I guess you've all heard," he said and the room fell silent. "The government's taken me in its grasp. There's a lien on my church and I've got to come up with some cash before I lose everything."

"What did the bank say?" a pained voice sounded from the rear. "There's got to be a better option than selling your homestead."

Mumbled corroboration followed.

"I don't see how that's possible. When the IRS got me, it got me good. And since we've been like family through the years, I figure an explanation is due."

"You don't owe us a thing," a young man with a dark beard shouted. "Forget what others think. I hope you can cash out with a profit. That's what we all deserve after the work we've put in."

Patch clenched his fists and muttered under his breath. He wondered if the world conspired against him. The things he loved most about Nikolai—the privacy and the sense that he'd helped shape it—were at risk.

"I want to be sensitive to everyone's worries," the Deacon said.

"Sure," the young man replied. "But I, for one, would be tickled to see there's interest in your land. That's a good thing, not only for you, but all of us."

Patch shuffled his feet and Emily tugged on the back of his sleeve to quiet him. Despite the admonition, he rose and turned toward the crowd. "What Kenny says is true," he said. "We've got a right to sell, but don't we have an obligation to the land, as well? We're too much a part of this place to hand it over to folks who can't appreciate it. It deserves better than the clutter of summer cabins and boats."

"That's funny," Ken said, folding his arms. "I remember how my folks prayed for others to come, so we could have a real community with schools and hospitals, libraries and such. But you're talking like you want it to be another bush village."

"No, I'm just saying we should look at our options. I suggest we buy the land and protect it."

The Deacon rubbed his bald head. "How would you do that?"

"We'll keep it just as it is. There'll be no development—not in our hands, anyway."

"That's not what I mean, Hoss. How would you pay for it? That's what I'd like to know."

Patch said he didn't know and that he needed time to make arrangements with the other homesteaders. A woman yelled, "You can count me out," and the discussion broke down into an unruly debate.

Suddenly an older man, short and stocky, stood and the room quieted again. "I'm embarrassed to tell you like this," he said. "But Mavis and I are getting too old for Alaska. We'll be out before the summer is over. I've cleared our last driveway."

Sounds of disappointment flooded the cafeteria and someone hollered over the noise, "I'll be glad to clear your road, Frank."

The man said he appreciated the sentiment, but he was seeing good money for his property and had to take advantage of what might be a fleeting opportunity. Patch asked if a specific offer had been made and Frank said he could get $23,000 per acre—even more for riverfront. A collective gasp rippled through the crowd. The Deacon smiled, as did Emily.

"That's a lot of money," Patch said. "I'm not sure we can raise that much. Maybe over time."

"It's a cash offer," the man said.

Emily lowered her head and stared at the tabletop in front of her. Patch wondered what she was thinking. Didn't she care about the traffic on the river? Wasn't she bothered by the imminent change in their lives?

"You'll be breaking up the land," he said. "Your riverfront—that place nestled by trees and moonlight—it'll end up a subdivision."

"You don't get it. I've already signed it over."

Patch's face went pale. He raised a hand as if to scratch his forehead. The act seemed innocent at first, until his middle finger, fully extended, rubbed the spot just above his brow.

A half-hour later Patch couldn't bear it any longer. He asked Rusty to take Emily home and he walked out. From the school he drove to the Rip Tide, a bar of uncertain lineage just outside of town. Made of old logs, it was marked only by an unlit sign and set back from the main road atop the bluff. He got the bartender's attention by raising a finger and immediately received a beer without mentioning a drink or brand. Alone under the glare of cheap fluorescent lights, he tried to dispel in a raised glass, all memories of the evening.

Patch returned home late—the clouds in his head especially dark—and figured Emily would be angry. Hoping to avoid a scene, he took a blanket from the hallway closet and returned to the great room. There he saw a letter taped to the TV. It was meant as an insult, he thought, suggesting he was in love with the tube.

He ripped off the note and read the words.

Patch,

> *I can't take it anymore. You're not the man I fell in love with. You've become melancholy and unresponsive. I could accept a need to blow off steam, but I can't tolerate the silence. You'll see me over the next couple of days picking up things, but I'm putting an end to us. Sorry you had to find out this way, but we don't seem to talk anymore.*

Emily

The following morning Patch heard the sound of a key turning in the entryway lock and sat up from where he'd spent a restless night on the couch. He shaded his eyes against the sunlight that gushed through the windows and saw Emily step inside. Patch chided himself, wishing he hadn't gone drinking and that he'd cleaned up. He had so much to say, but from the world of emotions swirling through him, he chose an expression of hope.

"Tell me you've thought it over and that you're not leaving."

Emily gasped as though surprised to see him. She crossed her arms and continued to stand in the entryway. "I've come for a few changes of clothes," she said. "That's all."

She looked away and her shoulders sagged. Patch took encouragement from the change in her attitude. He stood and ignored the sharp flashes of pain in his head and the jumble of incoherent thoughts fighting for his attention. "Don't go. If you're tired of seeing my face, I'll move out."

"There's no call for that—not now. I'll be staying with Linda for awhile."

Linda, Patch remembered, was the counselor they'd met after losing Amanda. For a year Emily had continued to receive counseling before she volunteered her own services to people in grief. "That's fine," Patch said. "Maybe we need some time apart, but promise me you won't make any hasty decisions."

"I've already talked to a lawyer."

Patch groaned, unable to think of Emily as an ex-wife. He recalled how some people mocked the value of marriage, saying a certificate couldn't make a union between two people any more genuine. If that were true, what could be said of a piece of paper that ended two decades of mutual commitment?

Emily stepped off the landing and walked toward the stairs. She climbed slowly, her hand alternately gripping and sliding over the rail. Patch followed her into the upstairs hallway and saw her hesitate in front of the bedroom they'd shared. She continued to the loft and gazed out over the living space, as though wondering if it were her last view of home.

As she turned away from the railing, Emily's eyes seemed to focus on a photograph hanging on the wall. It was of Amanda on the beach, hunkered over a starfish and smiling into the camera. A stiff wind whipped her hair across her face.

"It was always your favorite picture," Patch said. "You can take it with you."

"I'd like that."

"Go ahead, but I'm hoping it reminds you of our connection. I can't see you throwing that away."

Emily touched the photo and her breath caught in her throat. "A cynic might say the purpose of life is to replace itself. If that's true, we've failed even in that. Is that our connection?"

Patch tried to clear his head, not only of the sticky aftermath of his drunkenness, but of fear and self-loathing. Amanda, he remembered, couldn't have loved the ocean more if she'd been a fish. The unexpected gifts it offered, like the appearance of orcas in Kachemak Bay, had delighted her. She voiced interest in vocations that ranged from the humble to the prestigious, but were consistent in one respect: the requirement to be near water.

Emily, on the other hand, had never understood their girl's preoccupation. Even in calm weather she got sick in the boat. The smell of the sea, suggestive of something green and grasping, seemed to offend her. When Amanda asked for time on the water, Emily would answer in ways that made her position clear: The ocean was an inhospitable place.

"Let's see what the weather will be like."

Patch speculated: If a gale had blown on that day long ago, how better would our lives be? The question led to inferences that kept his mind busy. Who controls the weather? And did the master of sea and sky go to sleep at the switch?

"You blame me, don't you?" he said, wrapping his arms around Emily. "You think it's my fault for taking Amanda on the boat."

Emily shook herself free from his grasp and took the picture off the wall. "You harbored enough guilt without me piling on," she replied.

Patch watched her hurry down the hallway, her arms cradling the photo as if it were a child. He took a step in her direction and fell to his knees. "Don't go," he said, but Emily's pace quickened down the stairs.

Chapter 20

*While children invest in dreams, most adults
have already spent theirs.*

- From Kit Lerner's Journal

Evening came and Patch watched as Jesse tossed a salmon
belly—the oily silver strip he claimed to like himself—out the
door. Sasha emerged from shadows, chewed on the smoked
meat and swallowed.

"Does she do any tricks?" Patch asked.

Jesse pointed at the coyote. "That's it there. The
disappearing fish trick."

Sasha found a spot beneath the boughs of a large spruce and
licked her jowls. She made three revolutions before coming to
rest in a circle, tail over nose. Her fur caught a breeze, but she
seemed comfortable. Jesse went back inside and closed the

door. The stove crackled, leaving the cabin warm and smelling of spruce gum.

"No tricks, huh?" Patch said. "If she's your only entertainment, you must get awfully lonely."

Jesse took the remaining chair and sighed. It was the sound of frustration and forbearance. "No, there's plenty to do."

"Even in winter?" Patch searched the room for evidence of distraction. "Like what?"

"Well, there's my chores. And I read and study."

"Study what?"

"Lots of things." Jesse seemed to struggle for an answer. "Like your white god."

"White God?" Patch had seen a Bible on the table, but he hadn't asked about it. "You're talking about Jesus?"

"Yeah, I suppose that's him. I'm still reading the part where he's called Jehovah, or just plain God."

"And what have you learned?"

"He's pretty mysterious, I know that much." Jesse took off his glasses and began cleaning them. "Have you found Jesus?" he asked.

"Never felt a need for Him except as someone to blame."

"You blame the white god? For what?"

Patch looked out the window to where a sea of stars danced upon the night's dark blanket. Closer to home, a breeze disturbed the leafless branches of a birch. "If He was really so Almighty, you might think He'd pay attention to His kids instead of letting them suffer the way they do."

"But where would we be without the salmon that come to feed us? Their suffering is a part of our lives."

"Who ordained that?" Patch turned his palms up and the thought he'd wrestled with for many days found its way free. "There was an Anchorage woman," he said. "She passed away last winter, a few days' walk from here. I can't see any logic to that."

"What was she doing?"

"Preparing herself to do good things. She was looking for God."

"Alone?"

"Well," Patch said, reluctantly. "Yes."

"Then the white god didn't kill her. It's sad, but she killed herself. She did a stupid thing."

"But don't you get it?" Patch emphasized the question with a slap on the table. "She didn't have a choice. What she did was of no consequence. Her acts were overwhelmed by things only God controls."

Jesse looked confused. "A friend of mine says there's a reason for everything. Even mosquitoes have a purpose."

The lamplight flickered in Patch's eyes. He leaned forward with elbows on the table, a finger pointing. "If you see a reason for Kit's passing.... Or, for that matter, my..."

Patch turned again to the window and fought back tears. The night presented an explosion of stars, too many pinpricks of light to offer much solace. If he could search the entire universe, where might he find Amanda? Where would he even begin?

###

Why are you out here alone?

That was what Patch wanted to ask, but he'd come to know Jesse well enough to believe it would be met with ambivalence. Instead he contrived a similar question, one he hoped wouldn't irritate his host.

"Why don't you live in the village?"

They were walking along the hillside, looking for likely places to set snares. In the new-fallen snow Jesse pointed to a narrow trail recently used by rabbits. It followed a crease in the berm, ducked beneath the boughs of a fallen spruce and disappeared into the undergrowth. Jesse leaned over the lower branches of the tree, tied a length of wire onto a limb and fashioned a slip noose to dangle before an opening. Patch admired the snare's simplicity and thought how the end of things rarely came by complicated means.

After positioning the loop, Jesse stood. In answer to Patch's question he spoke of his life with nature and the joy he felt living on the fruits of his own labor. His arguments were convincing, because the sun was bright and the valley sparkled like cut gems. The weather was cold, but they were dressed for it and the cabin would be warm when they returned.

"Besides," Jesse said. "I don't belong in the village. A man can't live the way he should there—not like the god of the island or the old ones did."

Patch felt rare ease as he listened. "But don't you miss your family?" he asked.

"They're better off without me. I know that much. It's like that fellow, Shem."

"Who?"

"Shem," Jesse said. "He lived a long time ago—before Russians gave away this land they took from us. He was a healer, a man with power."

"A shaman."

Jesse nodded. "We Indians used to be the children of raven, because the bird made this world. Then Russians came and made us believe in the white god. Raven's children forgot the old ways and called themselves Christian, but they still went to Shem for his cures."

A ptarmigan, white in winter plumage, exploded out of snow-covered willows near their feet. It flapped away, wings pounding an alarm. Patch caught his breath, startled by the sudden flight and noise.

"You mentioned Shem," he said.

Jesse knelt to set another snare. "Back then, whole villages died from sickness. So when smallpox came to Tikchik Lake, Shem went with charms and medicines. The village, he saw, was bad off. A whole lot of people were dead and even more were sick. Shem used willow bark for fever, nettles for pain, bugbane for the stomach, and yarrow for strength. He knew a lot of secrets, but the sickness was strong. For days Shem worked his charms and sang to the gods, asking: Why do you give life, then take it away?"

Patch whistled low. "I wouldn't mind getting that answer myself, but what if there isn't one? Wouldn't we be better off ignorant than to think we're ruled by whimsy?"

Jesse didn't react, but continued with his story. "The smallpox killed babies and old folks, but with Shem's help, the village lived. Before going away he told the people to get the white men's shots. 'Do it, or die,' he said and he went home, tired to the bone. All he wanted was to sleep, but the priest asked for him."

"The priest?" Patch asked.

"Father Berezkin."

"What did he want with Shem?"

Jesse raised a hand as if to demand patience. "A long time ago," he said, "priests came from Russia to turn us Indians into white men. But why would we change, when the only thing the Russians did was get drunk and chase our women? Berezkin built a school, but not many kids went. And a bunch of times my people forgot the white god's ways. Berezkin said we were like children and didn't blame us much, but one thing he didn't like. That was the healers. That's why he told Shem to come."

Jesse stood up and walked again. Patch chafed at the break in the story. "What happened?" he asked.

"Shem went to the church, the biggest building in the village. Inside were many of his people, the children of raven, sitting and waiting. Then Berezkin came in and he was dressed all in black, like a big bird. He called Shem's name and said, 'We need to talk. You were in Tikchik and caused many deaths.'

"Shem couldn't believe his ears. Didn't he help the village? Why was the priest telling lies? 'No,' he said. 'I saved many people.'

"The priest knew of Shem's power, but that didn't matter. He said, 'The villagers believe in you and that's why they won't take our medicine.'

"But that wasn't Shem's fault. All the time he told his people to get the shots, but Berezkin wouldn't listen. 'Forget your ways,' he said. 'Stop using your charms. Show the people you have no power. If not, God will make more sickness.'

"The villagers whispered together. They had seen the power of white men—their guns and ships. They were scared of the priest, but Shem wasn't. He just opened his bag of charms. Inside were shells, a carving of a salmon, a pretty rock, and a necklace made from bear claws. He held them in his hand and asked, 'Didn't your God make these?'

"'God wants you to stop using them,' the priest said.

"'Is God angry with my healings? Does He want my people to be sick?'

"The priest shook his head, but didn't answer. 'Give them to me, or more people will die.'

"Shem looked around inside the church. He saw a cross and pictures on the walls. Why were they better than his charms? The carved salmon was a gift from his father. The shells were old-time money. The rock made him think of the good earth. The claws came from a bear that had fought even with a bullet in its throat. The charms were about good and simple things, like friends and courage. That was their power.

"Then Shem looked at his people and saw so much sadness in their eyes—like the sadness in his heart. Someday raven's children must live like white men. What else could they do? No one used bones for knives anymore, only iron. No one picked berries with willow baskets, or hunted with antler spears. No one made ropes or fish hooks. The old ways were gone. Even then, they were gone.

"Shem loved his charms, but he loved the village more. So he didn't make trouble and did what Berezkin asked. He knew people would hear what happened. The healer has no power— that's what folks would say. But because of what he did, they would learn to be more like white men.

"'Take care of my people,' Shem said, and he left the village."

In his mind Patch saw the story's final setting. He'd been to Nikolai's Orthodox Church once, driven there by a desire to see the inside of an ancient building. The priest had appeared from behind the altar table with its embroidered antimension cloth. Dressed in black robes, he walked past the iconostas hanging on the wall. He uttered strange words and performed a rite so foreign that Patch had never dispelled the image from his head.

"Is that it?" he asked. "Is that the end of the story?"

Jesse nodded.

Patch stared at the river, a dark strip separating Jesse's ridge from the valley and mountains across from it. "Shem gave up?"

"No, he gave in."

"What's the difference?"

Jesse stopped walking. "One means losing. The other is accepting what was always meant to be."

###

During the night their breath turned to frost and settled on hair and eyebrows. They slept late, curled in their sleeping bags, fighting the urge to pee. Shortly after the sun rose, the sound of an outboard reached Patch's ears. He leaped off the floor, just as

Jesse rushed outside. Both men hit the frozen ground, still slipping into boots and zipping up coats.

"Is it your niece?" Patch asked, rubbing sleep from his eyes.

"Could be."

Halfway to the river Patch saw Belle drawing up to the bank with Martin beside her. He yelled a greeting and continued downhill, but when another skiff came into view, he stopped in his tracks.

"Ezra Willis!" Jesse said, quickening his pace.

At the bottom of the slope, Jesse hugged Martin and lifted him out of the first boat. He held the boy in his arms as Ezra stepped onto shore and offered his hand.

"You've shrunk," Jesse said. "I wouldn't think you were a walrus today."

Ezra laughed and his voice echoed into the valley. "The Lord has rendered a mighty miracle. I've become as lissome as a maid." Hands on hips, he rotated to show he'd exaggerated, but not borne false witness. The black man was not only thinner, but he'd allowed his beard and hair to grow. The latter was just a fringe around his ears and the back of his head.

"What are you doing here?" Jesse asked.

Ezra wagged a finger. "First, I've brought back your boat."

"You didn't have to."

"Yes, I did. Your niece explained the importance of having one. But there's another reason I'm back. The Lord told me to exercise faith. 'Jesse is my child,' He said. 'See that you neglect him not.' So I've come to give you a final chance at salvation before returning to Detroit."

Jesse lowered his gaze. "You didn't get much done in Kaknu, did you?"

"Well, now. It depends on how you define success. I might not have thrust in a sickle, but I did plant seeds."

From an elevation above the others Patch listened to the friendly chatter. He saw Belle climb a few steps up the bank and touch her uncle's shoulder. There was color in her face and a sparkle in her eyes that hadn't been there several days ago. She turned to look at Patch and an odd phrase entered his head: My Savior. The thought caused him to marvel. Didn't I save her? And he tucked the notion away, as if it were a loose piece to a new jigsaw puzzle.

"I think introductions are in order," Belle said.

"That's not necessary." Ezra extended his hand to Patch. "This must be Brother Taggart, your rescuer."

"Yeah, that's him," Jesse said. "He blames the white god for all his problems."

Patch felt his face grow hot, surprised by the accusation and even more puzzled by his embarrassment. Hadn't he implied as much nights ago? He greeted Ezra, before turning to Belle.

"Are you still offering me a ride home?" he asked.

"We'll be leaving tomorrow. How does that sound?"

Patch grinned. "Like a plan," he said. "Like a plan."

While the sun began to set, they stood outside the cabin door and witnessed a remarkable scene. Sasha approached, less cautiously than usual, and took a caribou bone from Martin's outstretched hand. Ezra watched with apparent fascination and said he would add the memory to many others he would share at the Church of the First Evangelical.

"Can I pet the animal?" he asked.

"You can try," Jesse said.

Ezra stepped forward and the coyote crouched with her ears lowered and lips raised.

"You best not," Patch said.

They watched the animal limp into the trees with the meaty bone in her mouth and Jesse shook his head with astonishment. "I guess she knows the heart of the boy."

"Can I go play with her, Mom?" Martin asked.

"She's a wild animal, Sweetie, Sasha won't play. Besides, it's almost time for dinner."

"We made friends though, didn't we?"

Jesse smiled and said that nature was more of a partner than a friend. He put his hand on Martin's shoulder and led the boy toward the cache. Minutes later they returned with meat and, until dinner was ready, the two buddies talked about everything they'd done since spring.

Buoyed by thoughts of a hot shower and soft bed, Patch forgot his problems. He vowed to exercise enough dominion to breathe easy and relax for the evening. With a cup of chili and a fistful of game meat, he settled on the floor with his back to the wall. Across from him Martin slept on the cot and Jesse rested at the boy's feet. Ezra sat at the worktable and Belle joined him, holding her fourth beer of the evening. She giggled in the missionary's direction.

"You'll be happy to know Jesse has been reading that Bible you gave him."

Ezra's mouth stopped in mid-chew. "Glory be, is that true, Jesse?"

Belle didn't give her uncle a chance to answer. "He's been keeping notes, too."

"Oh? About what?"

Jesse gazed at the floor and his niece spoke again on his behalf. "It's mostly about things he doesn't understand."

"Can I help?"

"No," Jesse finally said. "I've been figuring things out."

Belle tapped pensively on the table. "One of his questions was pretty good. Who was that fellow we talked about? Abraham, wasn't he?"

"Abraham?" Ezra sat up straight. "That would be the father of the covenant people. You could certainly do worse than the works of that great prophet."

"He was a good man?" Jesse asked.

"Yes, sir, he withheld nothing from God, including his own child. He was willing to render any oblation—to offer any sacrifice."

"And that's good?"

"Let me put it this way. It's good to sacrifice whatever our Heavenly Father requires of us."

The look of assurance on the missionary's face was almost too much for Patch to bear. He suppressed a laugh and saw the others glance in his direction, but he decided not to speak of the notion unraveling in his head, like the tendrils from a noxious weed. God wasn't dead, only impotent. The Great I Am was incapable of willing an event.

Jesse engaged Ezra once more. "But isn't it wrong to kill?"

"Usually, but not when God commands otherwise."

Suddenly Patch couldn't keep from cackling aloud. How could God manifest His will when people saw divine purpose in everything? Rain was a blessing. Drought was a call to repentance—a flood, God's vengeance.

"What's so funny?" Ezra asked.

"Aren't we giving God too much credit? Think of what He's done: He chooses a favorite people and tests their faith by asking them to kill and displace others. He goes into cahoots with the devil to torment Job. His answer to disobedience is to flood the earth with death and destruction. Are those the works of someone to be revered?"

Ezra loosened the collar on his shirt and exhaled. "Well, I see you know the stories of our Lord, but you speak of them out of context. We should be careful of what we say. It might be taken as an offense."

"Why? Doesn't God prefer our honesty?"

Jesse looked from one man to the other, his eyes filled with apprehension. "Don't argue," he said. "We all believe the same thing: When folks die, their spirits live."

"Amen, brother."

"And maybe we'll become gods."

Ezra gasped and Belle nearly choked on her beer. "You? A god?" she said. "You don't even make a good honey truck driver."

Jesse stood and his face turned red and grim. His gaze rested momentarily upon each of his guests. Belle laughed until tears came. Ezra frowned and shook his head. Without saying another word, Jesse gathered his sleeping bag, along with two six packs of beer, and bolted through the door.

"Where are you going?" Belle shouted.

From beyond the cabin walls they heard the crunch of footsteps atop old-fallen snow. Ezra rushed to the entryway. "Don't go, brother, please," he yelled, but the sounds of retreat were swallowed by the night.

###

The cold seemed to freeze them in their places and arrest their tongues. A half hour passed and Jesse hadn't returned. "Will he be okay?" Ezra asked.

"He'll be fine," Belle replied. She was lying beside Martin on the cot, now.

Patch stood to feed the stove and Ezra stared through the pale light toward him. The missionary cleared his throat and spoke. "I might have said too much already, but can I tell you a story, brother?"

Though Patch was ready for rest—exhausted by thoughts of God and destiny—he couldn't deny Ezra a chance to speak. The man was a good sort, only misdirected the way Kit had been, with his self confidence standing in the way of meaningful learning. Patch shrugged an approval.

"I was a drunk once," Ezra said. "And I couldn't keep a job. So I resorted to theft—stole TVs, jewelry, anything to which I could place my hands. Afterward I would drink away the value of what I'd pilfered. One day, I woke up in a stolen car, unaware of what I'd done, the stink of alcohol on my breath.

"I hated myself and offered a prayer. 'Lord, give me a gun,' I said, 'that I might put an end to my existence.' I offered my petition throughout the day, but something unexpected happened. I didn't hear a voice, but I heard Him all the same. God took me—a common thief—and wrapped His loving arms around me. He told me I was forgiven."

Tears formed in Ezra's eyes. "Do you understand? You have to invite Jesus into your life. I'd done it all, disobeyed Him in every respect, broke all His commandments. But He took me from my life of sin, gave me hope and a new life."

"But why is He so fickle?" Patch asked. "Why does He save you and let others die?" He recalled a passage in Kit's journal and retrieved the copy from his pack. He turned to an entry she'd written after her kayak was damaged. "Tell me this isn't true," he said.

Ezra took the bound papers and read aloud:

> *The Bible says Jacob wrestled with the Lord and I suppose I've done the same. I ask God: "Where should I go? What must I do?" But He doesn't answer me—not anymore. Perhaps God wants something that I'm not willing to give and so I don't hear Him. All I know is that I'm lonely and hungry. Worst of all, I'm imprisoned by my need to know, held captive by a desire to follow.*

At this point I would give up my search only to be deliriously unaware of God's existence.

Through a microscope we're aware of tiny lives that would otherwise escape our notice. In the course of their short lifetimes these simple creatures may scramble the slightest fraction of an inch, but their progress is overwhelmed by the movement of tides and currents. Sometimes they're washed onto places for which they do not care. And that's what has happened to me. I'm an amoeba to God's greatness and He has left me spilled onto dry ground.

"Who wrote that?" Ezra asked.

"A young lady who loved her Maker more than life. And she's dead now."

Almost immediately Patch felt bad for his reply. The words extended the evening's row. The underlying message could have been: Don't you get it? Here was someone who invited Jesus into her life and do you see where it got her?

"There's much we don't understand," Ezra said.

"I hear that."

"But there's one important truth worth remembering." Ezra leaned, with elbows on his knees and his eyes earnest. "God loves us all," he said. "Sometimes I can feel Him nearby and a picture enters my head. I see a smiling father kneeling on one side of a large room. His arms are spread wide and He entreats me to take first steps in His direction.

"And when I stumble—as I'm likely to do—He forgives me more quickly than I can forgive myself. At times I'd rather lie on the floor to pout and be punished by thoughts of my stupidity. But He tells me to put away the baggage, to rise up and try again, to take a few more steps—awkward though they may be—toward Him.

"Do you see my point, brother? God already knows how to walk across the floor. It's we humans who have much to learn. And I can't imagine any condition for growth that's more important than the possibility—no, the inevitability—of sometimes falling."

Patch grabbed his sleeping bag and spread it out on the floor, wondering if he'd learned anything by surviving his days on the Killborn River. For that matter, how did Kit Lerner grow in the moment she left the world? That question led him to consider another passage from her journal, one that was odd, not only for its sentiment, but for its position among entries that dealt with little else but survival. What accounted for her apparent burst of energy? Was it an attempt to say goodbye?

> *In large inlets the tide rushes in from opposite directions and creates a line of ripples, whirlpools, and drift wood that fishermen refer to as the flood line. The flood line isn't dangerous, but it's an eerie place where the ocean speaks with the sounds of new birth— spitting and sucking—and it's filled with floating debris and tiny lives trapped by the incessant motion of currents and waves.*

I had a dream last night—or was it just this afternoon? I was with Jesus on a boat and as we traveled through a line of ripples and whirlpools, He shared with me a bit of wisdom. He told me that, like the flood line, life is a focal point where countless indomitable forces meet. And as participants in its motion, we find ourselves mated to a confusing mix of debris.

I believe that in some prior existence we chose to live in this world full of dilemmas and conflict. Without the flood line's aberrant behavior—without its eerie motion and its birthing sounds—we couldn't appreciate the beauty of Turnagin Arm, or a dozen other places of stark wonder. So opposition is necessary in order to provide a contrast.

Yet contrast constitutes a small part of its purpose. It's not an accident that accomplishment requires improvement and that improvement can only occur in less than ideal worlds. Someday, when my eyes blink their last, will I be sad to leave this imperfect place? Will I yearn again for its mix of good and evil? Perhaps. Because now I recognize this home as the perfect place to understand God's wisdom and appreciate His ideals.

###

Early the next morning, occupied by thoughts of home, Patch opened his eyes and took in his surroundings. The cabin was warm despite the lack of a stove fire, but moisture hung heavy in the air. Through the faint light he saw Ezra on the floor and Belle and Martin sharing the cot. Patch tiptoed to the window and gazed out at the mix of shadow and pre-dawn. Where the spruce had been blue the day before, a gray mist clung to the hillside and obscured the terrain.

He knew the weather was ripe for a change and that an early departure was in their best interest. Patch stepped outside and headed toward the smokehouse, where Belle's caribou quarters were stashed. He reminded himself that the meat had to be hauled to the boat, but another task took precedence—he needed to offer an apology.

Just as he'd thought, Jesse was inside, resting among fish scales and a pile of empty beer cans. The man was in his sleeping bag, open-mouthed and snoring like a chainsaw. Patch entered and the smell of alcohol and old smoke enveloped him.

"I'm sorry about last night," he whispered. "We were pretty noisy. I can't blame you for getting upset."

Jesse stirred and stretched. He opened his eyes slowly and looked up with a shout of alarm. "Oh, it's you" he said, slurring the words. "Did you guys kiss and make up?"

"We sure did. You're free to go back inside if you like."

Jesse said he would rather sleep, but Patch roused his wobbly-legged friend out the door. By the time they got back to the cabin Belle was up and making coffee. She rushed to her uncle, checked his hands and face for frostbite and chastised him for running off. Without acknowledging her, Jesse fell to

321

the floor. He slumped against the wall and chuckled for no apparent reason.

"He must have been drinking all night," Patch said. "When did he pick up that habit?"

"There were problems in the village. I guess he figured alcohol would help."

Patch believed he understood. Jesse was like a man straddling deep water, with each foot planted in a different boat. Unable to leap to one vessel or the other, he teetered between the two, always in the process of falling. Patch wanted to help, but he thought it best to leave the man alone. Unexpectedly a curious thought occurred to him: What happens when a fellow's ideals are unattainable? What else can he do but compromise himself again and again?

Just then Ezra sat up, yawning and groaning. He greeted the others, before glancing in Jesse's direction. "So the prodigal son has returned," he said, smiling.

"Probable what?"

The missionary laughed and rose to his knees. Still in his sleeping bag, he crawled across the cold floor and slapped Jesse playfully on the shoulder. At the same time sunlight trickled over the mountain and struggled through the fog, a reminder of how rare daylight was becoming.

"Guess I'll fetch that meat," Patch said.

Jesse struggled to his feet and almost fell. "Me too."

"No, we'll do it. You stay here and keep an eye on Martin. He'll be awake soon." Patch headed across the floor, hoping his drunken friend wouldn't follow, but he stopped when Belle squealed with delight.

"I see that Sasha helps herself now," she said.

Jesse elbowed his niece for a view through the window. A second later he snatched up his rifle and staggered outside. Patch asked what was happening, but Belle didn't answer. She followed her uncle, giving Patch an unobstructed view through the window.

Sasha was dragging one half of a ribcage toward the trees, but she dropped the stolen bounty and groveled when Jesse appeared from around the exterior wall. Patch raced outside, damning himself for not shutting the smokehouse door. He stopped at the edge of the frozen clearing and watched Jesse and the coyote face each other across a distance of several dozen feet.

"I'm your god," Jesse said, "and you tried to steal from me."

Sasha fell to her belly, blinked an apology and pawed at the snow. Belle turned to Patch with a hand over her mouth. "He's not going to shoot her, is he?"

Patch frowned.

"Don't," Belle said. "Please."

Jesse knelt with his 30.06 pointed in front of him, saying, "She needs to be punished."

The words echoed in Patch's ears and took their place beside similar phrases describing God's wrath: I will tread them in my anger, and trample them in my fury. Their blood shall be sprinkled upon my garments. The day of vengeance is in my heart.

"What's going on?" Ezra appeared at Patch's side. "Did he say, 'punish?'"

323

"That's right." Jesse checked his rifle chamber and locked the bolt. "I'm just like your white god. I'm going to fix this sinner."

"No, brother. You mustn't. God forgives the prodigal and so should you."

"The probable again, huh? I haven't read about that in your book."

Belle stepped between the coyote and rifle. She waved her arms in the animal's direction and shouted, but Sasha seemed confused. Jesse moved aside, raised his gun and looked through the scope.

There was no time for consideration. Patch yelled a warning and leaped. He fell to the snow with Belle in his arms. In the next instant the rifle barked. Ice and black earth showered several feet to the right of Sasha. With ears flat, the coyote stood trembling and stiff-legged. She looked in one direction, then another.

"Did he get her?" Belle asked, struggling to rise.

"Don't worry about the coyote. A bullet can as easily kill you." Patch kept the woman pinned to the ground. He looked back over his shoulder and the pitch of his voice rose. "Get that gun before he puts another shell in the chamber."

Ezra crouched next to Jesse and put a hand on his friend's arm. He reached for the rifle. "Perhaps this isn't the thing to do," he said. "You're not yourself now. The devil drink is controlling you."

Jesse jerked the 30.06 away and scowled. He extracted the rifle bolt and shoved it back. "What are you talking about?"

"You need not concern yourself with punishing this animal. That's not God's way. The God you've described is a human creation—a thing we've formed in our own image. Believe me, He wouldn't approve of what you're doing now."

"Listen to the preacher," Belle said. "Remember what you told me. This kind of killing isn't right. It has no purpose."

Jesse wiped the sweat off his forehead and raised his face to Ezra. "You're saying the Bible is wrong?"

"Yes, wrong when one takes license from it to cause harm."

The wind gusted and scattered snowflakes in its path. Patch looked up. A raven sailed against the gray sky—too fast to be in control of its destination, much less its destiny. To his eyes the smokehouse shifted and whirled. The coyote appeared caught in the movement. Patch felt sick, but managed to mumble under his breath.

"What?" Jesse said.

Patch answered only imperceptibly louder. "God must withhold His hand."

There was a pause. Jesse set the rifle across his lap. "Why is that?"

"I don't know."

"It's a mystery, right?" Jesse tightened his grip on the firearm and his words sounded like a chant. "She took what was mine. I was her god, but she stole from me. I have to smite her. I know that much."

"No," Patch said.

He rose to his knees, a spitting distance from the rifle barrel. The cold of the snow felt like a high-voltage shock, yet he remained kneeling. Another raven passed overhead and made a sound like dripping water. *Poi-ying*, it cried. Patch hugged himself and, rocked. *Poi-ying*, the song rang out once more.

"Don't shoot," he said. "It's no mystery."

Jesse rested the rifle butt on the ground and waited.

"I can see it now," Patch said. "God can't help one of His creations without doing harm to another. He won't stop you from killing Sasha anymore than He'll stop coyotes from eating. So it's up to you to do the right thing. You can believe in God—that's fine—but does He matter when His hands are tied? It's our responsibility to care for each other."

Tears broke in Jesse's eyes. "But I'm no good. I can't even watch after myself."

"That's not true. You helped me when I needed it. You're better than this."

Jesse took a deep breath and switched his gun on safety. He stood, using the rifle for support, and helped Patch rise. The two friends embraced, the shorter man's face buried in the other's chest. Across from them the coyote seemed to interpret the act as consent. She plucked up the meat and dragged it away, her faith apparently unshaken.

Patch felt weak with the weight of new thoughts filling his head. He stood with the others, unable to grasp their exchange of emotion and words. Some part of him, he sensed, wouldn't survive the dead of winter. It was already passing away inside of him and he wondered: Would its demise come as a relief? Or might it leave him a shell of his former self?

Belle led everyone toward the cabin and spoke as if trying to ignore what had happened. "Martin must have been tired to sleep so long," she said.

Jesse ran ahead, offering to wake up the boy, but he stopped at the open door and stared inside. "Where is he?"

Patch felt a shiver pass through him. He tried not to assume the worst, tried not to believe the boy was gone. He watched Belle go inside, hoping she would discover Martin in a clever hiding place, but she burst back through the doorway, screaming her son's name. With hands on her head, she hurried to one edge of the hill and looked over the river.

"Martin," she yelled.

They listened for a reply, but only her echo and the wind answered. Patch pleaded silently for the child's safety, struggling to believe someone had the ability to answer the petition. The others fanned out toward the edge of the woods, but Patch called them back.

"Let's not go off half-cocked." He squatted on his haunches and drew a crude map in the snow. "Martin wouldn't have crossed the river, so there's no reason to look the other side of it."

They crowded together as Patch described his plan. "Jesse and I'll hug the water and walk upstream. You two head the other way. Go about a quarter mile, then angle back and meet southeast of here. Whoever turns up signs of Martin should fire a shot into the air, so the others can follow."

Sheets of snow rippled across the ground and gathered into drifts, reminding Patch that any signs of the boy might soon be lost. He and Jesse followed the ridge upriver. They moved deliberately, calling down either slope and giving ear to every creaking branch and bird call. A half-hour later they curled southeast.

The terrain was dotted with a few stands of spruce and elevated hummocks of ground. Drifted snow filled the pockmarked landscape and covered an occasional fallen tree. The two men staggered through knee-high drifts, tripping over unseen obstacles. They hollered out Martin's name, but spoke to each other only to indicate the direction in which they should go.

With the sun beginning to set, they discovered the boy's tracks. Jesse pointed his rifle toward the sky and fired a round to signal the find. From the look of the trail Martin was struggling to stay on his feet. More than an hour had passed and Patch knew it was sufficient time for limbs to freeze. He reached within himself to find new strength and crashed ahead despite his exhaustion and cold.

The tracks led across a frozen clearing to a tangle of deadfall. Patch ran to it and knelt before an opening into a cavity. He expected to see the boy inside, but he was shocked by the sight of glowing eyes staring out of the darkness. Patch blinked and realized an animal occupied the space beneath the fallen timber.

He shrank back until his eyes adjusted to the murkiness and the outlines of a coyote became visible. In a bowl within the lair it lay in a half-curl with its head resting upon a dark mound. Patch suddenly understood it was the boy beneath the coyote and there appeared to be blood nearby.

"Get out," Patch yelled.

The coyote stood and dashed out of the cavity, passing so closely that its tail brushed Patch's face and upraised arms. It limped a short distance away and sat, waiting.

"Sasha?" Patch said, recognizing the coyote's gait.

He crawled into the opening, bumping his head and shoulders against the timbers above him. A thought resonated in his head: I should have let Jesse kill her. Coyotes, he knew, weren't large animals, but they could crush scavenged bones with their jaws. Patch came across a mass of chewed flesh near the boy and looked away from it.

"Is Martin in there?" Jesse asked, moaning and pacing before the opening. "Is he okay?"

Patch didn't know how to answer. He reached for the child's shoulder and turned him over. Martin's face appeared and his eyes opened, as if he'd been asleep. "Where's Sasha?" he asked.

Patch checked Martin for injuries, surprised to hear the boy speak. "Don't worry about the coyote. You're safe now. Where did she hurt you?"

"She didn't hurt me. She kept me warm."

"Sasha?"

"Uh huh. She brought me some meat, too."

Patch got a better look at the blood and torn flesh he'd seen earlier and realized it was part of the ribcage the coyote had stolen.

"I didn't eat any of it," Martin said. "It wasn't cooked. Where is she?"

"Outside—waiting for you." Patch backed out and pulled the boy to the opening. "You've got another friend here, too," he said, just as sunlight kissed the boy's face.

"Uncle Jesse!"

Martin scrambled to his feet and ran to his uncle. Jesse knelt to him, not speaking. They held each other for a time, until the boy raised his face from Jesse's shoulder and called out toward the trees.

"I'm okay now. They'll take me home."

"Who are you talking to?" Jesse asked.

Patch scratched his head, still puzzling over the memory of the coyote sharing her den with the boy. "Sasha kept him warm."

Jesse turned pale. "She did what?"

"Just like you told me before," Martin said, putting his hands on the man's tear-lined cheeks. "You can't change the nature of things. And she's my friend. I knew it right from the start."

Jesse held the boy to him and spoke in his ear. "Do you remember my stories?"

"About the god of the island? I remember."

"Good, then remember this, too: If he'd talked, he would have said we need to care for each other. That's what the old ones did."

Patch looked at the sky and decided there was enough daylight to guide them back to the cabin. His breath rose in a cloud and snow fell on his face, but he felt warm. He heard the sound of footsteps and knew without looking that Belle and Ezra had arrived.

"He's okay," Patch said. "The boy's fine."

They huddled together and the coyote sat a short distance away, sniffing curiously at the air. Sometime before Belle finally stood and suggested they go home, an idea occurred to Patch that caused his spirit to soar. Maybe I can't change the nature of things, he thought, but here I made a difference. That's when he made a decision: I'll box up my recriminations and self-loathing. I'll put the box away and never open it again.

Epilogue

Salmon are remarkable. Most of them are caught before they get a chance to spawn. Even the fortunate ones die soon after the act. Still, the salmon fill the river, undaunted. As a result of their sacrifices, they give life to a host of other creatures. Oh, that I were as steadfast!

- From Kit Lerner's Journal

For a month Patch and Ezra remained with Jesse and helped tend his trap line. Cold weather froze the surrounding muskeg and left a mantle of snow covering the underbrush. Over this platform they ranged through a plain so vast Ezra said he quaked to think an architect even greater had fashioned it. From the sweep of frozen earth they took beaver, fox, and lynx—also a few ermine and wolverine. Each night they retired to the cabin, stretched pelts and pondered the philosophical questions posed in Jesse's notebook. One evening Patch had an idea.

"Can I have a pencil and a sheet of paper?" he asked and immediately began to jot down a list of his own. At the top he wrote a heading: THINGS I NEED TO MAKE RIGHT.

Having delayed their return several times, the men strapped on home-rigged snowshoes and, ahead of the bone-splitting freeze of midwinter, they trudged along the river toward Kaknu. Three days later they crossed the frozen surface of Killborn Lake and stayed at Clarence and Belle's house.

They waited several days for the arrival of a skiplane and during that time Jesse fashioned more charms and taught Martin the stories of his people. The boy came home from school each day, searching out his uncle, but Patch taught him the most important lesson of their visit.

"What do those charms remind you of?" Patch asked within earshot of the entire household.

"My Uncle Jesse."

Patch slapped his leg. "That's where you find real magic— in the memories of those you care for."

When the plane finally arrived, Patch and Ezra gave each of their hosts a hug and took turns throwing Martin up into the air. They boarded the Cessna and buckled up for takeoff. From above the earth, they watched Jesse until he was a faraway spot on the ground, still planted to the runway and waving.

After that lazy beginning, the remainder of winter passed by in a frenzy. Patch returned home for a few days and arranged to have one of his planes leased to Fish and Game until spring. With the money he bought a ticket to Detroit and accepted

Ezra's invitation to spend a week there. He was amazed at the city's wide highways and the long rows of tenement buildings.

Patch had known Ezra would invite him to church and he planned to tolerate a session. As the only white man in the crowd, he discovered a taste for the ebullient singing, the hands waving, the ringing "hallelujahs," and the animated preaching. He also liked the parishioners, who treated him like a long-lost uncle.

The next evening he went to a special gathering where Ezra addressed the congregation. A placard outside the gray-painted church announced the topic. In hand-written script it read:

What I Learned from My Brethren
of the Bristol Bay Watershed.

Ezra Willis, Disciple of Christ.

The missionary addressed a full chapel and roused the assembly into loud adulation. Patch was proud to be there and committed Ezra's closing statement to memory: "More than anything else, I learned to recognize what was miraculous in daily life."

Time passed like a blur. At the airport Patch bid farewell, using words he'd rehearsed over his final days in Ezra's studio apartment.

"You've been calling me a name," he said.

"Have I?"

"You've been calling me, 'brother.'"

335

"Well," Ezra said. "It's not meant as a slur, I assure you. We're all members of God's family, brothers and sisters in that sense."

Patch nodded. There wasn't much he understood, but he could accept the idea of humanity being seed of one sire, subject to similar pains and limitations. Perhaps the assertion could be taken on faith. His next words, like the particle of belief he'd determined to hold dear, came without remorse or a contrary thought. He shook Ezra's hand, drew him close and wrapped an arm around the back of his neck.

"In that case," he whispered, "do you mind if I think of you in the same way?"

Each day offered additional opportunities to put things right. He visited his parents and grinned at his mother's familiar reference to the prodigal son. Later in Anchorage he called on Pamela Lerner and took her on a drive to farm country in the Matanuska Valley. Short on cash, he sold an acre of his homestead to a young family from Anchorage, saying he could think of no better place than Nikolai to raise children.

It was April before he gathered enough courage to perform the next task. At the borough building he watched for Linda, the grief counselor, to come out of a group session. He waited until she was nearly out the door before calling to her. She rotated on her heels and walked back into the commons area where Patch sat hunched on a chair. She didn't seem to recognize him at first, but gasped a moment later.

"My God. What are you doing here?"

"You remember me?"

"How could I forget? Our one meeting was a disaster."

Patch nodded. "I was hoping we could talk. I wanted to ask you a favor."

Linda crossed her arms. "What is it?"

Patch looked up at the ceiling and swallowed back the emotion rising out of his chest. "Amanda was my pride and joy. She deserves some tribute to her memory—even if it's just her dad mourning her to the end of his days. You won't mind if I come to your meetings, will you?"

Linda strode across the tiled floor and put a hand on his arm. "You're always welcome. Always."

Patch thanked her and started toward the door.

"And don't worry," Linda said to his retreating figure. "It may be awkward at first—with Emily in attendance at times— but hang in there, okay?"

Patch stopped, but he didn't turn around. He wiped his face with the heel of his hand. "That won't be a problem. I'll make sure of it."

Two days later with the sun promising a season of renewal, Patch appeared at the house he'd helped build. He looked into the trees and clear sky. The early morning seemed alive with bird calls and squirrel chatter. He unloaded twenty bags of concrete, some chain link fencing and a posthole digger from his pickup. He stacked the material on a pallet under the eaves of the house and went to the quarter-acre plot Emily loved.

It was still covered with melting snow. He knelt beside it, scraped aside a section of dirty ice and took up a handful of mud. Patch brought it to his face. He loved the feel of it dripping through his fingers. It was just like the bitterness of guilt and anger thawing in his heart, the part of him that hadn't survived the dead of winter.

Behind him he heard the turn of a lock. The front door opened and Emily poked her head outside. She stepped onto the porch, smoothing her disheveled hair and wearing a housecoat he knew from the thousands of mornings he'd watched her make coffee.

"Patch?" she said. "Is that you?"

"Last time I checked." He wiped the sweat off his brow and added with more contrition, "I'm sorry. I know it's early."

"What are you doing here?"

A soft breeze blew. Patch raised his face and took a deep breath. He could smell the river and fertile earth.

He answered, "Fulfilling a promise."

About the Author

M Alan Bahr is a former commercial fisherman and recovering investment banker. *Autumn Run* is his first novel and was a semi-final selection in the Faulkner-Wisdom Competition. It is based, in part, on Alan's experiences growing up in a small Alaskan fishing town. He can be reached at mabahr@ebbingtidepublishing.com.

CPSIA information can be obtained at www.ICGtesting.com

224258LV00004B/46/P